JAMES A MOORE

The Last Sacrifice

THE TIDES OF WAR BOOK I

ANGRY
ROBOT

ANGRY ROBOT
An imprint of Watkins Media Ltd

Lace Market House,
54-56 High Pavement,
Nottingham,
NG1 1HW
UK

angryrobotbooks.com
twitter.com/angryrobotbooks
The tide turns

An Angry Robot paperback original 2017

Cover by Alejandro Colucci
Set in Meridien by Epub Services

Distributed in the United States by Penguin Random House, Inc.,
New York.

ISBN 978 0 85766 544 7
Ebook ISBN 978 0 85766 545 4

Printed in the United States of America

9 8 7 6 5 4 3 2 1

Gripping, horrific and unique, James A Moore continues to be a winner, whatever genre he's writing in. Well worth your time."
Seanan McGuire, New York Times bestselling author of the
October Daye series

"James A Moore is the new prince of grimdark fantasy. His work is full of dark philosophy and savage violence, desperate warriors and capricious gods. This is fantasy for people who like to wander nighttime forests and scream at the moon. Exhilarating as hell."
Christopher Golden, New York Times bestselling author of Snowblind

"James A Moore keeps getting better. The cast of characters expands. Moore juggles them with ease, giving each one some background so that they don't all run together. And the battle scenes, whether it's individual combat or armies clashing, are riveting. Plus the intrigue keeps on getting more complex … Highly recommended."
Adventures Fantastic

"The prose is sharp, the pace wonderfully timed with great action tempered with some wonderful lulls to allow you to get your breath back. Back this up with some great characters alongside a world that is delightfully designed all round makes this a series that continues to go from strength to strength. Finally, and this is the clincher for me, Moore gives the characters a depth with their dialogue that not only shows their devotions but also gives them a roundedness that allows you to become fully immersed. Cracking."
Falcata Times

"James A Moore dedicates *Seven Forges* in part 'to the memory of Fritz Leiber and Robert E. Howard for the inspiration.' That dedication sets the bar high, and caused me a bit of readerly apprehension, because so many writers have imitated badly those two greats of the sword and sorcery tradition. Moore is far more than an imitator, though. He does some fresh, counterintuitive things with the genre conventions. More than once, he startled me into saying out loud, 'I didn't see *that* coming.'"
Black Gate

BY THE SAME AUTHOR

The Seven Forges series
Seven Forges
The Blasted Lands
City of Wonders
The Silent Army

The Blood Red series
Blood Red
Blood Harvest
Blood of the Damned

The Chris Corin Chronicles
Possessions
Rabid Growth
Newbies

The Serenity Falls Trilogy
Writ in Blood
The Pack
Dark Carnival

The Griffin & Price series (with Charles R Rutledge)
Blind Shadows
Congregations of the Dead
A Hell Within

Alien: Sea of Sorrows
The Haunted Forest Tour *(with Jeff Strand)*
Bloodstained Oz *(with Christopher Golden)*
Bloodstained Wonderland *(with Christopher Golden)*
Buffy the Vampire Slayer: Chaos Bleeds
Cherry Hill
Deeper
Fireworks
Harvest Moon
Homestead
Under the Overtree
Vampire: House of Secrets *(with Kevin Andrew Murphy)*
Vendetta
Werewolf: Hellstorm
The Wild Hunt

Slices *(stories)*
This is Halloween *(stories)*

This one is dedicated to EJ Stevens, Tony Tremblay, John and Roberta, Chris and Connie, Bracken and Heather, Hilary and Dave and Scott Goudsward. Just because.

Special thanks to Alejandro Colucci, who always makes my descriptions come to life, and to Marc Gascoigne for the beautiful design of my covers.

CHAPTER ONE
Four Coins

Home.

Was there ever a finer word?

Brogan McTyre and his cohorts had spent the last eight weeks riding along the Hollum trails and the plains of Arthorne, serving as guards and guides alike to the merchant trains. It was hard work, and it was unfulfilling, but it put enough coin in their purses to keep them through the worst of the winters.

Now, after two months' travel, they were heading back to where they all wanted to be – except for Harper, who seemed perfectly content wherever he settled. Back to their homes.

The leaves had started their slow burn, and to counteract the oranges and yellows that imitated a hearth's fire, the air had grown cold, and frost covered the ground every morning.

That meant the air was chilled enough that every breath offered a gust of steam and every intake sapped just a touch of the internal heat.

Still, they were heading home.

The Broken Swords were behind them. According to the legends Brogan's father had told him when he was a lad, the collection of mountains hid the remains of old giants, and the gigantic spears of crystal that thrust from the earth and stone of the area were supposed to be fragments of the giants' swords.

He didn't believe the tales, but he remembered them fondly and had shared them with his own children more than once.

A smile crept across his face as Brogan thought of his little ones. Braghe was his pride, of course, a hearty lad who at only five years was already an adventurer and constantly getting into battles with whatever monsters his imagination could summon. His daughters, the twins, were as lovely as their mother and happily too young for him to worry yet about the sort of lads who thought as he had before he married. Leidhe and Sherla were eight, and their hair was spun from the same fire as his. They had his locks and their mother's looks. A combination that would doubtless cause him plenty of grief, as they became young women. Also like their mother, they were fighters. When they weren't trying to be prim and proper they were out fighting imaginary beasties with Braghe.

Much to their mother's chagrin, they were seldom prim and proper.

His smile grew broader as he thought of their mother. Nora was reason enough to come home and the thought of being with her again took a great deal of chill from the morning.

"You're thinking of your woman again, aren't you?" Harper's voice cut through his thoughts and he looked toward his lifelong friend. Harper was the only man he knew who looked as comfortable on a saddle as he did on the ground. There was something of a cat about the man. He seemed perfectly relaxed all the time, until you looked at his eyes. They were constantly moving, roaming even when his body seemed incapable of doing more than stretching lazily.

"Why do you say that?" The thing with having Harper as a friend was you never knew when he was going to tease ruthlessly or try to provoke a fight. He looked perpetually calm – but that meant nothing.

"Because you've got that dreamy smile on your face again. You only ever get that smile when you've just been laid or when you're thinking about Nora."

"How would you know how I look when I've just had sex?"

"Because I've seen you *after* you get home to Nora as well as when you're thinking about getting home to her."

Brogan shook his head and smiled. If nothing else he could always trust Harper to observe the world around him very well.

"What are your plans for the winter, Harper?"

"I'll be finding a place to stay and a woman to keep me warm, I suppose."

That was always Harper's plan for the future. It was as reliable an answer as could be found in the Five Kingdoms.

Up ahead of them Mosely was rounding the final curve in the road leading to Kinnett. Not far from him stood Volkner, who owned the homestead nearest Brogan's.

The look on Volkner's face when he saw Brogan was enough to cause panic to set in.

Brogan urged his horse forward and kept his eyes locked on his neighbor, a dread sinking into his stomach that was deep and abiding.

Mosely looked back over his shoulder as Brogan rode forward.

Volkner's dark eyes were wide and filled with sorrow. "Brogan, lad, I'm so very sorry. We've been trying to reach you. I sent Tamra to find which path you were on. He must have chosen badly."

"What is it, Volkner?" His voice shook.

There are rules all people follow. Most of those rules are made by kings.

Volkner's hands were empty.

"There are coins, Brogan. At your door. Four of them."

"Coins?" Brogan frowned and shook his head. "What are you talking about?"

Volkner spoke again, carefully, with great emphasis, his eyes blinking wetly as he made sure Brogan was listening. "*Coins*, Brogan. There are *coins* at your doorstep. Four of them."

"No." Brogan could barely speak.

Harper came up from behind, his voice calm and cold. "Are you sure, Volkner?"

The older man looked to Harper and a faint contempt painted his broad features. "Oh, I've seen them before, Harper. Not as many as you, perhaps, but I've seen them."

Brogan's ears rang with a high, sweet note that tried to seal all other sounds away. "Have you looked in the house?"

"It's forbidden, Brogan. You know that." There was regret in the words.

"How long ago?" Harper again, asking the questions that Brogan would have asked if his heart wasn't trying to break.

Volkner shook his head and spread his arms in a gesture of his sadness and frustration. "Five days since, that I know of. I visited two days before that and all was well."

"Five days?"

The winter grew in Brogan's chest. Without another word, he drove his horse forward, brushing past all of them. The gelding charged hard and the familiar landscape nearly blurred but it was not fast enough.

His dismount was more of a leap than a proper climb from the saddle. Brogan only took five strides toward the door before he saw them.

He had heard of the coins before. Had seen one as a child, but only the one and he had never touched the thing.

That they were valuable was impossible to deny. Brogan could see the weight of them where they lay on the ground in front of his home. They were large and heavy and worth far more than he'd made in the last few weeks of travel. He stepped over them and opened the door, calling out to Nora and each of his children as he entered.

It was a good place. He'd built it himself with the assistance of Harper and others. The people around him had helped as he had aided them when the time came. The town was good that way. He left Kinnett and knew that all was well with his wife and children, and that people as good and solid as Volkner were always there.

But the coins were different, weren't they?

No one answered his calls.

No one was home. He'd known they wouldn't be. There were four coins, one for each of his children and one for his wife.

When they came, when they took from a family, they always left one coin behind for each person they stole away.

One coin for each and every sacrifice.

"No."

He backed away from the door and shook his head, that feeling of dread growing more profound.

"No. No. No. Nononononononononono…"

The coins.

He looked to the ground again and saw them properly. Four coins. Just as Volkner had said.

Without thinking about the possibilities, he bent and touched them. They were weighty, to be sure. The largest gold coins he had ever seen or touched. The metal was as cold as the air, colder, perhaps, as he held them in his hands.

They were marked with unfamiliar images and symbols.

As he held them, Harper dismounted and came toward him.

"Brogan..." Had he ever heard so much sorrow in his friend's voice before? No, surely not. Harper was not a man who held onto his grief. He was gifted that way. When his mother died as a child he'd cried for fifteen minutes then never again that Brogan knew of. When his father grew ill and withered five years later there were no tears at all.

"Harper." He could barely recognize his own voice. "You know the Grakhul. You've dealt with them."

"Aye." Harper did not turn away from him, did not flinch, but held his gaze. "What you would do, it's forbidden. You know this."

"Four of them, Harper? My entire family?"

"Brogan, it's the law in all Five Kingdoms. 'When the Grakhul offer coin it must be taken.'"

"My entire family, Harper." Brogan's voice was stronger now. Louder.

"Brogan."

"My entire family! How many do they take at a time?"

"Four. You know this, too."

The world did not grow gray, as he feared it might. It grew red.

"How long do they take to offer up their sacrifices?"

"How would I know that, Brogan?"

Part of Brogan knew Harper was trying to make him see reason. But where it mattered, Brogan did not care.

"Is there a chance that my Nora is still alive?"

Harper licked his lips. He looked as nervous as he ever had.

"There is a chance, yes, but it is slim." Harper held up his hand as Brogan started for his horse. "You don't know where they are, Brogan."

"No. I do not." He looked away from the gelding and toward his friend. "But you do."

"I cannot. You know this too."

"My entire family. All of them. Has that ever happened before?"

"No one knows how they make their choices." Harper shook his head as Brogan started walking again.

"Take me to them. Maybe I can make them change their minds."

He could see Harper wanting to argue again. He knew his friend well. They had fought side by side on a score of occasions and traveled together long enough that even if they had not grown together in the same town they'd have claimed fellowship.

"I have to try, Harper." His hands clenched into fists around the four cold, metal coins. They were of such a size that his fists could not completely close. "I have to."

Harper stood completely still for one more moment, then he sighed. "So let's go see if we can get your family back."

"I owe you."

"I've owed you for a lifetime." Harper shook his head and spat. He was not happy. There was nothing to be happy about.

Volkner was coming his way, his ambling stride leaving him swaying one way then the other. Brogan knew exactly how much the man ached inside for failing to stop Nora and the children from being taken.

"I am so sorry, Brogan."

"You could not have stopped them." It was all he could manage as a defense for his friend. It was the truth. No one could stop the Grakhul. They were called by many names, not the least of which was the Undying. Every story of anyone trying to prevent a family member from being taken ended poorly for the would-be saviors.

Brogan climbed back into the saddle and turned toward the Broken Swords. The sun gleamed off the distant shards in a display of colors that was the envy of rainbows, and Brogan did not care in the least.

Somewhere beyond those mountains his family was being dragged to their deaths.

He would save them or he would die trying.

Niall Leraby walked through the woods and let himself commune with the world around him. Not far away he could hear the Weeping River living up to its name, the waters sighing and crying as they pattered over the crystalline rocks and worried their way past the thick roots from the garrah trees that leaned over the river as if to protect their young.

A dozen paces away a doe looked at him and froze, waiting to see what he would do. He nodded in her direction and ignored her otherwise. He loved a good cut of venison, but he wasn't here to hunt for meat. He was looking for the proper herbs to satisfy Mosara's needs. The master gardener was not a hard man to work for, but he expected nothing less than perfection in what was brought to him. Less than that, he often said, would lead to a person dying.

There were some gardeners who tended to the trees on an estate or two, and then there were gardeners like Mosara, who handled the landscape at the palace. Some day, if he were bright enough and learned his lessons well, Niall would take his place there. For now he learned and in the process he wandered the woods outside of the city and plucked this root or that leaf or even an occasional berry, because Mosara told him he had to.

"All and well," he said to himself. "There are worse ways to spend an afternoon." That was the truth of it, too. He was happy with his lot in life. There were few who could say that in his estimation.

The deer was almost behind him now, and he had let her drift from his attention when she suddenly bolted, charging past him and leaping a distance that was startling to witness. She did not wait around, but continued her rapid escape from the area.

He turned to see what might have startled her, and saw the cloaked figure a dozen feet away.

Niall was not a fool. Upon occasion he was accused of being too trusting, but he seldom let himself get caught unawares.

His fingers tightened on the walking staff in his right hand and he made himself appear calm.

"Well met."

The cowl was filled only with darkness and whomever it was that looked back from under it made no response.

"Was there something you needed help with? Are you lost?" It happened from time to time, even away from the city. People could get lost. In the woods if they ate the wrong things they could easily get addled and forget where they were going.

Instead of speaking the figure tossed a glittering trinket into the air and Niall watched as the shining metal arced toward him. No. Not a trinket.

A coin.

The metal hit the ground in front of Niall and landed on its edge. The loam under his feet was soft, and the heavy coin cut the surface of the stuff and stood at a nearly impossible angle, like a dagger driven into flesh.

"What are you doing?" Niall asked, but he already knew the answer.

He took a step back and shifted his balance. The staff rose up from the ground and he held it in a two-handed grip.

"I do not follow your gods." He did his best to sound stern. "Find another."

The cloaked figure shuddered and came toward him, moving quickly. "No." The word was not spoken, it was hissed.

Niall brought his staff around in a brutal arc and aimed the thicker end of the hard wood at the blackness of the cowl's depths. Somehow he missed. His aim was good, but the stranger moved too quickly and dodged his attack.

Niall shook his head. He wanted this done and sooner rather than later.

While he was contemplating what he wanted something hit him hard in the back of his head. The wooden staff fell from his hands and he grunted then fell forward.

When he hit the ground, the cold coin of the Grakhul scraped along his jaw and narrowly avoided drawing blood.

There were more of them. Not one shape, but half a dozen or more, and they moved around him, cutting off any chance of escape.

He would have risen if he could have. The cloaked figure leaned over him and spoke again. "The gods do not need your faith. They need your life."

They fell on him then, their hands feverishly hot, their breath rancid and diseased. He did not know how many of them attacked; he could not tell for certain, but he saw their faces and knew a fear deeper than he ever had before.

After that the darkness swallowed Niall whole.

They rode hard, and as they went they gathered more riders to join them.

They did not manage an army, but there were enough folk who either owed Brogan for past deeds, had suffered from the same loss in the past, or would work for coin, that they gathered twenty in all. More would have been too cumbersome.

Harper led the way.

Harper, who could be so secretive and who had spent time among the Grakhul, protecting deliveries to their nameless keep in the forsaken northeast. The laws of the Five Kingdoms forbade travel to the area. It was the land reserved for the Grakhul, and unless those very people offered safe passage, the foolish that trespassed did not live long to speak of their journeys.

"We have to follow the proper passages across the land. Stray too far and death will follow."

Harper's words dragged Brogan from his thoughts.

"How do you know these paths?"

The man's smile was thin and unreadable. "I was trained to be here. I'm betraying a trust."

"Do you think I don't know what I've asked of you?" Brogan's voice was soft as the finest leather. "Do you think I ask it lightly?"

"If I doubted you, I would not be here." Harper did not flinch from his gaze. "She is your wife, and they are your children, but I've loved them too. They're as much my family as you are, Brogan."

"Why do they take them, Harper?"

"Why does the wind blow? The gods make demands and those who follow them obey those demands."

Really there was no more to say and so they rode on as quickly as they safely could.

The land they finally reached was bleak, a dismal collection of black rock and broken shale that fell toward a dim, gray shoreline of more shale and dark sands. The ocean beyond it was equally uninviting and violent besides. The waves at high tide slammed themselves furiously against the shoreline and dashed into the blades of rock with murderous force. The vibrations from the impacts could be felt through the leather of his boot heels.

According to Harper more than one fool had attempted to attack by that route but none had succeeded. Few had ever approached the nameless keep of the Grakhul and come back. Those that did were never the same. Strong men were broken by what they saw and their flesh sometimes withered where they had strayed too far from the proper path.

Harper pointed out the Gateway to them. The place that the Grakhul claimed led to the home of the gods.

At a distance the monolithic Gateway rose from the night time waters, a massive bridge of dark stone that sometimes was merely an arch and other times revealed the land beneath it. They had heard of the Gateway before, but only one of them had ever seen it. Few saw the Gateway and fewer still saw the keep. These were forbidden things, as ordered by the royal families of the Five Kingdoms. Those rare few given permission to visit were allowed only because the Grakhul deemed them worthy. Harper was one of the fortunate souls trained to find his way through what seemed like an unremarkable terrain.

None of them looked at the Gateway for long. There was something about that odd stone bridge over the waters that hurt the eyes and made the mind ache.

After a scan of the area Brogan McTyre pushed aside the idea of attacking from the shore below. There were other ways that might prove slightly less dangerous.

"Well, now we know why no one ever attacks this place." Laram scowled as he spoke.

The keep was built into the side of the dark stone cliff. Somewhere in the distant past madmen had decided to risk life and limb and carve the damnable place into existence. The very structure gave off a feeling of extreme age, even if one didn't take the time to notice where the winds had smoothed a few of the edges.

Brogan looked toward Laram and nodded. He felt exactly the same way. The difference was that he was the one leading the assault and couldn't actually voice that opinion.

He shook his head and spat into the cold sea air. If he thought too much about the dangerous air of the place, if he let himself worry, he'd lose his anger. He needed that right now to keep him warm and to keep him brave.

Unconsciously he let his fingers roam into the pouch secured on the inside of his broad leather belt, where the four coins rested. He did not need to see them. He'd memorized every detail of their surfaces. They'd been pressed between his belt and the fabric of his kilt for days, but when his fingers touched the heavy gold coins they still felt cold. He understood cold as he never had before.

"Enough. The sun's up in a few hours." He squinted into the wind and looked toward the east. "Though around here it might be hard to tell. Let's find a way in. We've bloody work to do."

A few voices muttered agreement but most were silent. They were here because they owed Brogan a debt or because they had experienced similar pains. Brogan couldn't hope to offer enough to offend the gods. Where others had allowed the old ways to continue, Brogan intended to get his family back or make sure it never happened again.

Harper spoke up, dark hair flipping lazily around his lean face, dark eyes staring intently at Brogan. "You are sure you want to do this? It breaks all of the laws."

Brogan knew the man was trying to be the voice of reason, but anger and reason have never been close associates. "I did not ask you here to stop me, Harper, and you know that."

His thin mouth broke into a crooked grin that made the man look younger by years. "I never said I would stop you, Brogan. Only that I would aid you in any way I can.

Sometimes that means saying the things you do not want to hear."

Brogan put a heavy hand on his friend's shoulder and nodded. "I thank you for that, but I mean to have my family today. Will you join me?"

Harper licked his lips. "I have never been one to turn away from blood. No reason to start now." The leaner man looked toward the shore and the odd, rough stone that marked the top of the Grakhul keep. "There is a pathway. It's right at the edge and it is steep. If you are afraid of heights, you might wish to turn back." Almost as an afterthought he added, "The horses will have to stay behind. They'd never manage to keep their footing."

"How do the Grakhul manage it?"

Harper looked at him for a long moment and barely even seemed to breathe. The man was seldom bothered by much. "They aren't human, Brogan. Make no mistake of it. They are not like us, no matter how much they might look the part."

Brogan spat again. "No turning back. Let's go."

Harper, the only one of them who knew the ways to enter the keep without dying for the effort, led the way with that same half-smile on his face.

Harper sighed. "No turning back, indeed, Brogan. No turning back now. Not ever again."

Brogan had heard the warnings before. They had all been raised on admonitions about what it meant to defy the Grakhul. Those had always been enough in the past.

Everything changed when it happened to your loved ones. He understood that now. There would be no forgiveness for whatever happened. For that reason alone he owed a debt of blood to each of the men with him.

They were mostly mercenaries. They'd fought at one time or another for each of the kingdoms. The thing about being sought for crimes was first people had to know you had committed them. None of them were foolish enough to admit to the crimes. Well, except possibly Harper, but he could only hope the man kept his tongue.

"Harper?"

"Yes?"

Brogan looked to his friend and took a deep breath. "I don't know what I'll do if we're too late."

"I'd say we should pray, but that might not go the right way. I mean who would we pray to?"

He could always trust Harper to find the most challenging part of a quandary. Who indeed?

The others would not talk. Like him they were here for personal reasons. Blood sometimes calls for blood.

Harper was right. Madmen had surely designed the slope down into the keep. The stone was slicked with algae and nearly too smooth to allow a man to walk. Instead they clutched at the wall of the winding, twisting path, and half-walked, half-slid toward the plateau below.

Brogan, a man bent on either salvation or revenge, could feel his heart hammering in his chest. After ten minutes of doing their best to keep their footing, Harper and the men he was leading made it to the flat land of the keep itself.

The ground here was just as damp, and the green slime that had been under their feet coated the walls of the ancient structure as well, lending it an unsettling level of camouflage.

The winds along the cliff face were rough and those men who had long hair and had not already tied it back began the task almost immediately. The sole exception was Harper, who remained as calm as ever.

For one moment Brogan pondered whether the man would betray him, then crushed the thought. They had grown up in the same town and been friends as long as he could recall.

Harper looked his way and drew his chosen weapons. In his right hand he carried a long blade with a hook at the end. In his other hand he gripped a thin sword that was perfectly designed for a man of his leaner stature.

Harper broke the silence. He spoke softly, but did not whisper. The wind would have stolen his words away too easily. The men moved closer to hear him. "We move around the first wall here, and we'll see their sacrificial pits. There are four of them. They are large, but they have no decorations to let you know they are there. Be very careful. You have already felt the surface of the ground here. Those pits, they are where the bodies go." He didn't have to say which bodies. They all knew.

The Grakhul had always come and they demanded their sacrifices.

The Grakhul did not ask. They took. They left only the coins. The weight of them pulled at Brogan's belt.

Harper looked his way and Brogan realized the man was still speaking. "Beyond the pits is the great hall. It's where the prisoners are kept and where all of the Grakhul feast." He looked at the ground ahead. Dark and green and damp against a gray sky that showed no sign of a sun. There were clouds out there, a gathering black bank that rose up the gods alone knew how far. The waves raged and threw themselves at the land.

Brogan knew how they felt.

"Lead the way, Harper. Let this be finished." His words were low, but heard by all.

Harper nodded, and that smirk marred his features as he turned and moved forward, sliding across the ground with a grace that Brogan envied.

Brogan strode across the level deck, with stone on three sides and a severe drop to the sea below on his left, and pushed his boots into the thick slime, balancing himself with each step he took. After only a few paces the slippery surface lost its coating of green and became a surer, safer footing.

Harper moved around the last corner and he followed. Five steps and Brogan saw the first of the pits. They were vast, indeed, and dark: cavernous holes large enough to easily swallow a fully loaded wagon and as perfectly round as anything he had ever seen. The walls were completely smooth and as far as he could tell no lichen or moss touched the stone. He had no idea how far they went down, but the cliffs ran for a few hundred feet before they met the ocean and he could feel a breeze rising from the pit. The breeze smelled of the sea and darker things.

Some moments take forever. There was so much to see, so much to absorb, and Brogan's mind was a sponge at that moment, thirsty for information.

No more than three heartbeats to take it all in, but only one was needed before Brogan was screaming.

There were four pits. The edges of three of them were coated in a residual wash of crimson that painted the dark stone.

At the pit closest to them a single man dropped a small, bloodied body into the well and looked up at the sound that came from Brogan's mouth. The shape that fell into the pit was tiny, no larger than a young boy. Brogan recognized Braghe's face before the figure dropped.

The second pit had already been abandoned, and the man who'd been standing there was walking toward the farthest of the four deep holes.

At the third, a man was looking down into the depths of the well – and turned toward the group as Brogan screamed.

At the fourth of the sacrificial pits seven men still stood. They held a woman by her wrists, by her ankles, to stop her from escaping. She tried, too. She thrashed and struggled and wailed at them.

Tears stained Nora's face. Through the markings they had painted on her flesh, he could see the tears as they cut at the colors that tried to hide her beauty from him. A hundred strides and more away and he knew Nora's face, her shape, as well as he knew his own hands. She was his world, his breath, his light.

"No!"

Brogan charged forward, barely looking at anything beyond Nora.

She looked his way, her mouth an open wound showing her pain. Despite it all, his warrior's brain calculated. There were four pits. Only one was still untouched. The sum was painfully simple. His children were dead. But there was still a chance, wasn't there? There was the possibility that he could reach Nora in time.

He ran for Nora, and Harper ran beside him and raised his chosen weapons. As a unit the rest charged forward, spreading out in an effort to block any attempts their enemies might make at escape.

The single man standing at the first pit looked their way. He was dressed in a dark tunic and boots. His head was shaved clean and his skin was pale. He stared without any comprehension, an expression so completely shocked by the appearance of strangers that it bordered on comical. His eyes flew wide, his mouth dropped open and his hands raised up to clutch at his chest. And while he goggled in their direction, Harper ran a blade from his clavicle up to his nose, splitting everything between in one stroke.

The dead man fell as Harper pulled the sword free, never missing a step in his stride.

Brogan ran past the corpse and continued on. There would be time to look at bodies when the living had been sorted.

The wind roared and threatened to push him aside. The

wind did not matter. There was Nora and nothing else.

As he went, Brogan pulled his axe from its sheath.

Four of the men around Nora came their way, most of them dressed much like the corpse left behind by Harper. Not a one of them was armed and as a whole they looked confused by the idea of anyone attacking them in this place of ritual and sacrifice.

Brogan sneered and raced toward them, his axe hefted up in his thick arms, his eyes locked on the closest of the pale bastards that had taken his family from him. He charged, a roar building in his chest. Four men stood between him and Nora. They would not stand for long.

The axe cut deeply into pale flesh and brought forth a river of crimson. He did not stop as the first of the bodies fell. The second man died where he stood. The next in line flinched back, tried to escape, but never had a chance. The blade cleaved through his chest and only stopped when it reached his backbone. A hard kick wrenched the body away from his weapon and Brogan roared again, the fury consuming him.

And up ahead Nora let out the smallest of sounds as a blade from the man beside her pierced her heart.

There was no thought left in him. Brogan smashed into the next fool between him and his wife and barged him into the pit. Another came too close and suffered the same fate as he reached for Nora.

The man who'd killed her – for even then, much as he wanted to believe otherwise, Brogan knew the truth of the matter – looked his way and tried to speak out a warning. His words were in a language Brogan did not know, but whatever he'd been saying in any tongue would have been wasted breath.

Brogan brought the axe up above his head and cut the man in two.

Whatever the plans, whatever possible ideas the Grakhul had in mind, they were forgotten when Brogan came forward. They fled from him, backing away and chattering in their foolish tongue as he dropped the axe from his grip and barely felt the sway of it on his wrist. Brogan moved to take Nora in his arms.

His wife looked at him. Her dark eyes rolled in their sockets and she looked his way, and whatever she might have wanted to say, whatever she might have been feeling, it faded from her, unuttered, as her ruined heart stopped beating.

There were only a dozen or so men. They never stood a chance against his gathering. If he had been alone Brogan would have died and never even noticed. He was lost staring at the remains of his beloved for a time. Who could say how long? Surely not Brogan himself.

He rose slowly, Nora in his arms, his axe swaying against his wrist, held in place by the heavy leather strap. It tapped against him several times but if it cut he did not notice.

Harper looked his way with haunted eyes and shook his head in sorrow.

"I am so very sorry, Brogan."

Brogan had no words.

Around him his men stood guard and looked on. Not far away the ocean roared and the wind howled and Brogan understood all too well their fury.

For a moment he considered the possibility of taking Nora's body home with him and giving her a proper burial.

Instead, he kissed her sweet face one last time and let her fall into the deep pit. A mother, he knew, would want to be with her children. "Let this be your last sacrifice."

Harper put a hand on his shoulder with great care. "Brogan, there are more of them. There is a *city's* worth of people here."

As he spoke, their enemies made themselves known. They came running from the great hall Harper had spoken of, most of them dressed much like the corpses around them. None were armed. None had even contemplated being attacked in this place.

The axe found its way back to his hands. It felt weightless as Brogan contemplated his enemies.

The closest of them bellowed in his gibberish language and Harper held out a hand, stopping Brogan for a moment.

He called to the strangers and they quickly exchanged words. Harper turned to his friend. "Truly I am sorry, Brogan. All of your family…"

"I know this." Four pits and now all four were painted with blood.

"They say the gods demand fresh sacrifices or they will tear this world apart."

Brogan's voice was hoarse with tension. "Let them."

The time for considerations and discussions was done. Brogan charged toward the speaker and cut into his stomach with one hard swing. Before him, the gathered men of the Grakhul stared, horrified, and did little or nothing to defend themselves.

Around him, behind him, he heard more battle cries. They owed him debts and so they came. They had lost to the Grakhul and so they shared their rage. They all had their reasons for breaking the laws and not one of them felt any regret.

The battle was brutal and fast; a reaping of bloodied wheat that fell to the stone floors without much protest and few attempts at defense.

When it was done, all of them were winded – murder is exhausting work – and Brogan looked at the corpses and frowned. It made no sense. These were not, could not be, the Grakhul he had heard so much about.

Laram said it for him. "These are the brutes who demand sacrifices?"

Harper shook his head. "No. They must be out and seeking their next sacrifices." He frowned. "The women, the children, they are hiding somewhere below. What do you want to do about that, Brogan?"

Brogan looked at the corpses. For as long as anyone knew, the Grakhul had come and taken and left their coins. For as long as he could remember it had not mattered. Now, however, his family, his entire family…

"We gather the children and the women. They come with us."

Harper looked at him with one raised eyebrow and that damnable smirk. "What will you do with them?"

"Give them to those who lost their families." He shrugged, not completely certain what he planned. "They can decide for themselves what should happen to scum who took their loved ones."

"And the bodies? What if the families see the bodies?"

His face in that moment, he knew, was not the face of a loving man. "Let them know my loss. Our loss. Let them grieve for their loved ones before they are given to the people who will judge them."

Laram spoke again. Laram, who was always a more decent man than Brogan. "We could push them into the pits."

Brogan shook his head. "No. There will be no more bodies in those damned pits. They've had their blood."

That was all there was to say about the matter.

The women and the children of the Grakhul did not go gently. They were not the least bit intimidated by the gathering of men and if they grieved for their loved ones they showed it by taking up weapons and fighting against the invaders.

The first attack came from a boy of perhaps ten who charged out of a darkened doorway with a knife in his hand and came at Brogan. One step out of the way took care of the knife. One fist to the side of the boy's head left him reeling on the ground.

The second attack came from the boy's mother, who charged at Brogan, swinging a small axe. Laram tripped the woman in midstride and sent her sprawling. She let out a cry and dropped her weapon. Rather than stopping, she came back up a second time with a dagger drawn from her belt.

Harper stopped her with a word. She froze and looked at the men around her, her eyes wide. By the time she was done assessing the situation Harper had placed the blade of his weapon to her throat.

Harper's words were a mystery but his tone clearly offered a warning. There were several exchanges between the woman and the soldier and when it was done he put away his sword.

"They'll come with us."

"What did you say to her?"

"They could come with us or they could die." Harper eyed the woman for a moment. "I also told her we'd make sure the children suffered before they died." The woman sighed, put her hand around her mouth to amplify her words, then bellowed out in the gibberish language of her people. Within minutes, a very large group was forming. Twenty men, all told. If the families got serious, Brogan's group would never have a chance, despite the fact that half the women had little ones gathering around their knees. There were twenty able-bodied and well-armed men. There were hundreds of women and children.

Brogan shook his head and spat. "If we're taking them, we need to be able to control them."

Harper shook his head. "No reason. They'll follow us."

"Why would they?"

The very woman who'd tried to attack him answered. Her voice was thick with the strange accent of her usual tongue, but he understood her well enough. "Because you have damned this place and the people here. Our only hope, no matter how small, is to be away from here."

She would say no more. Instead she soothed her child, the boy he'd punched in the head, and then she and the rest of her people followed after Brogan and Laram and the rest.

Harper and four others did not immediately leave. They caught up instead. Brogan noticed but said nothing.

Another exchange with one of the women and he and the others left again, coming back with a few wagons that had seen better days and horses to draw them.

One of the women led the horses and found a different route that wound upwards, to the top of the plateau. The exit point was nearly impossible to see and Brogan wasn't surprised that Harper had not known of it.

Within an hour they were on their way from the keep and moving in a very large serpentine across the nearly barren land. A few of the women had gathered possessions, but most did not bother.

As they left the sky roared with a hundred strokes of thunder and fingers of light ripped through the darkening clouds, cutting their way across the skies and bullwhipping strokes across the horizon. Brogan turned to look at the great Gateway. He watched as tongue after tongue of lightning stroked the thing but did it no harm.

"How often does that happen?" Laram was making conversation, nothing more. The woman with her son was walking nearby and looked at them but did not answer. Her smile was not pleasant.

The sea behind them raged on, hammering at the shoreline. The winds blew harder, as if inviting them to leave the area even faster than planned.

Brogan should have felt victorious. He had avenged his family and stopped the bastard Grakhul from ever doing to another what they had done to him. Instead he felt hollowed out and left to wither and die.

CHAPTER TWO
Traveling the Winding Paths

The attackers came fast and targetted the children. That was exactly the right thing to do if they wanted the women to stop defending the keep and themselves.

Myridia listened to the men as they spoke. Some of them were there for revenge. They'd lost family to the Grakhul, and like so many considered the people of the keep evil. They were wrong. They simply did not understand.

Myridia listened, and she learned.

The leader was a brute named Brogan McTyre. He was a large man with dark, reddish brown hair that was currently braided down his back. He kept his face shaved closely and he wore the clothes of a westerner; a loose shirt, a vest, a kilt. On clear days she and her family had seen hints of the distant mountains in that direction. The westerners were known for fighting and for selling their services to the highest bidder.

She remembered the sacrifices. That was part of her duties. She remembered them and she honored them. Judging by the way he was dressed she knew that most of the last moon's sacrifices were his people.

They had died honorably, even the youngest among them.

The children had all been placed in wagons. The wagons were drawn by a few old nags that were still around the keep. Mostly they were there as food, but the He-Kisshi – the rulers of the keep – believed that a few extra animals could prove useful. So did the raiders.

The children wailed and cried as children do, right up until Myridia barked an order at them to keep their tongues. After that they listened carefully and obeyed. They still stared out at the vast plain of Ulgrthh, but they no longer made noises. Myridia understood. They had never been away from the keep before. Until this very time she had not, either.

Unwynn, who was wiser by far in Myridia's eyes, spoke softly to the children, "We move on, little ones. This place is no longer safe for us, the gods have decreed that the land is now tainted."

"Why?" The boy who asked was only seven years old, and he blinked back tears as he watched the landscape moving.

"Myridia will explain to you." Unwynn looked at her for only a second, but the scolding was clear enough. She had lost her patience with the children over a trifling thing and now she would make it right.

"The gods sometimes punish foolish people. They have done so ten times before by reaching into the heavens and pulling down demons to make mortal people suffer."

"What's a demon?" The little girl, all of five, looked at her with utter fascination. She wanted to learn everything. That was the way with Grakhul women. Boys sometimes seemed slower, but they studied different things. They learned the methods by which the gods were observed and the women learned the history that the gods wanted preserved.

"The gods stride the universe. They walk between the stars and they seek places that they like to call their homes. Sometimes they meet other things that feel the same way and when that happens they must capture and defeat their new enemies.

"This has happened many times. The gods who we serve came here a long time ago and on the way they fought many demons and even other gods. Those they defeated they captured and put into special prisons. Those prisons are like bubbles in the water. They are there and they sometimes move around and we can even see them if we know how to look, but they cannot be touched by us any more than the bubbles in the water can be touched and captured. They're too different. Do you understand?"

It took a few seconds but the children nodded. Of course there was more to it than that, but it was a concept they could grasp.

"The demons are captured because they are dangerous, but they are kept because they have uses.

"We have always served the gods since they came here; they chose us as their servants. We did not want to serve them at first, but the gods reached up and plucked a demon from the skies and set that demon here. That is why the land here does not grow. We learned our lesson and served faithfully and so the gods gave us ways to have food and to live where no one else can without dying.

"Then they moved out among the people of this world and demanded sacrifices. They showed what had happened here, where once there were great forests and fields as fertile and green as any in the world, and they said, 'Do not fail us or this will happen to you.' Nobody listened. They did not believe.

"The people said, 'We have our own gods. We do not need you.'

"You should never say such things to gods.

"The gods grew angry and there was a great battle between the gods already here and the gods we follow. The gods we follow won that war and killed all the gods before them or drove them away. Then they took one of the demons they had captured in the stars and placed the demon on the ground for all to see before releasing it. The demon did what demons do and destroyed everything around it before the gods sealed it away again in its prison and told the people to listen to them. The people obeyed because they had no choice."

She paused a moment. "I see the look on your faces. You want to know what demons do. They can do many things. Sometimes they take the bodies of people and use them as puppets. Sometimes they suck the life out of the land and steal away whole cities. That is what they did the very first time a demon was placed here by the gods. There was once a vast city here. But the demon took it and used it as a toy. They took most of our people at the same time.

"The gods have punished this world ten times with demons. They have many more demons, but they will not use them again. The last time they said, 'The time for warnings is done. If we are disobeyed again we will destroy the world. We will be fed or all you love will die.' That is the truth as we know it."

The children were not comforted by the story. They were terrified, as they should have been. Myridia understood. This was all new to them, far from their life in the keep. To hear that the gods had no mercy in their hearts was not a comforting thing.

Next to her Unwynn was staring out at the plains, following the trail to the ocean. The land was exactly curved enough to take away all signs of the water, but the older woman stared just the same.

"What will happen when they get back?" Myridia suspected she already knew the answer, but asked just the same.

Unwynn didn't even turn to face her. "They will come after us, but it will be too late."

"Why too late?"

"Because you will be gone by then. You and the others. Leave the mothers. Leave the children. Just select the ones you know can fight. Then leave."

Myridia shook her head and frowned. "What if they decide to kill the ones who stay behind?"

Finally Unwynn looked to her. Fine lines showed around her eyes, but otherwise she could have been of birthing age. The sacrifices aged differently. It was one of the many things about them that was different. "We are already dead. All of us. Everything is dead. Never forget that."

Myridia nodded her head and forced herself not to lower her eyes in respect. There was no time for courtesy. "What would you have us do?"

"Escape. Leave here. Find the others if you can. They are far to the west, beyond the mountains."

Her throat worked. "And if we fail?"

"As I have said before, we are already dead. There is little chance that you can change that, but if you are fast enough it is possible." Unwynn looked away again. "When you are ready, I will make a distraction."

"To the waters?"

The older woman nodded. "It is your only chance. The plains are too open and they will find you. Head away from the keep and stay close to the shore. Avoid the rocks."

Myridia gathered the others quickly, fourteen in all, mostly using hand gestures. At least one of the men who had taken them spoke the True Tongue and that was one too many. She knew him. He had come and bartered with the people before. He was not trustworthy. Given a chance she would do her best to kill him, but that was not as significant as escape.

When they were ready, she spoke softly to Unwynn. "We are prepared."

Unwynn did not acknowledge her. Instead she spun on her heel and strode quickly up the column. She had promised a distraction. Now was the time to move.

Myridia waved her hands and the others joined her as she ran toward the distant surf. The dark shoal was slick, but there were none of her people who were not used to that. Walking above the keep, walking near the waters, the surfaces were always covered in algae or fungi and made slippery in most cases.

One hundred paces and they'd heard no alarm and Myridia thought for a moment that they would not be seen but there were sudden screams.

Male screams.

Hopefully her friend managed to kill a few of the bastards before she died.

The ground jumped and pounded with every stride she made. The men behind her called out. She heard them, but their words meant nothing.

Three hundred steps and her lungs were aching. Her feet throbbed. The land ended now in a sheer drop. That drop, she knew, led to the sea.

Another hundred steps and Lorae fell down. She was quick to get back up, skinned knee and all. The waters were close now, and the surf hammered the shore as it always had.

Myridia was the first over the side and she jumped and arched her body as she left the cliff side and looked down into the turbulent sea.

The water boiled with thick foam that ran furiously between long teeth of black. The teeth looked hungry.

The trick was not to let the teeth taste you.

Around and behind her the others were following her lead, as Myridia let out a call to the Masters and dropped into the water. The teeth had no satisfaction from her and she swam deep into the ocean. Somewhere up above it was possible that the men would come to see the bodies left behind. They would be disappointed.

The changes were subtle, but they were enough. Myridia gulped water and felt it expelled from her sides. The air she needed she pulled from the waters. The rest was waste. Her fingers and toes grew longer, a process that always ached, but in a pleasant way. The webs grew between her digits and she moved faster, swam deeper.

Around her the others called out in song and she listened.

The song was beautiful. It was dark and haunting and filled her soul with a longing she would never manage to recover from.

It was the song of the sea, and the sea was so very demanding.

Brogan looked on as the women ran. They charged for the sea and he let them go. They had a caravan of hundreds with them and near as he could figure a dozen or so women fled.

Part of him screamed that he should follow, that he should send some of the lads at the very least, but he did nothing. He watched them moving away and instead of acting lost himself for a moment in memories that he would rather have forgotten.

Dead. All dead. Every last member of his family.

No. He shook that away. Later, perhaps, when they were not dealing with the real possibilities of dangerous reactions to what they'd done.

Laram and Mosely had been forced to cut down one of the pale women. She'd come at them screaming and throwing stones with unsettling accuracy. Laram was sporting an angry welt above his left eye. An inch or so lower and he'd have been half blind for life.

He had no doubt she was meant as a distraction to allow the other women to flee. He'd have done the same. Harper looked on, his telltale smile faded down to a puzzled expression.

The distraction? It was what he'd have done. Tactics, and good ones under the circumstances. There was nowhere for the women to go, however, and he wasn't going to chase after them. It would cost too many hours and leave too many openings for others to try escaping the same way.

Escaping? The only thing below that cliff was angry water and daggers of stone. More likely they'd killed themselves to avoid being used.

He couldn't blame them. There were a few of the men talking about what they'd enjoy doing with the women. Only a few. Most were still trying to decide what they should do about being outlaws.

Not long after they'd started away Laram had come forward and pointed out something that was quite simple, really. "We are walking with prisoners. They are proof that we've broken one of the most important laws of the Five Kingdoms."

Brogan had almost asked him what he meant before realization set in. They'd been mercenaries on many occasions and most of the group had worked as highwaymen when the times demanded it, but the unspoken rule was to never leave proof.

The column of whelps and women behind them was proof that they'd been to the keep of the Grakhul and been about bloody business.

"Tell the lads to pull up their hoods and cover their faces. We get to Saramond in two days' time if we keep on. When we get there we sell what we have to the slavers."

"I thought you didn't like slavers."

Brogan found himself staring at the red mark on his

friend's forehead. "I don't." He gestured to the column of women and their young ones. "I like the notion of killing all of them less and I like being executed even less than that."

Laram nodded and started away.

"Laram."

The man looked back his way, his fine blond hair obscuring half of his face in the harsh winds before he scooped it away with his fingers again. "Aye?"

"Remind the lads that no one wants to buy damaged goods. If they're going to take what they want, make sure they don't do too much harm."

He'd have preferred the idea of them leaving the women alone, and the children too. He was not for the notion of taking from a woman simply because the desire arose. He was also not the one to stop the men with him.

They were not in a battle. They were there because he'd called them and they'd responded. What they did in their time was their own business, but he also knew most would talk and not react. They weren't animals, just killers and now, slavers.

When he closed his eyes, his rage wanted to do more. When he thought of his family and their deaths, he wanted to kill all of the survivors. He wanted them to suffer a thousand cuts for each second he would be without his family, but that could not happen. That way lay madness. The rage was there, still burning, but like a furnace he had banked that anger. He would use it if he had to, as a tool, not as the master of his world.

He spat again.

The affair was almost finished.

They would be riding away from this insanity soon enough.

Behind them the storms raged on, and the winds smelled of lightning strikes and the sea.

CHAPTER THREE
He-Kisshi

Rains hammered down on the landscape, and washed over Niall and the other three who were chained in place along with him. From time to time the ferocity of the storm calmed enough to let him think. Niall shivered and felt his eyes flicker open. He was tired and sore and the chill in the air had taken away what little energy he had.

He opened his mouth and captured rainwater, drinking it greedily. It was better than what his captors had offered. Cleaner.

Not that it mattered. He had never seen a member of the Undying, but he knew they were the ones that had him. There were enough stories of the fiends. They only came for one reason and that was to claim their sacrifices.

There were twelve captors, and they were loathsome.

They rode dark things. That was the only way he could explain them. They seemed horses most of the time, with proper tails and hooves and manes, but sometimes, when he looked at them from a different angle, the shapes were wrong. Also, after several days of travel he had never heard the things make a single horse-like noise. They hissed from time to time, and on one occasion he was certain the damned thing pulling the long flat wagon along had barked.

The platform he and the others rode on was long and narrow, and each of them was manacled at the ankles and wrists. Three men including himself and his neighbor's boy, Ligel. Ligel was to his right. To his left was the only girl in their gathering.

Their feet were kept on the rough wooden planks by short chains. Their wrists were held above their heads on T-shaped beams. Chained in place and made to stand as the procession continued. They were offered water to drink, but they were not offered food.

He had no concept of how long they'd been moving, how long he'd been locked in chains. His feet ached from standing, but his arms had moved past pain and into a numb, throbbing sensation a long while back.

The memories of when they came for him were fragmented and blurred, lost in the darkness of whatever it was they'd been using to keep all of them docile.

He'd been hungry when they started, but now he could barely remember what food tasted like and his stomach no longer protested. It was the water. He knew that much. The water they drank was not the same as the Undying consumed. It came from a different barrel.

Though he had never been the sort to deal in poisons, Niall knew enough about them. Before he was taken he'd been apprentice to Mosara the gardener. There was no better herbalist in the land. Before Mosara did any other training, he taught his apprentices about poisons and where they came from and what they did. The best way to avoid getting yourself killed when dealing with herbs was to avoid killing anyone by accident. The water had no unusual taste, but it made those who drank it sleepy and it dulled the reactions. His mouth tasted of water and ash. Mosara would have told him exactly what was causing the sensations, but he was a master and not a lowly apprentice.

Niall shook his head and took in deep breaths, the better to clear the fog from his mind.

The young woman beside him was whimpering softly. Her legs shook from a desire to sit, but the chains held her up and she either suffered from standing or felt the pain of her arms being stretched into a painful position. The dress she wore was plastered to her body and he could see her muscles tremble in the cold.

He frowned for a moment. The girl had been wearing proper shoes before, but now her feet were bare and the toes looked red and bloodied. It was hard to tell through the rain.

He looked up her lean body until he reached her face. Short blonde hair was glued to her skull and half obscured her wide blue eyes. She shook her head and silently begged him not to call attention to her. If she were up to something and their captors found out there would be no mercy. The creatures planned to sacrifice them as it was.

The Undying did not seem to care about the feelings of their guests, but if he had to guess they would be willing to sacrifice someone they'd already tortured. When he was younger he'd heard stories of the Undying. They once came to his family's farm and stole away three slaves. His father had been shaken by the incident, but forgave the sin because of the gold coins they left behind. Niall had seen the coins. They were large and surely worth enough to forgive a few thefts.

He looked back at the shapes ahead of them. Four of the forms rode their mounts and talked amongst themselves, uttering words that he neither understood nor felt comfortable with. The rest of them were out of sight. They'd moved ahead to prepare whatever needed to be done before the sacrifices could occur. The other four were here, he had no doubt, simply to keep the rolling platform on course.

One of them turned to look in his direction, as if it had somehow sensed his eyes on it.

It. The thing stood like a man. It walked like a man. But he knew better. The Undying appeared to wear cloaks and hoods, but he had been fighting against them when they came to take him away and the cloaks themselves were warm and had a pulse. The rains came down and no matter how hard they fell the cloaks retained their shape, unlike the garments he wore that had long since pasted themselves tightly against his body.

Where faces should have been, at the openings of the hoods, there was, instead, a wet, pinkish surface. The opening, Niall knew from having seen too much, was a mouth. There were teeth further back in that vile maw; teeth and other things that might have been tongues. Whatever they were, they moved and the breath that came from those "hoods" stank of charnel tastes.

Because he no longer cared, he spat in the creature's direction.

When the thing came back toward him he suddenly found reason to care again. Drugged waters or no, the monstrous thing was terrifying. "Oh, damn me." Too late, already damned. It was almost enough to make him laugh.

The Undying fell from the horse-thing and landed with ease before striding in his direction. There were legs there, at least, but he could not see the feet clearly. They might have worn boots, they might have had claws; whatever the case the thing squelched through the thick mud one heaving step at a time.

The creature came closer and he looked into the hooded face, his heart racing. The throat of the thing opened and closed as it breathed. He could see no eyes, no way for the monster to see him, but it did. It came closer then started walking backward, keeping pace with the wheeled platform. One of the hands reached out and grabbed his face. The flesh was dark and hot, and rough as the pads on the feet of a war dog.

When it spoke, the words came from deep within that throat. "Do not insult us. We have many ways to make you suffer that will not offend the gods."

In the distance behind the thing, a great stone arch rose from the waters beyond the edge of the cliff side. They seemed to have nearly reached the end of the world.

"Get your vile hand off me!" He tried to pull back, but the thing's hot grip was too firm and he shuddered at the hand holding his face. Whatever they were, the flesh smelled of cinnamon and other spices. It was only the breath of the beast that reeked of slaughter and decay.

The Undying squeezed and Niall moaned. The bones in his face felt like they would surely break.

The chain that whipped across the arm in front of him was enough to catch the thing's attention. Flesh, or cloth, or hide, whatever the fabric of the hellish beast, it broke as the links came down and scraped across the surface.

The Undying pulled back its arm and turned to face the source of its pain – and the girl beside Niall swept the long chain between her wrists around the creature's neck.

She spun her body and the chain wrapped around the Undying's hooded head. It let out a noise, possibly to warn the others ahead of them, but the sound became nothing but a strangled whisper.

The thing tried to pull back, but she was faster. Her body fell further away and the cloaked form staggered closer.

How had she escaped? Niall thought about her bared, bloodied feet and understood. She'd somehow picked the locks while he'd dozed in his drugged stupor.

The thing caught itself on the edge of the wagon and reared back, hauling the slight form of the girl toward it.

There was not much reach on Niall's chains. They weren't designed to let him move around comfortably. They were to hold him captive and to keep him in place.

The girl had managed to pull herself up the chains around her arms and had yanked them free. He could see that now. There was a hook that held the links. They were manacled and then the chains were lifted onto the hook, letting them adjust for the size of their captives.

Niall bent his legs as much as he could and jumped. The slack in the chains rattled, but nothing else happened. He squatted lower and did it again, whipping his hands hard as he rose. The chains did more than rattle this time. They fell loose.

He was hardly free. His ankles were still locked in place, but he had a weapon.

The Undying was pulling at the girl, a length of chain held in its left hand and the right drawing her closer. One hand stopped it from choking on the noose she'd wrapped around its throat and the other reeled in its prize.

Niall brought his hands together and swept the chains into the air, then brought the length of links down and crashed them into the vile face of the creature. Crude metal edges slapped into that hooded opening, cutting the rough maw until it bled.

The beast roared and threw its arms wide. Great flaps of what had appeared to be a cloak expanded into leathery wings and the nightmare lunged up onto the cart, its hands reaching for him. Niall fell back, a panicked scream ripping from his throat, and instantly saw the problem with his escape.

For just a moment he'd forgotten he was still chained in place.

"Oh, damn me."

"I will find another to take your place!" That vast, round

mouth with the shredded hood of flesh moved and snapped as the thing loomed over him. The wings were apart and revealed a thick, bloated body that he would have never guessed at. Bloated? There seemed plenty of muscle in either case. There was a thick leather belt with several tools on it. The creature did not bother with them.

The Undying had appeared large before, but now it was gigantic. Those heavy fleshy wings snapped in the rough winds and it lurched up onto the platform revealing the long-toed feet that had been previously hidden away. Each toe ended in a claw as thick as three of Niall's fingers. He had scant time to notice them as he was rolling away from the foot that tried to smash him into the splintered, wooden deck.

He pushed himself as far as he could away from the wooden post that had been at his back. It wasn't very far at all, and surely not enough to get away from the Undying. What had he been thinking? That somehow he could help the girl get away? That through some stroke of fortune she could return the favor?

For the second time he saw a necklace of chain suddenly lowered over the hood of the Undying, then it snapped backward with a strangled grunt. The thin girl had wrapped the chain like a noose, and now she hauled it backward as best she could, while her victim bucked and kicked and fought.

She was fierce, and used her entire body mass to pull, keeping the Undying arched back as it tried to force its hands under the links wrapped tightly around the neck.

Niall once again swung his chain up and over his head before bringing it down, this time across the abdomen of their captor.

The chain cut into flesh, tore at muscle and softer things, and the Undying rose into a sitting position, hauling the girl with it. While it once more launched for Niall, the girl took advantage of the moment and ran forward, bracing her feet on the broad back of the creature and throwing herself backward, the chains wrapped into her hands and around her wrists. Once more the hands of the Undying tried for the makeshift noose. And as it reached to defend its throat, Niall hit it again across the legs and lower abdomen.

Just that quickly it flopped down, shuddering. He did not know if he had struck something vital or if the woman fighting alongside him had managed to choke the nasty beast to death, but it shivered and let out a vile stench as it voided its bowels on the platform.

Niall panted. His arms ached. Not five feet away the young woman looked at him and nodded, her face set and determined.

As he looked toward the riders ahead of them, he gave silent thanks that they had not turned around to investigate. The rains were too heavy, perhaps, for them to have heard the noises. That, or they assumed their companion could handle the matter.

Whatever the case they were not coming back. Not yet at least.

Thin, nimble fingers worked at the chain around his wrist. He almost screamed. He hadn't expected the contact.

The girl looked at him and shook her head. "I will unshackle you but you can't fight me."

He nodded his head, speechless for the moment, and looked again to the Undying.

Ahead of them, ahead of the riders in the distance, he could see a barrage of lightning striking the coastline. The thunderclap was deafening and the light left him half blind for a moment. The horse-thing that pulled their platform seemed unimpressed.

He and the girl were both flinching and twitching and

Ligel, the neighbor's boy, all of twelve and already taken for this madness, shuddered and started awake.

The pressure of her hands fell away from his wrist, and took with it the manacle that had rubbed his flesh raw. He looked at her as she started on the other shackle and he reached down to work on his ankle restraint. There was only a metal post holding the parts together. It was snug, but with his hands freed he could pull on the lock and wiggle the damned thing free.

Up ahead the explosions of light did not abate, but actually grew more furious. The horse-thing no longer ignored the fiery display and let out a sound not at all horse-like. In the distance several shadow-forms rose into the air, one, two more, then another four – all of them with vast wings. They rose high into the electrified air and banked, turning, he had no doubt, back toward the other Undying.

That was all they could be. There had been nothing else to see on the desolate landscape.

The metal peg slid free and one leg was suddenly able to move. Niall pulled his ankle away from the chains and nearly sobbed at the pleasure of being able to move his leg properly.

The woman with him had freed his other arm and now she was looking at the skies, even as he reached for his last shackle.

"Be fast! They're coming!"

The flattened end of the metal, where they'd hammered it into the peg holes in the manacle, cut at his fingertips and he did not care. Niall let out a scream and pulled as the flesh tried to give way. A moment later, however, he was freed and standing up, staggering as he tried to regain his footing. The animal that led them was panicked now and he could see why. The skies were white and blue with fires that should not have existed. The horizon seethed as the earth exploded in wave after wave, shattered by the endless assault of lightning on the ground.

The girl grabbed his arm and tugged. "We have to go!" He knew she was screaming, could read her lips well enough, but there was almost no sound; it was hidden behind the shocking and nearly endless thunder rolling their way.

Ligel looked up at last, his eyes bleary with the poisoned waters they were fed, and stared at the blinding skies.

He was a good lad. Niall would remember the look on the boy's face for as long as he lived. The boy saw him, saw that he was free, recognized him and began to hope, even as Niall jumped down from the cart. Even as the horse that was not a horse reared up then bolted to the left, running in a blind panic that took it over the edge of the cliff and into the waters below.

Ligel looked at him the entire time before he disappeared.

It hardly mattered. None of it would ever matter, not until they were away from the destruction eating away the world ahead of them.

The girl ran across the ground, her bare feet saved only by the thick mud they had been traveling over. Niall ran with her. He could have easily run past her; his legs were longer and he had not spent countless hours using his toes to peel away the metal pegs that held his ankles locked in place.

He could have, but he did not. She had saved his life and he had every intention of returning the kindness.

CHAPTER FOUR
Dark Dealings

The man was carved from stone and dressed in satin. Beron was a slaver through and through, and he made no excuses about what he did for a living. There were plenty who opposed slavery, but none of them held any sway with Beron.

Currently he was facing off against Harper while Brogan watched. Brogan was a fighter, not a businessman. He could haggle if he had to, but had no idea how much slaves sold for, nor any interest in learning.

Beron looked his way several times, but always looked back to Harper. There was no doubt who was in charge when it came to final decisions. That was why Brogan was there. But Harper spoke for him in this.

The voices were kept low enough to avoid anyone listening in. It depended on which kingdom as to which laws applied when it came to selling slaves. Most lands did not allow the sale of newly captured enemies as slaves, but Saramond was the exception. Saramond had a king, but he did not rule the land and that was common enough knowledge. King Frankel wore the crown, but it was Beron and his ilk that truly ruled. The Slavers' Guild made most of the money that filled the royal coffers and for that reason

51

alone they were beyond reproach.

Beron's voice had a musical quality, Brogan thought. The accent from his native tongue. Beron came from the far south, the very edge of the Five Kingdoms, from one of the islands where it seemed all the slavers were raised and trained in the art of taming slaves without killing them in the process. "Where do they come from? I've never seen their kind before."

"From the other side of Trant's Peak." Harper kept his face perfectly straight as he told his lies and for that reason most believed him. If Harper had ever been beyond Trant's Peak he would have been one of the few. The peak was the edge of the world for most people. After that the cold was too fearsome and there was nothing to find but wind and ice. The people over there, the few who lived in the vicinity, were normally pale in color. It was enough.

Beron nodded. "That would explain their color then."

Brogan resisted the urge to call the man an idiot and instead looked around them. The city was clean, the people well fed and mostly disease free. Even the slaves were relatively well tended. Better than some he'd seen in Hollum. There was a town full of the worst people around. He should know. Half of his crew had just come from the place when he decided to either save or avenge his family.

He had hoped for salvation. Instead he settled for revenge.

Brogan slid his eyes over to the men and their haggling. Harper slapped the slaver's arm amiably and offered his half grin. "You are a hard man to bargain with, you bastard."

Beron's satisfaction hovered around him like an odor. "It is my duty, boy." The slaver stood up and Brogan understood why the man was in charge. Even in a town where physical prowess was not as valuable as a good mind, the man was a staggering sight. Taller than Brogan by a full head and almost half again as broad, sitting down he looked like a bull. Standing he looked like a boulder granted life.

The man bellowed and four of his associates slipped out of the shadows. They set down a substantial fortune in coins. It spoke highly of Beron that none of the people around them looked twice or even considered counting from a distance.

That didn't stop Brogan from preparing himself. The locals respected the slaver. That did not mean they thought enough of Brogan or his men to avoid trying to kill them for a fortune.

Harper slipped two fingers into his mouth and blew out a piercing whistle. Three of the lads came forward to help with the payment. A score of men were suddenly wealthier than any of them imagined. He wondered if any of them would seriously consider the slave trade when they saw their earnings from the raid.

Not for long. They'd know what Brogan already knew: the money was good but most raiders didn't go into Grakhul territory and literally steal away all the women and children.

Harper's expression was unchanged. "We could have bartered for more, but it's enough, I think," he told Brogan.

"More than enough. We're all of us rich." The words tasted like ashes. He was glad they'd made their plans earlier. Laram and a few of the others were up and out of sight on the rooftops. They watched over everything that happened. And they waited, with weapons at the ready. The roads and alleys of Saramond might stop many things, but an arrow could still drop from the skies and kill with ease.

He looked over his shoulder and, knowing he should not, let his eyes move over the pens where the remaining Grakhul women and children were now gathered. An unsettling number looked back at him with dark expressions. They were not a hopeless lot, which was what he supposed he'd expected. Instead they had a cold air about them, like anger simmering under the surface. It was a feeling he knew well enough to recognize it in others.

The slavers had them properly surrounded. He looked away, refusing himself the luxury of guilt. Had their ilk not taken his family for the damnable sacrifices their men would be alive and they would still be free. That was the end of it.

Harper chuckled and tapped his leg lightly with the tip of his hooked sword as he and Brogan made their way through the alleyways to meet the rest of their men. "That didn't take long."

The hooked blade flickered lightly to the right and when Brogan looked he could see the first of their stalkers.

It was a lot of gold and silver. Someone was bound to try for it.

"Are we ready for them?"

"Your decision of course. We can make a spectacle or we can simply cut them down."

The other men with them were still carrying the sacks. Brogan forced himself to remain calm. Part of him wanted to lash out, to strike down any fool wanting to take from him, but he crushed that notion.

"Let Laram and the archers take care of it."

Harper nodded, sheathed his sword, then made a dozen quick gestures that involved tapping his wrists, his chest and his chin. The last gestures all pointed the way for the archers.

They were discreet, which was what Brogan wanted. That didn't mean they weren't efficient. Seven arrows fired. Seven stalkers died. Left where they fell, they served as warning lest others had the same inclinations.

Unless the slavers reneged there likely wouldn't be any

more attacks. It was one thing to try for five armed men. It was another to try for twenty.

While everyone watched, Brogan sorted the coins into piles. As the leader he could have taken a larger cut. Instead he let the others choose their stacks first and took the last allotment of coins for himself. As the scout, Harper was also entitled to an extra cut. Neither of them took it. There was plenty for all and none of them needed to get greedy.

That night the men took turns and slept in shifts. There were no disturbances.

Four nights after they left their homeland, Myridia and her small group rose to the surface and climbed from the waters. She looked to the north and saw the storms building.

Waves that were stronger than she'd expected hammered the shore, but the sand was soft and they managed to step away from the water easily enough. The tide was out and the damp sand gave easy footing. Ahead of them the sand gave way to smaller cliffs than those they were used to, and beyond that the lights of a town burned and painted the underbelly of the clouds.

As she walked she looked at the others, marveling as always at the transformations and how quickly they happened. The webbing slipped away from their hands and feet. Their fingers and toes shortened, and the shimmering scales faded quickly enough. There were many tales along these shores that spoke of water nymphs and other creatures that haunted sailors. Myridia and her kind knew the origins of those tales.

"Will they come for us, Myridia?" Lorae's voice was soft and uncertain.

"The He-Kisshi? Or the men who came for vengeance?"

Lorae shook her head. Her eyes were wide and showed that even after they'd been travelling for days, she was still afraid. The moon was bright and the clouds were finer than they had been. They had moved beyond the fury of the gods. The winds from the north, however, smelled of rain and rage.

"I don't know, Myridia. I can't think."

"So I will think for you." She kept her voice low and soft and touched her forehead to the young girl's brow until she had no choice but to look at Myridia and share her breath. "If the He-Kisshi come, they are our allies. They might make demands, but they will have their reasons. If the others come, we will kill them. We do not have the children to consider any longer. We will do what we must."

Lorae took a deep, shuddering breath and nodded, forcing a brave smile. "We will do what we must," she repeated.

Not far ahead of them, Lyraal kept low to the sand and looked carefully for signs of anyone else. The beaches here were often deserted, but it was best to be safe. Lyraal was a prize to have with her; the woman was a seasoned fighter and furious over the deaths of the others, as she should be. Her husband was among them, and he had been a kind, gentle soul.

For the last four days Lyraal had sung her rage into the waters, and the storms almost seemed to promise her revenge.

Myridia knew better, of course.

The sacrifices had not happened. Even if the He-Kisshi had managed to bring fresh sacrifices to the pits, they would not have known the proper way to prepare the flesh, or cleanse the spirits of the chosen.

A body could not merely be cast into the pits and accepted as an offering. There were stories passed down from the old times that said offering anything unclean to the gods was an insult and would only anger them.

"Where do we go from here, Myridia?"

"We have a great distance to travel, little one." She put her hand on the younger girl's arm and moved it slowly up to her face. "We have to travel to the other side of the Five Kingdoms."

Lorae nodded and looked to the evening skies. "Will we get there in time?"

"We must." She frowned and watched Lyraal move up the soft embankment to the road they knew was above. The winds were blowing colder than they should have and for a moment Myridia lamented the loss of her clothes. They would have helped against the chill, but in the waters they'd only slowed her down.

Four sleepless days of travel under the waters had placed them well beyond the reach of the humans they'd escaped from, even if the men had chosen to come after them, which she suspected they had not. Now it was a matter of getting to the Sessanoh, the Mirrored Lake, where the other pits lay unused for as long as there had been Five Kingdoms.

None of them had ever been to the Sessanoh. There were no maps, but there were the songs of their ancestors and tales they'd learned throughout their lifetimes, and there was the pulling sensation that roiled and tugged at her insides and she knew if she followed that pull, she would find her way.

They had no choice. If they did not find their way to the Sessanoh soon enough, the gods would not be appeased and the rage that was already showing itself would only get worse.

He-Kisshi. The word, roughly translated, meant Divine Collector. There was little of the creatures that most would consider divine. There were twelve. There had always been twelve. The gods made their decrees and the He-Kisshi obeyed. For that reason there would be twelve again

The corpse of Ohdra-Hun lay where it had fallen, where the escaped sacrifices had left it. The flesh was wounded in a dozen places, bruised and slashed by chains.

Because the He-Kisshi demanded it, the weather calmed down, allowing them to do their solemn duties in relative silence. For the moment at least the gods were done with their tantrum.

"Ohdra-Hun, you always let your temper get the best of you." Dowru-Thist looked at the body and shook its head. Then carefully, it bent down and grabbed the flesh, peeling it slowly back. Long, curved claws caught the hidden flaps where the flesh sealed and pried them open. The skin did not part easily. It never did.

The hooded form opened, the heavy hide peeling away from the body underneath. The human under the hide was dead, of course. She'd been dying for a long time but the beating administered by the desperate escapees guaranteed that her life would end sooner rather than later.

Three of the others gathered around, all of them looking down at the ruined flesh, watching as Dowru-Thist removed the heavy, leathery form.

"Are there any nearby?" Dowru-Thist's voice held no sign of the strain of lifting the heavy, shapeless mass.

"Bogrun-Nisht brings a new host." Ellish-Loa pointed to the skies and the slowly descending form. Wind-riding was always a strain, but doing so while carrying a struggling human made it harder. Just the same Bogrun-Nisht managed and dropped the screaming shape into the mud only a dozen feet from where Ohdra-Hun had fallen.

The girl was young, no older than fourteen years. Perfect.

She looked at the He-Kisshi and reacted exactly as they would have expected, by staggering to her legs and starting to run. They did not stop her. There was no reason. There was nowhere for her to go and they knew that better than most. The great citadel of Nugonghappalur was gone, destroyed by the gods themselves when the vile humans who'd committed their wanton slaughter failed to offer sacrifices.

Petty gods. Hungry gods. Angry gods.

And they had to be appeased.

Dowru-Thist listened to the girl as she ran, her breaths rapid and fearful. Her body was strong and she moved quickly across the great, muddied field, wisely heading away from the waters. The sea was enraged and the waves would have shredded her as easily as they had destroyed the other sacrifices who had escaped earlier.

The runaways had not been forgotten, but they were not important at the moment. "It is time, Ohdra-Hun. Time to be reborn."

The great collection of hide whipped and thrashed in its arms and so Dowru-Thist let it go and watched as the winds caught the remains of its sibling.

The wind was slave to the He-Kisshi, whether or not they were intact. The thick caul of flesh rose into the air and steadied itself for a moment before moving toward the fleeing child in the distance.

She ran well, but the mud was tiring her out and she, foolishly perhaps, looked back in an effort to see whether or not she was safe. That was what cost her the most.

Ohdra-Hun caught her easily and wrapped itself around the girl, staggering her with its surprising weight. Long, thin legs buckled at the knees and she fell forward catching herself on her hands and screaming her fright to the uncaring skies.

Ohdra-Hun did what it had to in order to survive and opened itself completely, revealing the fine layers of thread-thin tendrils that quickly pushed through the girl's flesh and insinuated themselves deeper and deeper into her body. Her screams only stopped when she fell face first into dark mud.

For several minutes she lay where she was, her body shivering in the heavy protection of the thick hide. And then she rose, standing with ease, her slight form completely lost within the depths of Ohdra-Hun.

The scream that cut from Ohdra-Hun was not human.

The He-Kisshi gathered together around their brethren and examined it from the crest of its hood down to the mud-painted legs and long, curving toes.

"Nugonghappalur is gone."

"I know." Ohdra-Hun took in great breaths of cold, damp air, and bellowed out gouts of steam. The body burned hot as they often did when first taken. Deep inside Ohdra-Hun the girl continued to fight. She was strong and she was suffering. Ohdra-Hun was pleased by her struggle. As she resisted, the thick blood of the He-Kisshi slowly sealed her properly within the body. She tried to scream and drank deep of the blood, speeding up the union of bodies with each thrash and moan.

The gods were kind in their ways.

"Ohdra-Hun, we must go."

"Go?" The entire body shook with rage. "I will find them! I will have them! They are mine!"

"There is no time for this," Bogrun-Nisht warned.

Instead of listening, Ohdra-Hun extended its great wings and caught the winds, rising fast into the clouds.

Bogrun-Nisht looked at the other He-Kisshi. "We go on. Ohdra-Hun will follow or not, but we cannot delay any longer." They all agreed. The gods made demands and the He-Kisshi did as they were bid.

As they rose into the air the storms began again, no longer restrained by their will. In the distance, too far away now for human eyes, the Gateway stood against the raging lightning and watched on blindly as the shoreline shook and began to split.

The gods would be appeased, or there would be nothing left of the world.

CHAPTER FIVE
Unexpected Company

As soon as Niall was sure that they were out of sight of the monstrosities that had kept them captive, he made the girl stop long enough to collect the rain waters and rinse the worst of the muck from her feet. When he was done, he tore his tunic into strips and wrapped her damaged feet as best he could. She did not need to die of infection, not so soon after saving his life. After that, they moved as quickly as they could, often crawling or hiding when they could find a place to shelter and keep them from view.

Each night they hid in the mud. When the darkness came they slathered themselves in the stuff, constantly fearing the Grakhul would come for them and desperate to find ways to hide themselves. They slept fitfully, exhausted and unable to properly recover.

As he feared, she took on a fever. She was strong, and her body fought against the illness, but it came back again and again.

He would not leave her.

On the third morning she found mushrooms but he warned her off them. Mosara would have been proud. Those particular fungi brought about severe stomach cramps, vomiting and diarrhea. There wasn't much left of Niall's clothes, but he managed to wrap a few of the mushrooms into a pouch just the same.

There was always the chance they'd get captured again. Best to plan for the possibility.

On the third afternoon they ran out of mud and rain. They'd managed to stay ahead of the storms mostly by running and walking fast. They'd used the rains to their advantage, drinking what fell from the sky and cleansing from their bodies whatever venoms the bastard Grakhul had forced on them from their bodies.

They did not speak. Instead they focused on moving and when one of them fell, the other was there to help them back up and to urge them on silently.

On the third night, they found actual shelter in the form of a lodge.

It was not a large structure, but it was sound and there was a roof and a pit for fires. Lodges were scattered into every part of the Five Kingdoms, and they were considered safe places, though the perception and the reality often differed. Most looked close to identical, and all of them had the same symbol carved into the stones on the eastern facing side: a long staff crossed by two broken arrows. No one had any idea what the sign originally meant, but over the years it had come to symbolize hospitality.

Niall didn't know which of them wept more loudly when they came upon the place.

There was no caution involved. They ran toward the stone building and entered it without checking.

Niall had never stayed in a lodge before. As often as not they were maintained by the slavers, and as a result it was best to stay well away from them. Custom said no one bothered anyone in a lodge, but slavers were not notorious for sticking to custom. At that moment in time he would have gladly allowed himself to be locked in a pen and sold into servitude if it involved being out of the rain and the cold.

They found the place blessedly abandoned.

They also found food with only a little searching. Not a great deal, but someone had left behind a satchel filled with nuts. Niall broke the shells against the edge of the fireplace and the two of them ate with all the civility of hungry sharks.

When they'd finished the small meal – which after the last few days was enough to leave them both feeling sated – the girl scooped the nutshells into the fireplace and used them as kindling to start a proper blaze. There were enough logs near the hearth to fuel the fire for a few hours.

Exhaustion won quickly when the warmth filled the room and soon enough they were both on the edge of sleep.

"What is your name?" Niall asked as he started to drift into slumber.

"Tully," she answered.

It was not the name he would have expected, not common at all in his part of the world and hardly the sort of name he thought belonged with her features, but it suited her well enough.

In the morning, Tully was shivering violently, despite the increased heat in the lodge. The fire had done its job and warmed the hearth and well beyond that point. Both of them had stayed within range of that warmth, but the girl was far hotter than she should have been and while she moaned and shivered in the pleasant, baking heat, Niall unwrapped her feet and saw exactly what he'd feared. Her toes were swollen and red, and there were open cuts from where she'd managed to pull the bolts from her ankle manacles. The skin was raw, and seeped pus and trickles of dark blood.

The mushrooms could not be ingested without risk of

killing the one who consumed them but that didn't mean they couldn't be useful. Niall went back out into the rains and set a cast iron pot at the closest gutter, letting the rainwater gather quickly then bringing it back to the hearth.

Within half an hour the waters were warm enough to let him steep the mushrooms Tully had planned to eat not that long ago. He did not remain idle while he cooked. A little inspection of the lodge found an old cloth that would suffice for his needs and little else that would be useful. Still, one found fortune where one looked.

He tore the cloth into strips and soaked those in the boiling waters, letting them take in the essence even as he took the pot from the fire and started the cooling process. The rags were drawn from the mushroom broth and left wet as they cooled. When the rags could be tolerated against the inside of his arm, where the skin was more sensitive, he knew her feet would also survive the coming tortures.

Tully screamed when he placed the hot rags on her feet, but there was little she could do besides that. All the fight she'd shown before was lost for now, hidden in the fever and the infection, and he took the time to settle his weight around her legs before he started.

She yelled just the same and made a few pointed remarks about his heritage in the process. Niall ignored the comments, and managed to avoid getting his manhood crushed by her thrashing knee. It was a close thing.

They spent the next day with her in a fever and him eventually leaving her just long enough to scavenge for food. The area they were in was still soaked by rains, but by the light of day he could actually see well enough to find the woods not far away and to forage properly.

Well before she was recovered enough to do much more than eat broth, he'd found a few onions, harmless mushrooms and leafy plants that could make a decent stock, and fortified it with eggs he plucked from a nest – there was no sign of the mother bird, though the eggs were still warm. He made Tully eat, despite her protests. She spent most of the time between small sips gagging and trying not to regurgitate. Sometimes she succeeded and other times she did not.

For three days he watched over the young woman who had saved his life. He cleaned her wounds, and cleaned up after her when she soiled herself or when what little she ate refused to stay down.

Three days where he managed a little sleep and three nights when he kept the fires burning and listened to the raging storms as they first approached then overtook the area, and wondered exactly how and when they would get out of the madness of the lodge that was lost in that very same storm. The walls wept precipitation and the air was cold and wet, but the fires burned well enough and eventually even the wettest logs would catch fire.

He could have run. He could have left her behind. There weren't many who would blame him, especially if he never told anyone. But three days was not so high a price to pay to someone who'd saved his life, even if it was mostly by accident and coincidence. There was a life debt to be covered.

Life debts were the ones you had to pay if you wanted to face your own reflection in the light of day. Niall always paid his debts.

Even when they cost him in the end.

Their fourth day in the lodge started with Tully finally winning her fight against the fever. She was awake when Niall roused himself from sleep and when he looked in her direction she was sitting up and looking at her feet, the latest bandages peeled aside to allow her a proper inspection.

She looked up at him and nodded carefully, a small frown

on her face. "Your doing?" She pointed to the bandages.

"Yes. They were badly infected."

"At the very least you saved my feet."

Niall nodded and shrugged and looked away. "Yes, well, I'd have gone over the cliff with the others if you hadn't freed me." He thought back to the look on Ligel's face as the boy vanished over the edge, and his insides twisted themselves.

Tully moved her foot into the air and flexed the toes, and Niall caught himself admiring the shape of her calf, the play of muscles along the back of her thigh, before he looked away.

"How long have we been here?" Tully's voice was soft.

"A few days. You couldn't be moved."

When she stood up, it was on uncertain legs. He braced in case he'd have to catch her, but she held her own.

"We should move on. They might come for us."

He nodded. "They might. But we've no horses and little by way of food." He pointed to the latest collection of fungi and moss he'd managed to gather, amused by her expression of dread. "It's tastier than it looks."

"I hope so."

"Before we go anywhere we need to do something about your feet. You can't walk on rags." His own boots were far too large and he'd need them himself.

Without another word, the girl looked around and nodded. He settled in and tended the fire while she roamed the lodge, presumably in the hopes that she'd magically find a set of boots waiting for her.

When she came back it was without boots. He was not surprised by the lack of new footwear. He had seen nothing even remotely suitable during his many examinations of the place.

Outside the rains continued. The constant patter of water

against the roof and sides of the lodge perfectly masked the sound of the wagon pulling up outside until they actually heard voices approaching the door.

They only had a moment to prepare themselves before the first of the newcomers walked through the threshold and looked at them, a surprised expression on his round face. Thick white hair and a wild beard the same color surrounded blue eyes and the thickest eyebrows Niall could ever remember seeing.

"Well then," the stranger's voice was loud and jovial. "What a delight! We already have a fire going!" He stepped to the side and a lanky woman with hard eyes and a thin scowl entered. Her hair was short and dark, slicked to her head by the water dripping from her.

Two more people followed on, both of them younger, both just as cheerful as the man who'd come in first. They seemed far likelier related to him than to his female counterpart. Both were stout and smiling and seemed delighted by the thought of a fire.

"With your blessings, we'd join you for a while." The white-haired man's words were spoken with warmth but were also formal. That was the most standard greeting when a person ran across someone else at a lodge. At least according to Niall's mother, who had traveled to several different lodges in her youth.

"You are welcome," Niall said. "We were planning to leave soon and you will have the lodge as your own."

The group moved in, pulling a few items with them, bedrolls and standard supplies.

Despite a dour expression on her thin face, the older woman was sharp of eye and quickly realized that Niall and Tully had virtually nothing by way of food or supplies.

She looked from one to the other and shook her head. "You'll not go anywhere without a meal in your stomachs," she commanded. There was no second guessing the tone.

Niall found himself nodding and Tully nodded as well.

The older man boomed laughter and shook his head. "You'll be thinner than Doria if you don't eat something and she's only skinny because she never stands still." The two younger ones laughed at the notion and the room that had seemed cold despite the fire was suddenly warm.

Sometimes you meet strangers on the road. Sometimes you meet family you never knew you had.

The town of Muaraugh was not one the women had ever seen before, but they were as prepared as they could be and they had no intention of staying long.

Night had fallen several hours earlier and the long, deep dark of early morning surrounded them.

The rains were still coming down from the skies, but this far inland they were weaker.

Myridia was tired of walking. She was tired of shivering in the nude as well, a victim of the weather's whim. She was not alone and she knew it. Lorae, who was thinner than most of them, trembled violently from time to time as she adjusted to the cold.

They crouched near an outcropping of rocks and waited for Lyraal to return. Lorae shifted nervously, swaying from one leg to the other in her lowered position until she nearly made the older ones around her dizzy. Lyraal was scouting their way, of course, because she was the best choice.

They would fight if they had to, but their weapon selection was small and they had no armor. Most had no clothes. Perhaps that would distract an opponent, but best not to plan for it. They had little experience with the humans, aside from preparing them for sacrifice.

Their scout came back and sighed as she squatted with the rest of the group. "There are horses not far from here. There is a smithy. It is closed, but I suspect we can find weapons. We should go soon. The longer we wait, the greater chance someone will awaken."

Instead of speaking, Myridia gestured her consent and a moment later they were moving, walking softly and quickly toward the smithy.

There were a few voices, but none of them close by. Attacks might happen in many of the larger cities but apparently no one was interested in what Muaraugh had to offer that night.

Myridia did not understand that at all. The buildings were made of wood and shingled with thatch, and the roads were even and holding up under the constant assault of the rain.

The gods did not slumber nearby and demand sacrifices. Under different circumstances she might have liked to meet the people of the town. Of course the people of the town, if they knew what she and her companions had done in the past and planned to do in the future, likely would have burned them in rage.

She made herself remember that as they moved along.

Myridia looked at the smithy and pressed her lips together. Perhaps there wasn't much theft in the area, but the smith or his apprentices knew better than to keep the area unsecured. The door was thick oak, braced with bands of iron, and there was a lock.

"What now?" Lorae's voice was soft, but in the silence it was almost as loud as a scream.

Myridia let the water take her. Beneath the waves their bodies were different, stronger and more resilient. She did not like changing in the air, and had it not been raining enough to keep her skin soaked it would have been harder. She shifted quickly and beside her Lyraal did the same. They moved together, battering the heavy door with their shoulders, and promptly slid backward in the watery muck that puddled at the door's edge.

Lyraal chuckled. "So perhaps we brace ourselves better?"

They motioned a silent count, planted their feet securely, elongated toes burrowing through the mud to find better purchase, then hammered the door with their bodies. The door did not break, but the hinges holding it did.

The entire affair fell into the smithy far too quickly for them to catch it, not that either of them cared. Lorae moved past them and into the darkened interior of the shop. A faint light came from the forge, a bloody glow that made it possible to see well enough. It brought with it warmth enough to elicit sighs. The younger girl searched through the shop and gestured the others forward. There was no time to relax.

Her drying skin itched as Myridia moved into the area and looked carefully at the weapons. Several blades were there, true, but most were meant for other than combat. They were designed to reap wheat, or cut back the woodlands. Still, they would do.

And there were others. There were several good blades. Short swords of the like that were favored in the area, and one weapon that was entirely different, a much longer sword, with a straight edge and a broad blade. The weapon was sheathed in a black leather scabbard, trimmed with silver. The damnable thing was nearly as long as she was tall, and despite herself, she was drawn to it.

Without waiting to see if there would be debate, she grabbed the weapon.

No one protested.

Lyraal hissed, "We have to go, quickly. The horses," and Myridia realized she was talking to her. The rest of them had already left the shop.

She nodded and moved, crossing the threshold with quick steps and following behind the others.

Lyraal was already well ahead of her and moving toward the largest building in the area. Around them the smaller structures were dark.

"What are you doing here?" The voice was loud and harsh and Myridia spun quickly into a crouch, facing the source of the words.

The man in front of her was heavy with muscle and flab alike, but in the important places with muscle. One look at his arms and she knew him to be the smith. Scars old and new adorned his hands and arms up to his elbows, and here and there bits of metal scarcely larger than grains of sand had fused with his flesh. His beard was short and his hair was long. His broad face wore an expression of confused anger and he took a step toward her.

"I'll not have you stealing from me, lass." He was not surprised by her appearance, but it was dark and the rains were falling. Perhaps he did not see her scales clearly. Perhaps naked women were common enough here. She did not know.

She spoke their languages. She understood his words. She did not have time to explain to him that they were trying to save the world, or that she and her sisters had to take from him in order to do so. He would want to debate the merits of their needs and he would demand payment that she did not have.

The sword came from the scabbard with a soft whisper. The blade was as keen as she had imagined it might be and the metal itself bore a deep pattern that resembled scales. She knew from the weapons she'd trained with that those marks were simply where the metal had been shaped and forged, but it was a pattern she admired even as she swept the sword around her in an arc to feel the balance of the piece.

'"Don't make me take that from you girl." He growled low

in his chest as he spoke; likely she was meant to take the noise as a warning. He spread his arms wide and crouched himself, prepared, perhaps, to bat the sword aside if she should attempt to feign an assault.

So instead of feinting, she attacked. The sword was well balanced and she took advantage, spinning her body to gain momentum then bringing the great sword in a hard arc that came down between the smith's shoulder and neck and cleaved deeply into his chest.

The edge was excellent, and despite a jarring impact she cut the man in two.

And then she very quickly followed after her kin. They had spent far too long getting to Muaraugh and they had so very far to go.

They rode as a unit from Saramond, leaving early. By the time the sun was heading for its zenith, they split apart and went their own ways. There were Five Kingdoms and most of them had homes in one place or another.

Harper, Laram, Mosely, Sallos and Brogan rode together, heading for the west and their homes. Strength in numbers meant that for the time being they continued together. After only two days of hard riding they finally outraced the storms that threatened to overtake the city before they left.

Mosely was a kinsman, however distant. Brogan was broad and well-muscled; Mosely was much the same, but tended to the fatter side of the equation. His hair was lighter in color and showed more gray though he was a few years younger than Brogan. He was also a singer. Not a good one, but what he lacked in talent he made up for with enthusiasm. They listened as he bellowed out song after song, and now and then they even joined in.

All save Brogan, who could find no reason to sing within him at the moment. Every breath reminded him that Nora and his children were dead, and every exhalation reminded him again. Not even the gold in his purse made a difference and it was a great deal of gold.

They were wealthy, every last one of them, and they were wise enough to hide that wealth away, in some cases packed into hidden pockets, or small coin pouches, in others tucked into boots, vests, and places on the saddles of their horses.

For eight days and nights they traveled and mostly the group got along fine. It was on the ninth day that Sallos would not stop looking over his shoulder, until finally, as they climbed into the foothills that marked the start of the Broken Swords Mountains, Brogan looked over his own shoulder to make sure that they were not being followed.

Most times the approach to the mountains stopped people from looking behind them. The crystalline formations that broke through the earth's crust and reflected the sun in a thousand brilliant spectacles was enough to ensure that. Not so with Sallos.

"What?" His voice was sharper than he meant, but not enough that he corrected himself. "What is it, Sallos? Are we being followed? Because I don't see anyone."

The younger man looked at him and scratched at the growth of beard he hadn't shaved since they'd started on their way. His blond hair was tightly braided and stayed away from his face, but his beard was like moss on a stone surface: patchy.

As with many of the westerners, Sallos Redcliff was often introspective. Getting him to offer information was a challenge. Hazel eyes regarded Brogan for a long moment and finally Sallos pointed to the distant horizon. "The storms aren't going away."

Brogan looked back and stared at the gathered clouds. They'd gone a goodly distance and passed several small towns along their way. The land was mostly flat across the Plains of Arthorne and from their current height it was easy to see Saramond, Hollum well to the south and a scattering of villages. The silvery threads of the Three Serpent Rivers spread across the plains from their origin point in the foothills of the very area they had just invaded in an effort to save Brogan's family. It was also too easy to see the great black veil of clouds that hid away most of the horizon to their north. The clouds were towering affairs and their shadow loomed ahead of them, half obscuring Saramond. "Storms along the ocean are not unusual. What of it?"

Sallos shook his head. The lad was younger, true enough, but he was also a seasoned fighter and experienced enough to pay attention to his environment. "They haven't broken up or scattered away since we were in that damned place. Not at all. But they're coming this way. Moving steadily. I've never seen storms do that before."

Brogan stared at the distant bank of dark clouds. While he looked he could see strobes of white and blue flashing through their black depths.

He chewed at his lip. Those clouds were serious business. They were days and days away and yet he could see them. Somewhere beyond them the coastline he'd left behind was buried in darkness and lost in raging storms.

"All the better that we've finished our business, then, lad."

Sallos looked at the storms again and slowly nodded his head. He'd lost his father to the Grakhul when he was five years younger and had never forgiven them. Like most of the men who'd joined in the fight, he'd have gone without promise of money.

It was Harper that added to the worries. He was toward the end of the group riding for home and he'd listened in on the conversation long enough. He stopped and joined them in looking back toward the black cloudbank slowly swallowing the distance.

That damnable half-smile of his remained on his face as he turned to look at Brogan. "What do you suppose would happen if they were right all along and the sacrifices were the only thing that kept us safe from the anger of the gods?"

Brogan tried to ignore his words. Rather than replying, he turned back toward the west and started riding again. Home was still a few days away at the least.

Still, despite a silent vow not to, Brogan found he kept looking back at the slowly gathering storms and in the back of his mind Harper's question echoed again and again.

Another five days' ride got them through the mountain paths and heading toward their homeland, Stennis Brae. The mountains did not so much go away as become more level and less maddening. The Broken Swords were behind them, and the great outcroppings of crystals that made the area so treacherous were to their backs as well. Ahead were low hills and farmland, and the forests and rivers that had marked the best possible place in Brogan's eyes.

Most every time he'd gone away he'd come back and stared at the rolling hills and felt his heart swell. This was where he would normally be riding harder, eager to take the last day's ride at speed, the better to see his wife.

He could almost imagine the sounds of his children calling for their father.

Instead of moving faster, he scowled a bit and rode on at the same speed.

There was no wife to lie with. There were no children to sweep into his arms and swing in great circles while they giggled. There was no one he could entertain while he talked of the great merchant trains that he'd guided past the worst areas. He would not tell Nora about his adventures or about how so many of the women in Saramond dressed in clothes that made less sense than a sunset in the middle of the day. They wore sensible garments in Stennis Brae, pants and tunics and kilts and cloaks. In Saramond they wore clothes that showed off their bodies in the oddest ways and offered little by way of protection. Every time he told his family of the latest odd garments in Saramond they'd laugh and he'd draw images, or describe the stuff while demonstrating with gestures.

None of that would happen again.

The slow, dark rage grew in his chest. He had wealth, to be sure. He could live where he pleased and how he pleased, but he would not be able to bring his family back and that fact fed the growing hatred in his being.

There were five of them and only Harper seemed in a good mood as they moved past the great cairns at the edge of Brundage and continued on for Kinnett.

Home.

Mosely had stopped singing and instead whistled softly between his teeth. For Mosely that was as close as the man usually came to agitated unless there was bloodshed to be done.

They came to a fork in the road and Laram looked to the others, slapping his hands against his thick thighs.

"That's it. I'm heading for Brixleigh. I'd say it's been a pleasure, boys, but we know that would be a lie. Profitable? Yes. Pleasurable? I fear not."

No one climbed down from their horses, but Brogan looked his way and let out a great breath. One heavy hand rested on his friend's shoulder and he smiled. "I can never thank you enough, Laram."

Laram jingled the edge of his cloak, where a small portion of his vast fortune lay tucked safely away. "You already have. I expect I'll be buying myself a castle somewhere soon." He paused a moment and a smile lit his face as surely as if the scattered clouds had decided to let the sunlight through. "And I do believe I'll ask Old Slattery for his daughter's hand again. I believe his answer might just change this time around."

He waved once then turned away, heading for the town where he lived and where he preferred to stay. It was only for Brogan's sake that he had left and that fact weighed heavily on Brogan. Laram had killed and traded in slaves, two things the man did not want to do. He had tried and failed to be Brogan's conscience and that, too, now stood between them. They had been friends a long time and he feared that time was now passing.

The world he'd known was gone. He was going to have to face that knowledge.

They rode again but not very far. Half a league down the Brundage Highway the road cut through a narrow passage between two large mounds of earth. The road tapered down to half the regular width. If Brogan were planning an ambush it would have been in exactly that sort of spot. He wasn't too shocked by the horsemen that blocked the way.

It could have been twelve men, or a good twenty. Either way, armed men were coming their way, sporting the colors of the king. Bron McNar was a good king. He kept the peace better than most and worked to ensure prosperity. He was, in short, what Brogan thought a king should be: sensible. That was not the case with all of the Five Kingdoms to be sure. The king's men rode steadily forward, and as was tradition Brogan and the others moved off the main path to let them go past.

Brogan frowned a bit, not used to seeing the king's men heading for the Broken Swords.

The man at the head of the column was familiar to him. He didn't know a name, but he recognized the face. Dark, braided hair, a thick beard and a heavy build. The man was strong, he had authority and he knew in his heart that he was better than those he addressed.

Brogan had never liked him much, even when they'd fought together against the Mentath.

The same was apparently true in the opposite. The man looked at him for a moment and nodded. "You'd be Brogan McTyre?"

Brogan nodded and paused a moment when the men behind the speaker reached for their scabbards. They did not draw blades, but they prepared themselves.

His hand touched the haft of his axe. One loop of leather was all that prevented him from pulling the blade free and he knew exactly how to handle that loop with his thumb.

"And who am I speaking with?" He kept his voice civil but it wasn't easy. He was tired and the man was asking questions with an authority that he took too easily.

The man spoke again. "Have you been away from Stennis Brae?"

"I have." He didn't like the tension in the air, and knew without looking that the others with him felt the same way. He was also annoyed by the lack of an answer to his simple question. It showed a level of disrespect he did not want or need.

"And have you been far to the north, perhaps taking yourself into territories that are forbidden?"

He thumbed the leather strap aside.

"In what ways forbidden? And where are you talking about?" Harper's voice carried clearly and the man leading those facing them looked his way.

"There are few lands forbidden by the whole of the Five Kingdoms." The man leaned back in his saddle and crossed his thick arms. They were heavy with muscle. "Last I heard they were called 'up north, where it's forbidden to go'."

"Well, we've only just come back from Saramond, where

we had dealings." He had to give that to Harper: the man was calm and friendly and it didn't seem a ruse. Of course, he had seen Harper looking exactly that calm when he slipped a dagger into a man's neck.

Brogan looked at the others with him. Mosely and Sallos were both tensing already. They knew the situation as well as he did. They would be "escorted" to see the King or one of his men. Along the way they would be searched for weapons, and in the process, if it were discovered that they had secreted a fortune on their persons, the question of to whom, exactly, that fortune belonged would arise. Four men versus a dozen or more. The odds were not good.

Each of the four carried enough money to make the soldiers with them wealthy in the extreme.

Harper's words brought Brogan back to the situation and out of his considerations of strategy.

"We cannot go immediately. Perhaps in a day?" Harper's voice continued on smoothly.

"Don't confuse my polite tones with a request." The man was annoying. When he smiled, as he did now, it was a baring of teeth that had nothing to do with friendliness.

"If that's your polite tone, you need a lesson in manners." Brogan rested his hand on the haft of his axe. Enough.

The man turned his head sharply toward Brogan and prepared to speak. The thin blade of Harper's sword sprouted from the roof of his head like a hard steel sapling.

An instant later Harper was charging forward even as the man started to slump.

Brogan didn't wait for an invitation to join the fray. His knees urged his horse under him forward and it obeyed. There was much to be said for a well-trained warhorse.

The brute pushed past the dead man's horse even as the animal started adjusting for the weight of a corpse falling from its back. It was too much for the animal and it reared up, dropping its dead rider and separating Sallos and Mosely for a moment.

After that Brogan didn't have time to think about his friends. There was death to be taken care of and no time for much else.

The axe came up and swept in a hard arc, cleaving the air between him and the first man facing him. The fellow had been focusing on Harper and did not live to regret it. His lower jaw and his neck split in a wash of red as Brogan continued forward.

The sounds of an animal screaming behind him became just another noise. The next man in line was armed and ready, prepared for the axe. He raised his sword and blocked the first swing from Brogan, but lost his balance in the saddle in the process. Brogan took advantage of that, clenched his knees on the horse between them and used his free hand to shove the man in the chest. The swordsman went down hard even as Brogan and his horse were pushing against his mount. Brogan's leg was crushed for a moment then the horses shifted and he was past, knowing he was lucky not to have been injured by the impact.

And then the axe was up again, swinging for a man's face. The man leaned back in his seat, narrowly avoiding the blade. Brogan swept the weapon around his head and slapped the man's horse in the flank, opening a painful but not fatal wound. The horse panicked, exactly as he'd expected, and bolted toward the road ahead, taking his opponent along for the ride.

Either Sallos or Mosely would take it from there with any luck.

A sword came up fast. Brogan barely blocked it with the heavy haft of the axe. Had it been mere wood his weapon would have been lost, but metal bands and studs saved both the weapon and his life. The impact ran up his entire arm and nearly unseated him. These were trained fighters and he'd been lucky so far. He knew better than to expect luck alone to keep him alive.

Harper's hooked blade caught a rider at the back of his neck even as the man was starting a hard charge for Brogan. The soldier didn't have a chance to scream before he was dropping his sword and trying to pull the bloodied barb from the back of his skull. Brogan hacked into the man's stomach and pulled back. Likely he wasn't dead, but wishing for the pain to end. Brogan pushed on and watched as Harper released the sword. It would be there when they were done.

Three more men before him, so he rose up in the stirrups and roared a challenge. A goodly number of men would have turned and fled from the sight of him. Only one of these looked panicked.

He took aim and hurled the axe at that one, reaching for his sword a moment later. He did not see the axe hit, but he heard the man's scream. The sword was free and by the time he was looking at the men again, they were in front of him, swords at the ready.

Two swords to his one and the men were prepared.

He charged harder, lowering over the horse and making them seek a target to hit. The men were expecting him to continue his mad bellowing and by the looks on their faces they were surprised that he did not.

On his left the sword rose high and the rider charged forward. Brogan cursed, as the sword was in his enemy's left hand.

A hard nudge and the horse under him moved right and smashed into the piebald mount of the other swordsman. The blade on his left hit his arm, cut into the meat of his shoulder, but not deep enough to stop him.

Damned lucky.

The man on his right was properly staggered by the impact and desperate to keep his seating. While the rider waved his arms and pushed his body where it belonged, Brogan hacked a deep slash into his thigh, then swept the sword into his stomach and chest.

The sword rammed between two ribs and refused to move from where it was. Brogan either had to let it go or lose his own seating.

The sword stayed put and Brogan moved on, pushing through the end of the gap that narrowed the road and coming out on the other side, where once again there was room to maneuver easily.

No axe. No sword.

He turned the horse around as the only warrior who had hurt him so far came back around from the other direction. Harper was already there and he was grinning like a wolf. Without a word he unsheathed a dagger that was nearly as long as Brogan's forearm and tossed it in his direction. Brogan would catch it or go weaponless. He managed to catch the blade by the hilt and only scrape a few layers from his palm in the process.

Three of the riders were coming toward them now, and they were coming hard, furious at the attack that had already killed several of their fellows.

One of them turned his horse for Brogan immediately. The one who had cut him across his shoulder. He wanted to finish his kill.

Brogan lowered over his horse and charged, not thinking about the chances of failure. The man rode just as hard, holding the blade across the front of his saddle, to brace it. At a guess, he intended to ram the blade clear through Brogan.

Brogan rose up in the stirrups and thought about the dagger in his hand. The sword was coming at him at a serious clip.

Sometimes being crazy is the only way.

He kept the boot closest to his enemy in the stirrup and then raised his other leg to the top of the saddle. He could see his enemy's face well enough to know that he was puzzled.

Good.

As they came closer Brogan jumped from his horse, throwing his entire body mass at the rider. The sword tip stayed where it was, rather than rising up to impale Brogan. As he'd hoped, the man was too shocked by his desperately stupid move to retaliate.

The horse took one look at the maniac leaping for it and swerved hard, sending its rider sailing through the air, sword and all.

Brogan did his best to roll as he hit the ground, bouncing and flopping wildly before he slowed down. His chest hurt and he felt as if he'd been kicked in the guts, but he managed to stand up.

His right hand still held the long dagger.

The other rider was already picking himself up. The sword was no longer in his hands.

Brogan charged again, on foot this time, and drove the blade through the top of the man's head.

The bastard screamed, but did not die. Brogan tried to pull the dagger out and stab him again, but it was seated properly and did not want to be pulled loose. The man screamed some more and reached to stop him, so Brogan stepped back and drove a fist into the damn fool's face again and again until he stopped all his yelling.

He looked around and found the man's sword. It would do. He reached for it and missed, reached again and grabbed the blade up.

And by the time he was done with that Mosely was riding his way.

Sallos was directly behind him.

"They all dead then?"

Sallos spat. "Not hardly. Mostly just so broken they can't get themselves up and start fighting again."

Harper came closer, still riding his horse. His face was once again smirking.

"What do you suppose that was all about?"

Brogan looked back at him. "Seems the king would like to talk to us about murdering some folks."

Harper shook his head. "And what do you plan to do about that?"

"What else? We're going to talk to the king."

"What do you plan to tell him about this?" He gestured at the wounded and dying.

That was a problem.

"Whatever we have to." He looked around the area for a long moment. "We hide the bodies."

"What about the ones still alive?" Mosely meant well.

"We've just committed an act of treason, lads. We hide the bodies."

Mosely opened his mouth to protest and Harper spoke up. "They'd have taken our money and killed us to keep us silent."

Mosely closed his mouth.

A moment later he was off his horse and moving closer. "What about the ones who are still alive?" Perhaps the lad hoped for a different answer.

Harper stared hard, that same damnable half-smile in place. "We hide the bodies. *All* of them."

Brogan knew the man was right. He'd have answered the same way. That didn't make him feel any better about it.

In Saramond the weather had soured. Rain was bad, but this was not merely rain, it was accompanied by wind and lightning and the endless roars of thunder.

B'Rath was a free man and he owned the stables at the northern end of town. The money was enough to let him have a comfortable life, though he knew he'd never get rich from it. What helped him stay more than merely comfortable was the information he shared with the right people. For a few coins he reported whenever someone new came to town. Not every person passing through, merely those he suspected were important to someone.

The day was growing old and the sun would be setting soon enough – albeit somewhere behind the clouds – and B'Rath closed the doors of the stables and locked them properly. Horse thieves were not a large problem in Saramond, but they were a problem. He had four servants – his brother Uto among them – to watch over the animals and they did their job well enough, but he did not like to tempt the hearts of thieves.

As he headed back for his small house in front of the stables, the lightning flared and lit the northern road for a moment. He was looking in that direction as luck would have it, and so he saw the shapes that fell from the sky at the edge of town.

They descended like fruit dropping from a tree and only as they should have struck the earth did they suddenly slow and settle themselves.

When B'Rath was much younger his family had lived on the coast near Adimone, and his father had worked on the docks, paying for the fish brought in by the boats and selling them to those who wanted to feed their families on the fruit of the sea.

There had been a fish called a sea cape. The great thing had a wide body and, instead of fins, had massive, fleshy wings that it used to swim at great speeds. His father had favored the meat and often brought them with him for the family to eat. B'Rath had always been fascinated by the things and remembered them well.

The shapes that fell from the sky reminded him of sea capes, and he watched as the wings of those shapes wrapped around the bodies until what he saw looked more like a man draped in a great hooded cloak than anything else.

He didn't need to know more than that. B'Rath hid himself against the side of his home as the forms walked closer.

The hooded shapes drifted across the muddied ground, their heads lowered and their faces hidden in shadows. As he watched, the two at the front of their short column dropped lower and their cloaks slithered and folded around them, moving across the muck of the street much as the wings of the sea capes had slithered through water or sand. The mass of their bodies nearly seemed to float, while the wings suspended them.

The heads lowered further and even through the downpour and the rumbles of thunder, he could hear the wet, snuffling sounds of the creatures sniffing the ground as if they were a pair of hounds on a trail.

One of them rose and nodded. The other stayed low to the ground and the group moved forward again.

He had seen them before, of course. Most people had seen the Undying before, at least if they lived in one of the cities instead of in the silent places where farms were more common than people.

Saramond was a large city and he lived on the outskirts. He stayed hidden as the shapes moved past his house and he whispered silent prayers to the gods. The Grakhul came for their sacrifices when they chose and he prayed desperately that his family would be spared. He had never heard of any member of his family being taken by the hooded shapes and he hoped to keep it that way.

Sometimes the gods offer favor.

The dark forms, eleven all told, moved slowly down the road and into Saramond proper.

B'Rath considered the coin he could earn by warning the slavers.

He considered his wife, his children and his ailing parents who had given up the sea and moved with him to Saramond.

He did not need the coin enough to risk his family.

CHAPTER SIX
Chains

Beron walked with his hands on his hips, scowling his disapproval to the men he'd left in charge of training the newly acquired slaves, women and children, the best sort to sell to the pleasure markets. "It's not sorcery, you idiots!" He did not speak, he roared. "Find common words! Speak to them! Use whips if you must, but make it clear that they are now property and must behave as proper servants!"

After a week of attempts to teach the new acquisitions, it had become unfortunately clear that they had no desire to be instructed. Just the same, he would have them broken and trained. They had cost him dearly and he would not tolerate this foolishness longer than necessary.

He watched on for another half an hour as the men working with him did their best. The words failed. The whips were employed. Only on the women, because children often broke under the severe beatings and dead slaves did not sell. The whips failed, too. He watched one of the pale women, one who seemed frail in comparison to most, take a dozen lashes that left her bloodied across her back and shivering from the pain. She did not cry out. She did not beg for mercy in any language. Instead she simply stood her ground, cried silent tears, grimaced and finally warned her child back when the boy became agitated and tried to come to her assistance.

He had known plenty who broke well before a dozen lashes. The whip was a great ender of arguments.

"Argus!"

The man came at the sound of his harsh voice.

There were few men who could match Beron in size. There were fewer who remained unimpressed by his voice, his temper or his combat skills. Argus was bigger, meaner and deadlier straight across the board. The only reason he listened to Beron was because the slaver paid so well.

"You bellowed?"

"Of course I did! I want them trained!"

Argus crossed his thick arms and eyed the man who employed him as if he'd caught a particularly foul fart. Beron had no idea where Argus came from. He only knew the man was pale before his body was covered with tattoos, and that he was capable of any number of dark deeds that left him apparently unworried and little concerned about any possible punishments in this or the next life. The tattoos, according to Argus, kept him safe from sorcery. When Beron expressed his doubts the other man pointed out that they'd never run across a single sorcerer since he'd allowed the first tattoo to be put on his body. It was a hard logic to deny.

"They're being trained. They're just stubborn."

"Break their wills." He looked out at the crowd of pale women and children, his eyes drinking in their shapes. They were healthy specimens to the last. That would change if they didn't start eating.

"We've talked about this. You want me to break them I can do it physically, but a lot of them will suffer before anyone breaks – or we can do it by taking the children."

Beron snorted as he looked at the pens. The children

currently stood near the adults. Separating them would be hard.

"Move them into smaller groups," he ordered. "Smaller pens. Then take the children. I know a few who would like the younger ones. They're easier to train as whores."

Without saying a word to Beron, the brutal, tattooed man gestured and several of the slavers moved to him. When he spoke they nodded and obeyed.

Beron walked away from the area, knowing that he would be obeyed and not caring beyond that simple fact.

By the time the sun was descending, the separation of women and children was nearly finished. A few of the women had to be subdued, as he expected, but overall the process was smooth.

The women, who had been docile before, now bared their teeth at the slavers who touched their children or dragged them away.

Beron contemplated their change of demeanor and smiled. He had not been aware of how unsettling their silent stares were until they replaced that placid demeanor with anger.

One of the most hostile actually growled at him.

"You would like your children back?" he asked, not expecting an answer.

She continued to stare at him with rage. But another, only a few feet away said, "You are being foolish. You don't know what you're doing."

Beron shook his head and smiled. "I am making a profit. How I make that profit does not matter to me. You can behave and follow orders and I might let you keep your children with you. Or you can ignore simple orders and I can send them to Torema, where young children get a fine price as concubines and whores." He paused as the woman considered him. "It is a long trip. Likely many would die, but you are pleasantly different in color and I think the remaining ones would fetch a fine price."

"You do not understand. The He-Kisshi are coming. They will ruin you for this." She looked him over, head to toe. "You are large and you are strong. I can see that. The He-Kisshi will kill you just the same."

"I have never heard of these 'He-Kisshi,' and I remain unimpressed."

She smiled. It was as cold a smile as he had ever seen. "You sometimes call them Grakhul."

That got his attention.

"You call them Grakhul. They are not Grakhul. We are. They are He-Kisshi. What you call Undying. They are the Undying. The Servants of the Gods."

He thought a great deal about that. Finally he nodded. "If that is true then we will move all the faster."

"What do you mean?" It was her turn to frown and that pleased Beron immensely.

"I have spent too much coin to let you go. You and yours have cost me a fortune. Enough to buy a country. I do not intend to lose my investments."

He paused a moment then bellowed for Argus. The man came over at his usual saunter. Beron looked at the skies above them and saw the bank of black clouds rising to towering heights to the north. They were the sorts of clouds that promised horrifying weather. Lightning flashes danced deep within them, lighting shadows that looked like the monsters from nightmares he'd suffered from as a child: grim things that ate the feet of sleepy children. Those demonic looking clouds were two days away at the very least. They would need to expedite matters if they wanted the slaves on their way before the storms hit.

"I need you to prepare the children for travel. Leave by tomorrow morning at the latest."

"Why the change of plans?"

He gestured to the pale beauty he'd been talking with. "My 'friend' here just said we have reason to worry. I intend to take her at her word. By the dawn and no later. I am trusting you. Do not disappoint me."

Argus nodded his head and eyed the pale woman. The wind from the north ruffled his short blond hair. "By the morning then. What of the women?"

"Leave them. I have a different destination in mind for them."

"You're taking our children from us?" The woman's voice was surprised.

Beron looked her way. "You have not cooperated. Your strength of will can only make them less controllable, so yes. They will be taken and trained to pleasure their new masters." He smiled at the horror on her face. "You did this to them. Remember that."

She looked to the clouds and nodded. "And what comes for you? You did that to yourself as well."

By the time the sun had set, ten of the King's Guard had shown themselves. They marched in unison and presented themselves to Undenk, the eunuch who protected the front of the enormous house where Beron lived. As always, they came prepared to escort him before the king – as if the man had any authority that Beron did not give him.

Beron sighed. He'd been half expecting them.

"Lord Beron, sir, King Frankel calls you to his court."

"Later than usual for that." Beron was sitting in his offices. He chose to eat there most nights, as he could see all that he owned from that position. Currently he was eating slabs of pork with hard bread and cheese. He looked at the food and then at the soldiers and continued to eat.

"Lord Beron, the king was most insistent."

"He always is." Still, he sighed and stood and the men who were there to escort him backed up a few paces. Beron was not the largest man in the city but he was definitely one of them.

He took his plate with him and continued eating as he walked the road to the palace. On some occasions he took a horse, but there wasn't time and horses did not do so well on darkened streets.

By the time he'd finished his food they were entering the palace. Beron walked with head high and shoulders squared and made his way to the throne room easily enough. It was a vast room and adorned with many magnificent works of art and sculpture. There were even a few suits of armor, none of which Frankel was likely to ever wear. He had never been in combat. He had sparred a few times when he was younger, but these days he sat on his royal ass and did nothing else without the express permission of the slavers. Except, occasionally, when he called the slavers before him to ask questions and politely make requests.

It was simple math. The slavers made the majority of the money in Saramond. The only other industries worth note involved several drugs that the slavers imported, and farming. The slavers allowed the necessity of farmers making a living. If they hadn't, there likely wouldn't have been any farms in the region, but nor would there have been food for the slavers.

Frankel was not smiling when Beron entered the room. That was a rarity. Most times the king was delighted to see the head of the slavers, because he was very happy with their relationship. Beron paid him enough to ensure he was happy, and in turn the king signed the papers that ensured the slavers were content.

"Beron." Frankel rose from his seat and gestured to a gathering of travelers to one side of the room. There were no religious orders in Saramond. Beron and his people made sure of it. Religious sorts tended to argue the rights of slaves. That would never be allowed in Saramond so long as Beron was alive. Still, the men looked like religious sorts. Like the sort of penitents he had heard of in Hollum, always ready to beg a coin and tell a person how to save themselves from the wrath of the gods.

Beron felt his skin tighten, the hairs on his neck rise, but deliberately relaxed his entire body even as he became more alert. Tension was a mistake too many people made. He seemed as relaxed as ever and looked slowly at the monks.

"These folk had some questions about a great deal of people brought into the city to be sold." Frankel allowed himself a smile that was awkward and devoid of warmth. The king was terrified and Beron knew it.

He assessed the penitents.

The throne room was well lit. A fire roared pleasantly in the fireplace and several torches hung along the walls. There was enough light to read a manuscript with ease, but the competing light sources left each form with several dancing shadows.

Beron knew instantly these were not penitents. They did not wear robes. It was flesh, the pelted flesh of–

Grakhul. No, he corrected himself, *the Undying*. The women, their children, they were the Grakhul. These were He-Kisshi, according to one of the women. They were the very source of half the nightmares known to the Five Kingdoms.

Despite himself, Beron felt his skin crawl. There was little he feared, but only the foolish felt calm in the face of the Undying.

"How can I be of aid?" Beron kept his voice calm.

The closest of the He-Kisshi rose in height until it was as tall as he was, and turned the blackness of that cowled face in his direction.

The voice was cold and dusty. "We seek our people. Our servants. They have been stolen away from us."

"How many people are we talking about?"

That darkness was as blank as any shadow but he could feel the gaze of the thing. "Hundreds. Women. Children."

It was close to a thousand, actually, but he wasn't going to disagree with the thing.

"I will keep note and bring any news I have to King Frankel. Is that acceptable?" He tried to keep his voice pleasant, tried not to panic at the thought of the Grakhul looking for his newly acquired stock. What he did not do was consider releasing the new herd. "I will also spread the word. Is there a reward for anyone who finds them?"

"Life will be the reward. Death the punishment for liars."

"If someone bought hundreds of slaves, they would have invested a great deal of money."

"Let them seek the ones who sold our servants." It paused a moment, then brought one hand from the folded flesh of its "robe." The hand held one of the heavy gold coins that the Grakhul left for every soul stolen away. "One hundred coins for the slavers who took our servants. Bring them to us alive."

Beron nodded his head slowly. "I will let all of the slavers know of your generosity."

Frankel spoke up, which was surprising as he usually only spoke in public when Beron had given him a script.

Frankel said, "Perhaps it would be best to call for a council meeting, Beron. That way the words of the Grakhul cannot be misunderstood."

Beron stared at the man for a moment and kept his face neutral. Frankel would be taught his place again but not today.

"An excellent idea. Would you like them here tonight? Or do you prefer the morning?"

Frankel opened his mouth to speak, but the Grakhul spokesman interrupted. "Tonight. Time is limited. There are great forces at play. The gods want this handled."

"I will summon them immediately. We will meet here within the next two hours." Beron turned and headed for the door. The king was a puppet. He had served his purpose.

The Grakhul did not bother turning to follow his progress, but instead spoke calmly in the unsettling quiet. "Until we receive our servants, this city is not safe. There is a great storm coming that will wash Saramond away if we are not satisfied."

Beron stared into the darkness where a face should have been and nodded slowly. He did not like threats. "Well then, I expect we should find your satisfaction."

Without another word he was on his way, and without his plate no less. There were more pressing concerns.

Twenty minutes later he was back at his offices and roaring orders to Argus. "We have been cheated. Get the children on their way now." Argus nodded and scribbled a note on paper, with a coal stick. "The very finest women are to be separated out. Prepare them for travel, set them in cages and set the cages on wagons. The rest of them must be hidden as best we can. Find places where they can be locked away. Find places where they can be tied together and gagged if need be. I will not lose a fortune over a lie."

"Why the urgency?"

"They belong to the Undying. We will not give them back. They are bought and paid for."

For a moment Argus looked like he wanted to argue, but finally he nodded his head. No one wanted to fight the Undying. Easier to face off against kings, as they already knew. Frankel was given his fill of women and the powders that made him happy. In exchange he followed orders. The Undying might not feel the same way. They weren't even human. Having seen them, Beron now understood that.

"Put out the word. That big bastard and his salesman. Brogan McTyre and Harper Ruttket. They are to be found and brought to me. I will take back what they received through their lies. Then I will skin them alive."

Argus nodded. "Where are you going?"

"I have to meet with the others. We have to prepare for a confrontation. The Grakhul..." A sigh. "The He-Kisshi will not get what they want from us without a fight."

"They are called the Undying, Beron."

"I don't intend to kill them. I intend to lie to them and if that does not work I intend to bring the Slavers' Guild down upon their heads and wrap them in enough chains to hide them from the sun forever."

Argus nodded, but Beron could see that he was not convinced.

Not that it mattered. Argus served. Beron ruled. There was a reason for that.

Their capture was inevitable and they did not resist.

Brogan and the rest of his band hid the bodies as best they could, and hid their treasures in a different spot.

The guards took their weapons, as they were not idiots. Not one of the four looked anything less than dangerous.

"This will go poorly." Harper was being optimistic. There was a very strong chance they'd be dead within the next few hours. Bron McNar did not send twenty men out after four unless he planned to honor them, or see them in chains, or beheaded. Brogan did not think the men they'd encountered had been an honor guard.

Brogan nodded his head. The men with them were silent and grim. They'd asked the same questions as the previous group and all that Brogan answered to was his name. The rest, he'd declared, would be discussed with the king. There were areas where that sort of response would end with a pike through the guts, but Stennis Brae wasn't one of them. Mostly at least. A man spoke his mind if he was so inclined and lived to tell the tale. The kingdom was not known for diplomacy. It was known for strong people who worked hard. That was enough to earn respect from most who lived in the area.

It was a long ride, several hours, to get to Journey End. It was not really a sizable town, but unlike most of the other settlements in Stennis Brae it came with a very large castle. Stoneheart lived up to its name. It was built of stone and it lay at the very heart of Stennis Brae, a massive affair built to house thousands if it came to that. Guarded by enough soldiers to keep the king safe and to defend against any who would attack. Brogan had never in his life had reason to step past the stone walls surrounding the castle. In a different time he might have been impressed, but he had seen palaces and castles before and then he had reason to study them. They were tales to tell the children and his wife. Now? Now he was here because his king demanded.

There were no chains. Had any of them resisted the second group – and had they been defeated – the four men would have been bound in irons, but as they offered themselves freely they were allowed to enter as free men.

The men who led him along did not wear their own colors. They wore the colors of the king. Some might have been related, but all were in his service. They were clean and they were uniformed. In comparison Brogan, Harper, Mosely and Sallos had been on the road for a long while and all looked forward to the idea of bathing away the dirt and sweat of their journeys and finding cleaner garments.

They did not look their best when they were brought before their king. They remained tired, road worn and dirty from their labors.

Bron McNar was their king. They respected him. He had earned their respect by building roads and keeping the peace in the area against all enemies. He was an honorable man, or, as Harper put it, as honorable as a king could be. He charged taxes but they were not too heavy, and he listened to complaints from his people with fair regularity.

The king was a big man. Not a giant as he had been described, but certainly a man of presence. He had fought hard to be where he was. There had been a time when the Mentath to the west of the mountains had tried their luck at taking Stennis Brae. That time was long past as a result of the king. He was a warrior, a diplomat and a good and wise ruler. He was also, currently, an obstacle.

The king sat on a throne carved from a single piece of the Broken Swords. The base was hard, brown stone, but, higher up, skilled craftsmen had carved one of the pieces of crystal into a wide seat. From what Brogan had heard, the stone took ten horses to pull from the mountains to the castle. The throne room was large and wide, built of granite blocks. The fires from hearth and torch alike offered light to the throne and made it glow with warm illumination.

Bron McNar leaned forward on the furs that lined his throne's seat. Heavy arms rested on knees that were bare. Like most of the men in the area he preferred a kilt to standard pants. He wore the same colors as his guards, but no one looking at him would have mistaken him for one of his followers. He was larger than life and even if he had not been a big man, he would have dominated with his presence.

He nodded as the men came forward, but his lined face was not kind under the heavy brown beard.

"You are Brogan McTyre?"

Brogan nodded his head.

"I like a man who owns his name. I like a man who tells

me truths and comes of his own volition when his king calls."

"I am honored that my king calls, but puzzled as well. What have I done to gain your attention?"

The king rose from his throne and stood to his full height, which was nearly eye to eye with Brogan himself. He stepped forward, his dark eyes locked with Brogan's.

"We'll be discussing that." He looked to Harper next. "You are Harper Ruttket."

"Yes, my king."

"I know you. I've met you before. I knew your mother and father. They were good people and I was sorry to hear of their deaths."

Rather than actually answer, Harper merely bowed his head in acknowledgement of the words. He was not comfortable with the passing of his parents or how they died.

"Do you know what makes you different among your peers, Harper Ruttket?"

Harper looked at his three companions and shook his head. "I do not, my king."

"You have not trespassed where you were not permitted."

"I do not–"

"Two scryers have told me what I need to know."

Harper shut his mouth immediately.

"You were smart to come peacefully. Your friend was not as wise."

A quick gesture of his hand and two of the guards brought Laram from where he'd been sitting in the shadows. He was in chains, his hands and ankles manacled and his face swollen from several blows. That he did not look pleased was a given.

Laram stood on his own feet, but he wobbled a bit.

Brogan shook his head. "What have your scryers claimed?"

The king didn't seem to take any offense at his lack of formality. Brogan knew he wouldn't. He was not the sort of man who measured another by their use of pretty words. It was one of the things Brogan respected about the king.

"They've told me that you have been busy, Brogan McTyre." The king's eyes were hard as he moved in front of Brogan, pacing like a war dog barely kept to heel. There had been a time when the man was called the Dog of Kinnet for a reason.

"Way I hear it," he continued, "you've gone to the far north and tried to stop the Grakhul from handling their tasks."

Brogan nodded but said nothing and after a moment, the king continued: "There are laws in all five kingdoms about the Grakhul. Those laws are passed down from ruler to ruler and they cannot be broken, not even by kings or queens. They must be obeyed."

"Why?" Brogan looked back just as hard, unflinching before his king. It was not bravery. It was anger, rage, a slow-burning fire in his chest that grew hotter every time he thought of his Nora.

The Dog bared his teeth and growled low in his guts. "Because it has always been that way, you damned fool! Because centuries ago the kingdoms all made arrangements with the Grakhul to keep the world safe from their gods."

Brogan took in a deep breath and held his tongue.

Harper did not. "My liege, the Grakhul–"

"Were upholding their part of the *bargain*!" The king's voice was a harsh bark that echoed through the chamber. Several of the men sitting around the room – men who were, no doubt, important if only in their own eyes – stirred nervously at the tone.

"What possible reason could five of my people have for breaking sacred laws?" Bron McNar skewered each of them with his gaze, his large, scarred hands curling into fists as he walked in front of them.

"There was one scryer I have met before who came to me and offered up her tale of Brogan McTyre breaking the sacred laws. And another who came and told me there were more who rode with him. Free men, guards and others like him, mercenaries, travelers who are seldom home, but lived under my laws and my rules." He paced, the king, and as he paced Brogan understood how it was that men would fear him. He was a large man and his confidence in what was right and wrong was absolute.

The scryers served all the kingdoms. According to Harper their sole purpose was to make certain that the laws of the Grakhul were honored.

The four men with him looked his way. Ultimately, Brogan knew, the answer had to be his. He was the one who'd called to them and placed them in this position.

"The other men here, they came when I asked. They followed. I led. If someone must be punished let it be me."

"That's not for you to say, McTyre! You've broken laws not easily ignored! You've put my kingdom at risk for your foolish notions! By rights I should lay the lot of you down on your funeral pyres and burn you alive!"

Brogan reached into his belt, and the king's eyes flickered down and watched. He did not tense, but he watched. A wise man knows to look for weapons.

They had been stripped of their weapons, of course. They had hidden away their newly acquired wealth. The one pouch Brogan had not worried over was the one he knew no self-respecting soldier would ever touch.

It was said that to steal the coins of the Grakhul was to risk their wrath. No one willingly angered the Undying.

Brogan held the coins in his hand and one by one he tossed them to the ground before the king. The first fell and

he said "Nora." The second fell and he called out, "Sherla."
The third, "Leidhe." His eyes were wet but he did not shed
the tears that stung them. Finally, the last coin. "Braghe."

"What?" The king's eyes widened in horror.

"My wife! My children! The whole of my family! All at
once! Taken by your precious fucking Grakhul!" His body
trembled with fury.

Bron McNar looked from coin to coin and then slowly he
looked up at Brogan.

"Tell me you would have done differently! Tell me man
to man, husband to husband, and father to father that you
would do anything differently to save your family!"

And there it was, the secret shame. Brogan did not have
to say a word, he made no accusations, but many claimed
the families of the kings and queens of the Five Kingdoms
were spared by the Grakhul as part of that ancient bargain.

"I was trying to save my family!" Brogan's teeth clenched
and he did his best to force his jaw open, that he could
speak clearly. "I called in every debt I had in this world,
every favor owed, every coin owed, and I asked that those
who call me brother help me in my time of need. I still lost
them. I saw them slaughtered. I failed!"

Bron McNar, the king of Stennis Brae, looked at Brogan
McTyre and slowly nodded his head.

"I'd have done the same." His voice was low and soft.

Brogan did not relax. He was not so foolish as to think
he was free of punishment, but perhaps he had saved his
friends.

"I would have done the same, Brogan McTyre. I would
ride to the Edge of Star End to save mine from that sort of
fate and so I understand your actions." He looked away for
the barest second, eyeing the rest of the would-be saviors.
"I ache for your loss, lad. But I cannot forgive your sins
without my kingdom paying the price."

"I will take all the fault."

"If I could I would let you. I cannot. But I will not kill a man who sought only to protect his family. I am a bastard, but not that vile."

Bron McNar gestured to the ground. "Take the coins. I've no desire to see them. Put them back in your purse and get out of my sight. Leave this kingdom, Brogan McTyre."

The king sighed, not happy with his declaration.

"You are banished. You may never return. You have until sunset tomorrow. All your lands are stripped from you. Any titles you may have are taken from you. Your families may stay, if you are fortunate enough to have any left, but each of you men is banished. It is done. Leave me before I regret my mercies."

They nodded their heads, even Laram, and as Brogan took his coins from the ground, the guards removed the chains from Laram's limbs.

McNar looked at the guards. "Give them back their weapons. They are free to go. Should they be seen after the sun sets tomorrow, they are to be killed without question."

And so it was that Brogan McTyre became a man without a country.

The Plains of Arthorne were not a kind place to begin with, but the women felt the heat more than most and their skin was not the sort that took in sun well. They did their best to cover themselves with what they had managed to scavenge or steal.

After ten days, Myridia thought they would all surely die, but the gods offered them relief in the shape of a river. They'd have missed it completely but the horses knew better and left the trail they'd been following.

The horses trotted to the waters, completely ignoring the riders on their backs. To be fair, the riders were too busy holding on for dear life to consider protesting or trying to rein them in, even if they'd known how.

The horses were large animals and much healthier than those they had known in Nugonghappalur. These animals carried them with ease and the women did their best not to anger the beasts. So far none of the horses had thrown them. It was the best they could hope for.

Back to the north and east, the storms roared and the skies were black with the fury of the gods. The only saving grace from that anger was the sweet waters washing across every gully and crevasse to be found. Streams became rivers. Rivers became flood zones as the water fell from the skies.

They rode through a desert that was taking in water like never before. The heat of the area had gone from arid to humid and the winds from the east blew colder than they had in lifetimes.

The gods were angry and, in their anger, kept their children safe from the worst of the desert's threats. The river was all they needed to survive.

Lorae dropped into the waters and spread her feet, getting her balance. She stood still after that and only moved when a fish came by. At those moments she was so fast that she blurred. Each fish she caught was thrown to the shore, where it gasped and danced and slowly died. The river was fast and the fish were careless. In minutes she had enough for all of them to eat.

When they were sated the lot of them moved into the river downstream from where the horses continued to stand and occasionally drink. The waters were sweet and soothing and they cleaned the grit from the ride off their bodies.

"Does this river take us where we need to be?" Lyraal's voice was deep and soft, a whisper in comparison to some. She spoke clearly enough however, and she looked to

Myridia when she talked.

"For now it goes in the right direction and we are ill-prepared, without water and food. We'll follow as long as we can."

She looked back over her shoulder toward the northeast and saw the titanic black wall of clouds running along the edge of the world, moving slowly in their direction.

"Have the gods spoken at all? I heard that they can. That they sometimes make their desires known." Lorae's voice was weak and insecure. She barely dared speak, as if Myridia would lash out at her. Fear made some strong and some weak. She was worried for Lorae. She was not the strongest of girls. She had youth on her side. She was resilient. If she were lucky the gods would make her strong enough.

"The gods speak to the He-Kisshi. They have never spoken to me. But I know what they want. The old tales have told us that if our home was taken we had to go to the Sessanoh, and so we will."

"The world is so large…" Lorae looked around, her eyes scanning the horizons. On one side there were the clouds. Far in the distance there were mountains, in the west, that shone with the oddest light in some places. In between there was the seemingly endless stretch of scrub grass and dirt. If not for the river there would surely be no way for them to survive the trek, not unless they found supplies.

Sometimes the gods offered aid in the strangest forms.

There was a caravan heading their way. At first they were only distant marks on the western horizon. Those forms followed the river and would soon come across their paths.

"Be aware, sisters," Myridia cautioned. "We will soon have company."

They came in wagons painted in a dozen garish colors, with horses of their own and gatherings or items stacked to preposterous heights on each of their wagons.

The women stayed where they were, and watched as the wagons came closer.

The man riding in the first wagon tipped a hat to them. He was tall and thin and his hat was much the same, dressed in red ribbons that flapped in the light breeze. As he finally reached their location, he slowed the wagon to a halt and the others followed suit. No one came from the wagons nor did he move from his spot. There were no threatening gestures made. He was wise enough to know that strangers could be dangerous when startled.

He was tanned where they were pale. He smiled as he saw them, then frowned.

"You are not in the right place. Your skin is peeling. Do you have clothes enough?"

Myridia looked at her body. She had a thin shawl wrapped over her shoulders and back, and there were strips of that same shawl over her feet. Aside from that the only clothing she wore was the occasional shadow that fell to shelter tender, sunburned skin. Most of the others had a bit more. She made sure they were sheltered properly.

"What you see is what we have." She stood taller and let the shawl fall back. He was a man. His eyes flickered over her body then back to her face. Then they moved to the dirt nearby where the remains of their meal sat raw and stripped of flesh.

"Then you are in a good place today. At least one of you knows how to fish and that is something we cannot do. So I propose a trade. You catch the fish..." He looked at the raw remains. "We cook the fish, we share the fish and we find you clothes to wear."

Five words in their native tongue and Lorae and Memni – slightly older than Lorae, and far too brave for her own good – were in the water, fishing.

"I am Myridia. We will have fish for you soon."

The man smiled, his long features seemingly designed for that purpose. His hair was cut short and his clothes were dusty but well kept.

"I'm Garien. We are entertainers, heading for Saramond."

Myridia nodded. "We head for…" She paused a moment, trying to remember the words in the tongue of the stranger. "We head for the Mirrored Lake. It is across the mountains and far to the south."

"I can't say as I've ever heard of it."

"It is hard to find."

"On a long journey then?" He looked back the way they'd come. "I know you would like to follow the river, but I'll recommend against it. There are others following us who are… unkind."

"Unkind?"

"We are entertainers. Minstrels, dancers, puppeteers. We like to make people happy and we spread the news from one place to another."

His eyes did not show happiness when he spoke again, as if a light within him had been dimmed. She preferred the smile.

"Those who follow us prefer to make bad news happen. I would avoid the night people."

"The night people? Why do you call them that?"

Garien stared at her for a long moment, not even breathing. His eyes took in details and catalogued them. She saw it in the way he stared. He was not a man who missed many details. "Because they only travel at night. I daresay no one has ever seen them by the light of day. I don't know if it hurts them, but I know they hide from it."

"Where do they come from?"

"I cannot say, but they have followed us from the tail of the Broken Sword Mountains. And that is far to the south of here."

"You have been far south of here?" She paused as Lorae called and pointed to a large collection of fish. Garien looked at the fish and nodded before looking back at her.

Garien nodded again, slowly. "Many times."

"Is there a fast and safe way to get there?"

"Head across the plains for the base of the mountains and stay there as you go south. There are a few small towns but they are not as regularly bothered as some."

"Bothered by who?"

"There are always raiders. Sure as there is a sky above us, there are raiders. They look to take what they can from anyone who looks weak."

Garien looked past her and pointed. "And now my question for you. Do you have any idea what is making that happen?" He paused as she turned to look at the towering wall of clouds in the far distance. A hundred bolts of lightning that danced and shivered, half hidden by the rains and the distance, cut the blackness but it was easy to see that the storms were violent.

Garien continued, "I have never in my life seen a storm like that." The plains were a wide open area and even from a great distance it was easy to see that the storm bank was vast.

She could have lied, but did not think she would be doing him or his a kindness. "The gods have been angered. They have sent the He-Kisshi to find the ones who interrupted the last sacrifice."

"What are the He-Kisshi?"

She frowned. "What you call the Grakhul. They are the Undying. They are the voice of the Gods and the Anger of the Gods."

"Cloaked fellows? Take as they want and leave coins behind?"

"Yes." She nodded.

Garien frowned again, this time in concentration. "I suppose I owe Em an apology."

"Em?"

"She is our acrobat. A better tumbler and climber you will never meet." Garien shrugged. "She also swore that the Grakhul were real. I have never run across them in my life, but she has."

Myridia nodded. "He-Kisshi. They are not the same thing. The Grakhul do not take people from their homes."

"And how do you know so much about them?"

"I have… met both before."

Garien smiled and nodded and his entire face was made brighter. "I have seen much of the south and you much of the north. I suspect we have seen a great deal of the Five Kingdoms between us."

Myridia did not smile. Instead she squinted back toward the storms. "You should turn back."

"Whatever for?"

"The world could end soon. The north is not a safe place for anyone."

Garien climbed down and waved to the wagons behind him. "We can discuss that after we eat. I have not had fresh fish in a very long time."

After his gesture the rest of his troupe came out of their wagons, moving cautiously, but smiling as they gathered.

One man and one woman moved toward the collection of fish. In moments they were cleaning the catch and preparing them for roasting.

CHAPTER SEVEN
The Undying in Their Rage

"We're from Mentath. That makes us stubborn as a people."
Scodd's voice boomed warmly. It seemed the only way the
man could speak was with great, bellowing words. Despite
that fact, Niall liked him and his entire family: Doria, his
wife; his son, Doug; and Temmi, who was at least as loud
and boisterous as her father. They'd stayed two days at the
lodge, while Doria insisted on fixing him and Tully as if
they were badly broken. She fed them enough for twelve.
What they could not eat the family took care of without
issue. Though it took some doing, the woman even found
shoes that were small enough to fit Tully's feet. They had,
according to Temmi, belonged to her before she'd grown
breasts. When she mentioned her breasts, the girl lifted
them in their bodice, with her hands to show Niall. Not so
much because she was bragging – though she was ample
– but because she loved the look of discomfort on his face,
and she laughed herself red at the expression he managed.
It seemed to be a point of pride for the family to be brash
and unashamed in all of their actions.

The family came from Gaarsen, a rather substantial city
on the other side of the Broken Swords. The best way to get
across the mountains was the Crystal Pathway, a natural

opening in the mountains that was named because it was lined with the selfsame crystal. Had the stones been worth anything they'd have been picked away generations earlier, but they were only quartz and not a very fine grade in that area.

In any event, the family were travelers and they sold wares. They'd planned to sell them to the Grakhul – they were among a small handful that were permitted – but the storms were too intense and they chose to ride them out in the lodge. Two days later the storms were only getting worse.

The next day Niall finally told them what had happened with both him and Tully.

The Gaarsens were horrified.

"I have heard of people getting away before." Scodd waved that part away. "Now and then someone outsmarts the cloaked ones and escapes. There are always replacements. That isn't the part that confuses me here. It's the storms. My family has made these trades for generations. My father, his father and his father before him. Longer back like as not. I have never heard tell of storms like these. Something has gone very wrong."

Scodd looked to his wife. "Do you think you should?"

Doria scowled even more than usual. She always scowled, or so it seemed. Apparently her mood could be positively joyous and she still scowled. The only time that changed was when she laughed. When laughter finally came, her face was fifteen years younger and bore a powerful resemblance to the constantly smiling Temmi.

"I'm not even certain that I can anymore."

Niall looked at the woman and found himself frowning. Mysteries had never been something he enjoyed. He preferred finding the answers to reading the riddles.

"Doria was a scryer before we were wed," Scodd explained.

Doria looked toward Niall and shrugged. "Sometimes the gift stays and sometimes it goes. I chose to leave that behind and have a family." Niall nodded as if that meant something to him but she saw right through his attempt to bluff. "Scryers have to stay in one place. They are to be at the beck and call of their nobles, the better to let the royal families know if the gods are angry."

"Is that what scryers do? I thought they only told fortunes."

Doria smiled. "That is not at all what scryers do. We only study the portents sent by the gods. If there are problems, if there is a failed sacrifice, we are there to let the royals know. If the royals have questions for the gods, we answer them as best we can."

"You actually speak to the gods?" Tully sounded astonished.

"No." Doria shook her head. "We listen to them. They do not speak to us or to anyone. We are the method they use to let their will be known. Even if a king asks a question, we do not speak to the gods. We merely send the message onward."

"The royals can't ask for themselves?" Niall asked.

"The gods cannot hear them. They will not answer unless the royals ask a scryer."

"So you used to be a scryer and quit?"

The scowl deepened and Doria shrugged, then scratched at her short hair. "Like I said, I chose to be with Scodd."

Tully looked to the older woman with wide blue eyes. "So, are you going to ask the gods what is happening?"

Doria looked at her husband and then at each of their children, then at Niall and finally at Tully. "I think I must." She shook her head. "I am not sure I will like the response, even if the gods do answer."

Without another word Doria rose from where they'd all

been sitting and moved over to the supplies they'd brought inside. A great deal more was out in their wagon, secured then hidden as best they could from prying eyes. What they'd brought in was what Scodd considered necessities. Niall had never owned that many "necessities" in his life. Then again, he was one man and not a family.

Within minutes Doria came back carrying a mortar and pestle along with a small package of dried herbs and plants.

She saw Niall's expression and nodded her head. "They'll help me attain the right way of thinking. I'm out of practice." He couldn't promise he'd kill to know what herbs went into the mix, but he knew at least a few gardeners who would.

Who wouldn't want to touch the mind of a god and hear the thoughts of the creators of the universe?

Doria very deftly cut open her palm and watched blood flow into the bowl before she ground the herbs and blood together. The mixture looked darker than he would have expected. When she was done the paste went into her mouth. Her expression said all he needed to know about how vile it tasted.

Moments later she was on one of the cots and laying back, her eyes closed and her face slack. He'd have thought she was asleep, but her hands moved. Making very meticulous gestures.

Scodd leaned in close and spoke softly. "It's been years. She used to be able to do this without any sort of assistance. Now we're not even sure if she can get an answer."

He gestured to her hands. "There are a couple of hundred ways she has to move her hands. She said it's like a prayer and a way to clear her mind. Best we stay quiet and let her think. Then we can find out what we need to do."

They were silent for a while, but the simple fact is that sometimes silence is boring, and so they moved out of Doria's earshot and talked softly among themselves.

The winds hammered against the door of the lodge, shaking the structure in its frame. Sadly the noise was no longer unusual. The storms were not slacking off at all, but staying consistently miserable.

The fireplace hissed and crackled as a thin stream of water sought to get in and douse the flames. With a solid series of coals burning in the base there was little threat of that, but the fact that water was managing to trickle in spoke volumes of the storm's intensity.

The door thudded hard in its frame, hard enough to make Tully jump and then giggle nervously.

Tully opened her mouth to speak and Doug looked toward the shaking door. Doria sat up at that exact moment and screamed, "He's coming here! He is so angry!" Her voice was stricken with panic and her eyes were wide.

The door shivered once more then was ripped from its hinges and hurled out into the storm. Water splashed in and the wind came blasting through. A heartbeat later a silhouette came to the threshold, a black shape that looked like a man bracing against the wind. It was not a man, and despite knowing that he had killed the damned thing, Niall recognized the monster that came through the door.

That dark, hooded face looked at the ground initially, but soon rose to scan the room. It took in Doug and then Doria, body moving with the head, the cloak-like form shuddering with each bellowing breath, buffeted from beyond by the gale.

Tully, who had been sitting cross-legged before the fireplace, did her very best to stand up and force herself through the closest wall, facing the nightmare that had previously tried to kill her.

"We killed you!" Her voice broke and her skin, already pale, grew paler still. Her eyes were wide and in that moment Tully looked all of twelve.

Niall rose as quickly as he could, searching in vain for a way to get past the hellish thing blocking the doorway with its body.

"I am Undying, you foolish bitch!" The He-Kisshi stepped into the lodge. Lightning tore at the ground behind it and backlit its shape as it slipped into the place that was supposed to be a sanctuary.

Scodd spoke up, forcing a smile across his round face. "This is a place of shelter. No one is supposed to be attacked here." His words were nervous. He knew what he was facing. He understood that the thing was a He-Kisshi. He'd been the one who had explained to Niall and Tully the difference.

"Be silent!" The monster's words were a whip crack in the air, followed by the thunder that always chased after lightning. "Do not speak and I may yet spare your lives!" The clawed finger of the thing jabbed at each member of Scodd's family, then turned to stab at Tully and Niall.

"But they are forfeit." The words were softer now, hissed. "I will have my satisfaction."

Gods be praised, Doug and Scodd both stepped forward at the same time and spoke as if they were one. "No. You will not!" Scodd's thick, booted foot kicked upward and slapped across the demon's cloaked legs.

Doug aimed higher and his heavy fist – complete with something in it – smashed into the cowl as if striking at a face. The hooded shape staggered and fell, and for a moment Doug looked pleased.

Then the thing rose up as quickly as any man ever had and ripped its clawed fingers across Doug's face, tearing trenches down to the bone beneath his flesh.

Doug fell back shrieking in agony and Scodd screamed in denial, shaking his head, horrified by what had happened to his son.

The big man's teeth were clenched and his eyes narrowed in fury as he slammed his mass into the He-Kisshi. The first attacks had been fairly successful but his latest attempt may as well have been thrown at a stone pillar. The nightmare did not move. The arms of the thing reached out and grabbed at Scodd, hoisting him easily from the ground despite his weight and throwing him toward the fireplace and the blaze it held.

Niall stepped in and pushed, knocking his recent companion away from certain death.

Tully was no longer screaming, but instead was crouched low, her legs wide, her knees bent, her eyes locked on every motion their enemy made.

Outside lightning ripped across the skies and sent rumbling growls across the air. Inside the lodge, the storm crashed into every living being.

Doria bellowed out words that were not her own, spoken in a tongue that was utter gibberish to all of the listeners save one. The He-Kisshi made the same words, the same proclamations, in the same tongue. Niall could not tell if the words came from the woman, the creature or perhaps from the gods themselves. Whatever the case the guttural sounds were unsettling.

The young woman who had moments before been chuckling over making him uncomfortable with her body was now screaming at her brother, trying to get him up from where he lay on the ground, clutching at his ruined face.

Scodd was hauling himself back to his feet, glaring hatred at the cowled thing that had tossed him aside with ease.

Tully threw the contents from the pot boiling above the fire onto the cloaked nightmare and set it screeching in agony. Hot liquids, hot stew and the bits of meat and vegetables they had been planning to eat spilled down its front and side.

Niall followed her lead, reached for the small shovel for removing ashes from the fireplace. He quickly filled it with hot coals and hurled them into the face of the thing.

A trail of red flashing stars filled the air between monster and shovel, raining down across its face, its side and the ground. The monster screamed again and Doria continued her rant.

Scodd ran toward the family's supplies and drew a short sword from its scabbard, hurling the cover away and charging toward the cloaked demon.

When it turned toward the man, Scodd carved away a part of its arm with a sweep of the blade and sent it staggering back.

"I'll *kill* you!" Scodd roared as he moved forward, swinging the blade again. The second blow was just as solid but not quite as successful. Flesh was stabbed but the demon grabbed at Scodd with its other hand and sank long talons deep into his forearm, hooking meat and scraping bone.

The jovial man was gone, replaced by a killer. Rather than stop attacking because of his injury Scodd hurled himself at the thing harder, pummeling the hood of the creature with his free hand.

The third time his fist drove into the hood, the beast bit down, clamping its teeth into the man's flesh. Having had the misfortune of seeing the rows of sharpened fangs, Niall couldn't help cringing. Scodd let out a horrified squeal and tried to pull his hand away, but instead came back with a bleeding stump. Part of his hand was still there, but what remained had been crushed and torn, broken and shredded.

The hooded thing spat out lumps of meat and bone and dove forward, the vast, bloodied mouth snapping at Scodd's face. There were more things than Niall had first realized about that face. There were appendages almost like fingers that came out and tried to pull the man's head closer in.

Niall clasped his small iron shovel and rammed the blade into the furred back of the He-Kisshi, drawing blood and scraping skin away from what lay beneath.

The thing whipped around to face him and the whole of the body moved along. The "cloak" opened and revealed the same hellish shape he had seen before. One wing slapped around and struck him above the eye, sending him staggering back to land on his backside.

Tully buried a blade in the shoulder of that unholy shape, blood slopping free as it arched its back and screamed again. The mouth, so like a cowl, stretched wider than usual and it staggered toward the open door, running from them, both hands trying to unseat the dagger wedged deep into its unclean flesh.

The pelt of the damned thing smoldered and burned where coals had seared their way into the hide of the beast.

The great wings of the He-Kisshi flapped madly for a moment and then it was airborne, rising higher and higher into the air, its shape highlighted by more lightning strikes.

Doria finally stopped speaking her unsettling gibberish. Her eyes remained wide and horror-struck as she looked around the waterlogged room. Rains slashed through the doorway and soaked the ground, extinguishing the coals that still glowed on the floor.

Scodd was on the ground, holding what was left of his hand. Temmi was cooing to her brother, who softly sobbed as she pressed cloths to his ruined face to staunch the blood. Tully calmly stomped out the few blossoming flames that the rains missed.

Niall stared after the horrible beast and then moved to Scodd. The hand was a ruin, but his life could still be saved.

Outside there was one last scream of outrage as the He-

Kisshi rode away on the wind.

Doria looked around slowly, but Niall doubted she saw anything at all.

"We are doomed," she whispered. "The gods have no mercy. They will end the world unless we find a way to stop them."

Bron McNar sat on his throne and brooded. He was not a man given to brooding. Brooding required a level of deep thought he was not usually fond of. He preferred action. There were those who claimed the crown was a burden. Bron did not agree. It was a privilege that came with many rewards. He had a wife who was lovely and two young children. He had more money than he would ever be able to spend and he had a country that looked to him favorably rather than wishing him dead.

Every three years there was a gathering of kings. During the last two there had been peace among the kingdoms – save for the inevitable arguments between families on the borderlands that happened no matter what state the kingdoms were in. Bron felt a part of that and even got along well enough with Mentath and King Parrish, the man in charge there now, who was as insane as his father had been before Bron put him down. If there was ever a man who should have hated him, Parrish was the one.

The world was mostly a good place. He believed that in his heart. There were monsters, to be sure. There were things that moved through night and day alike that would kill anything they could touch, but they were the reminders to be grateful and nothing else.

And then there was Brogan McTyre. Bron closed his eyes for a moment and relived the confrontation, felt again the shame and horror as each of those massive coins hit the floor not fifteen feet from where he was currently sitting.

His shame was matched only by the fury he faced in the other man.

He would have done the same. He tried telling himself otherwise, but to have anyone come for his wife and children, why, the only possible answer could be blood.

He let them go. Five men he should have held for the Grakhul or the vile things that came seeking sacrifices. Bron was not completely certain there would be consequences but he suspected there was a good chance.

He was still brooding, elbows on knees and chin resting on heavy fists, when the seer came back to him. Mearhan Slattery was fairly young and pretty enough in her way. Heavy freckles, red hair and crooked teeth. Big blue eyes and a buxom shape. She had a sour look on her face, not because she was angry but because she would be bearing bad news. She was also feeling the burden of her own place in the world as surely as he was feeling the weight of his crown. Mearhan had confessed to feelings for the young man who'd fought against coming back. Laram his name was. He'd apparently twice before proposed marriage to her father and been denied.

He sat up straighter as she approached. There were places where protocols stopped people from speaking to their leaders. Bron did not abide that. Certain times of the day he sat on his throne and waited for people to talk to him. It was part of his duty as far as he was concerned and if someone came from halfway across the country it seemed only proper to see them.

He wasn't a fool, mind you. They had to come with empty hands. No weapons. Words, however, could be quite as cutting.

"King Bron."

"What brings you back here, Mearhan Slattery?" He rose from his throne and looked around the room. His closest advisors, men he knew he could trust, were still close at hand, though not a one of them looked comfortable at that moment

She lowered her gaze for only a moment before looking back at him. "I bear a message for you, my liege."

He had asked for possible solutions to the dilemma before him as a king before Brogan McTyre had come to him and offered himself for judgment. In all the chaos, he had forgotten that he'd spoken to the young woman and to his most often used scryer, Eida Minster. He supposed Eida would be upset about it but there was nothing to be done for that now. Eida was a proud old woman and well paid. She would survive any unintentional insult.

"Speak your piece, Mearhan, as I know you must."

"The gods have spoken again and they are angry. You have released Brogan McTyre and the rest. They want them captured and brought before the mirrored lakes at Sessanoh."

"Never heard of the place. Wouldn't know where to find it." He crossed his arms. One thing to be given a warning. Another entirely to be told what to do by gods to whom he owed no allegiance. "Perhaps they should speak to their Undying about how to handle the matter."

Mearhan shook her head. "I've no say in this, my king. I only give you what I have been given. The gods say that the world will end if this thing is not done. They are ending it now." Her voice shook. "They are destroying the world, King Bron."

Tears started in her eyes and the king was reminded that under the burden she carried she was still only a slip of a girl, younger than he was when he took his crown and younger by far than he was when he married. "They are killing the world, my king. They have started already. Before the week is done the Undying will destroy Saramond for taking what belonged to the gods, what was sold to them by Brogan McTyre and his men."

Bron shook his head, his brow knitting. The gods were not to his liking but that hardly mattered. Scryers did not lie. To do so was to risk the fury of the gods and there were stories aplenty of what happened when they tried to pervert the words they uttered to their own benefit.

The woman stepped back, her hands clutching at the area over her heart. Her man, Laram, whatever else happened his fate was the same as Brogan's. "I know their reasons, but it does not matter to the gods. They will destroy everything if Brogan McTyre and his men are not captured, chained and brought to them. They showed me a sign that proves how unworthy the men are, my king."

"What sign would that be?"

"You sent out an escort to bring Brogan McTyre and his men to your throne. They did not come back with him. That is because he and his men murdered them all and hid their bodies. I have been told where you will find those bodies now, my king."

He had indeed sent out an escort. They'd not returned, but there were several roads and he'd assumed they had taken a different path. "Show me."

"Have you a map?"

Bron shook his head. "We will take horse right now. Come and show me."

It was very possible that she did not want to go, but that hardly mattered. When a king spoke he expected that he would be obeyed. That was the price for all a king did for his people.

Four hours and most of the daylight gone found Bron, Mearhan and a dozen of his soldiers standing around the spot where combat had occurred and not far from the spot where the bodies had been thrown.

The area was mountainous. The Brundage Highway was only a dirt road, but it was paved and well oiled, the ground strong enough to resist the rains and the run off after the winter alike. With winter not far away, Bron had made certain the road was coated with oils again in preparation and next year cobblestones were to line the way.

The cairns were a landmark to be sure. Three times the height of a large man and ten times that wide, fitting a road between them had been a challenge but it was the best way to mark the path in the distance. What secrets they held were something that none could answer, though many had speculated upon. Ultimately, they were landmarks and little else. Too far in one direction and you ran into part of the Broken Swords where the ground could be treacherous. Too far in the other direction and there was a cliff that fell a few hundred feet down to the Mentath River. Anything dropped there would be lost for certain, unless what fell was caught in the rocks below.

The rocks loved to eat. That was what his father had said when Bron was a lad.

Looking down he could clearly see several bodies a hundred or so feet below. They were dead. They wore his colors. It was enough.

"The gods claim Brogan McTyre and his followers did this?"

"Yes, my king."

Behind him the head of his personal guards, Ulster Dunnaly, sat on his charger and watched. Ulster was not a giant. He did not need to be. He was one of the fiercest men Bron had ever known and had saved the king's life on several occasions during various skirmishes.

"Ulster?"

"Aye, King Bron?" Ulster was one of only a dozen who he would have called brother.

"Gather fifty men. Take hounds and good trackers if you

like, my friend. But whatever the case, I need you to hunt down the bastard Brogan McTyre, and either bring him to me or bring him to this damned mirrored lake."

"I don't know where—"

"Just make it so." He looked to the scryer. "Mearhan here will go with you. She'll make sure we keep the gods as pleased as we can."

Mearhan slumped a bit in the saddle. Still, she nodded. A king must be obeyed or there would be consequences.

"This goes poorly, Brogan." Harper rode his horse as if there was not a care in the world. Brogan knew better. There were cares aplenty. They had been forced to leave their homes and money or no, a man without a country to call his own was a man set to swimming in a sea of worries.

"I had noticed that, Harper."

Laram looked around from ahead of them and showed his bruised and hammered features. He was scowling. Or maybe that was just the swelling in his lips.

"Mearhan was the one who told the king's guards. Who told old Bron himself."

"Mearhan?" Brogan frowned. "You mean old man Slattery's daughter? The one you wanted to marry?"

"Aye. That very one."

Harper shook his head. "Why would she do a fool thing like that then?"

"What choice? She's a scryer."

Harper shrugged. "Well then, don't go taking it personally. She had a job to do."

Laram nodded. Before they'd left the area he and the others had gone to where Laram had hidden away his gold. None of them were foolish enough to get caught on the road with that much wealth. Now all of them were once again riding with fortunes wrapped in cloaks, sewn into hidden pockets and stashed on their bodies where they could make room. Money enough to buy castles and keeps and not a bit of it mattered as they rode away from Stennis Brae for the last time.

"Where are we going?"

"Well away from Saramond." Brogan looked to the east in the direction of Saramond. It was too far to see even a smudge on the horizon from their current distance. But he could see the banks of storms that rode like a cresting wave over the place where the slavers did their business. "By now I expect they've found the truth of the matter and we will not be welcomed with open arms."

Harper nodded. "I imagine they'd gladly open throats for us, or bellies."

"I should rather not consider that," muttered Mosely.

"I'm sorry for this, lads. I mean that truly." Brogan spoke softly but they all heard him.

Harper spat. "You can take your apologies to your grave, Brogan. We all knew what we were doing. I warned each and every man who rode with us after they agreed, just as soon as you weren't there to cut my throat for it."

Brogan cast an eye at each of the men aside from Harper and all of them nodded their agreement.

"We all of us knew the risks. It wasn't just you I told to consider the consequences. I could do no less for hardworking mercenaries." Harper stretched, his eyes roaming the far off horizon. "Besides which, the general consensus is you'd have returned the favor."

Brogan shook his head. "I may not have been completely sane through this."

"Few would be, you damned fool. Few people are ever sane when they lose as much as you have."

There was silence between them before Brogan gestured. "South, I suppose."

"Giddenland or Torema?" Harper's eyes slid to look at him, half his mouth lifted in a smirk.

"They are the same place, Harper. Torema is in Giddenland." Laram scratched at his chin as he spoke.

Harper's smirk became a smile. "Spoken like a lad who has never been to Torema. There was never a finer city for spending a fortune on your dreams, my lad." Harper spread his arms wide. "Torema is the place where you go if you want to forget your sorrows or buy a few fond memories. I'm for both, myself."

Brogan nodded. "You can have anything you like in Torema, provided you have coin enough. Currently you could buy a new life there and still have enough left over for a house the size of a castle."

Far to the east there was a sustained blast of lightning. It was bright enough to light up a portion of the horizon perhaps even a hundred miles wide. They were weeks away from that spot but the light was bright enough to make them squint and left even Harper unable to come up with something to say.

When it was done, they waited in silence and Brogan found himself counting as he'd been taught to do, to estimate how many leagues away the lightning might be. It was a vain effort as far as he could tell. The light show was far too distant.

"What was that?" Sallos's voice broke.

"Possibly the largest stroke of lightning ever seen by a living being." Harper's lips were pursed into a small *o* as he spoke. He whistled softly between his teeth.

"That couldn't have been lightning." Sallos's tone said what they must surely all have believed.

Harper shrugged again, his face worried. "'And the world was born as it will end, in a great storm that forged mountains from islands and lifted the land from the seas.' I believe that is what the gods wrote once upon a time."

"Fuck the gods." Brogan spoke clearly. "They've nothing they can say that I want to hear. They're vile things that take instead of give. I do not want them. I do not need them."

Brogan looked at the area where the fearsome white-blue barrage had finally settled down, and shook his head. "South. We go south. It's as good a direction as any for the present time."

Instead of heading down into the plains immediately, however, they stayed in the mountains and wove their way across the paths that existed there. For the present. Brogan's mind would not leave alone the notion that they had gotten away too easily and it would be a great sight harder for anyone to follow them through the mountains and foothills than it would to follow them on open ground.

The winds picked up from the east and it sounded like the sky was roaring in the distance. Part of him wondered if the turmoil in the air was caused by the electrical storm. He suspected it was, and that notion left him cold. Or maybe it was winter's teeth sinking in. They were due for bad weather and it looked like they'd have it one way or another.

Beron's house was a small castle. That was the truth of the matter. He had a score of men working for him, each well trained and well paid. They were the ones who made sure every man coming in for the meeting was on his best behavior.

The Slavers Guild had five people in charge of it. The head of them was Beron. He earned the most and he demanded the strictest rules. All were tied together by mutual need, the need to keep the slave trade alive in a time when many countries frowned upon it.

The good news was that people always needed slaves. The better news was that those who mattered in making decisions could always be bought or threatened. Mostly they were bought. When Lord Harrington of Adimone – who publicly condemned slavery and pushed for the end of the trade – was found tied to a post, his body cut deeply in a hundred and seventeen places and then flayed as a message, the hint was received by nearly everyone in the Five Kingdoms. Better to deal with the slavers than to risk their ire. More profitable, too.

Ellis sat to the right of Beron at the small table. His face was long and dour, his hair was longer still, even drawn into hard braids, but he was a shrewd man who understood that strength was heightened by joining forces rather than arguing. Ellis was by far the most adept "breaker" they had. Currently the fifty most stubborn women among the new slaves were in his stables being softened. In time they'd come around or they'd die. Long before the time came for death they'd wish for the caress of the Taker.

Levarre sat on Beron's left. He was a businessman first and often offered advice on how best to stay ahead in a market that changed as often as the moons. Levarre was also the man who'd suggested handling Lord Harrington as a method of making a statement. He was not to be trifled with. As thin as Ellis was, Levarre was thick. Most of him was muscle but not all. He had a belly that shook when he walked. He also had four wives to keep him satisfied, all of them slaves he formally owned.

Lexx was the fourth of the guild leaders, a lean, seasoned warrior who'd run the wagons to the south for fifteen years and never once lost a slave on the arduous rides. A few people claimed that was not true, that he replaced the slaves who died along the way, but no one could say for certain and Beron didn't question the matter as long as the money showed up when it was supposed to. Lexx had scars on his face from a few personal duels. He'd won them of course, else he would not have been at the table.

Lastly there was Stanna, who was easily the scariest woman that Beron had ever met. She shaved most of her dark hair away and what was left fell in a wave across the top of her head and then down into a braided mass. She was as tall as he was and heavily muscled. She likely weighed half as much as he did but she made up for that in ferocity and her skills in general. She carried a sword she affectionately called "the bitch." It was well used and according to some it actually screamed when in combat.

Beron had no desire to find out for certain.

"Let's get to business, shall we?" Stanna leaned back in her chair and planted her booted feet on the top of his table. It was not a very fancy table and he didn't mind. Even if he had, he'd not have mentioned it to her or anyone else. Stanna was one of his best allies. Why ruin that over a little mud on the wooden table?

Beron smiled and nodded. "On to business, then. It's been three days and the Grakhul are losing patience."

"How go the plans?" Lexx leaned over the table and planted his elbows. "How many are away?"

Levarre answered that one. "The most valued of the lot are already gone. We've trains to send the rest of them out in the next two nights, all except those that Ellis deems unbreakable."

"They'll break. For now they are hidden in the cellars. They won't be found." No one doubted Ellis's word.

"So." Lexx leaned back and crossed his arms. "We do this tonight?"

Beron spread his arms. "No choice in the matter. We've all seen what is going on outside. The storms are only getting stronger."

"How is it that little cloaked men can hold back a storm?" Stanna shook her head. The Grakhul had said the city could only be spared if the white skins were returned. To make their point they'd gestured to the window of Frankel's castle and shown the approaching storms. With a gesture the one in charge – Dowru-Thist – had stopped the storms from approaching the city's perimeter. Now, three days later, there was a half circle of area around the town where the clouds and storms were held at bay. The rest of the system stretched out on both sides, winds raging and lightning clashing constantly, but Saramond was unmolested. Around the city waters rushed and washed away trees and bushes and even a few huts from near the edge of the city, places where the poorest tried to eke out a living on farms they built for themselves. Those farms were gone, washed away with their owners in most cases. Plantations where the slavers grew the crops to feed themselves and their charges were out there, too, and many of them were already ruined by the storms.

Beron shook his head. "They say they do the will of the gods. I have seen no gods in Saramond. They are likely sorcerers. When we are finished with them they will not be able to cast any spells."

"They are called the Undying." Levarre's tone was conversational.

Beron spoke softly. "They are not called unimprisoned. We are *slavers*. If anyone can wrap a living thing in chains and hold it forever, it is us." He too leaned back from the table. "We have a plan. We have discussed it long enough. We have to act, or we will lose all that we have fought to make ours. I do not intend to leave this world a poor man or a prisoner." His eyes narrowed as he looked at each of his companions. "I have been both in my time and I found the experience unpleasant."

"So we start now?" Stanna took her heels off the table then rose from her seat. The chair sighed with relief. "Then let us do this thing."

"Are your people in place?"

"They will be in twenty minutes."

Beron nodded. "Let's do this thing, indeed."

The false king sat on his throne and gulped nervously at his red wine. A hundred tempests raged nearby and he must have known how close he was to those storms tearing his kingdom apart.

"Why are they not here yet?" Dowru-Thist spoke softly. It seldom needed to raise its voice.

Frankel looked toward him and took another quick sip of wine.

"I. That is. They said they would be here before the sun set."

"The sun has already set." It pointed to the window facing west, where the storms were not yet hiding away the world beyond. The sun had indeed set, leaving only a thin line of light on the horizon. In minutes the stars would show themselves.

"Perhaps I should have them brought here?" The man managed to flinch with his voice.

"I wonder how it is that you have remained king for so long?" Dowru-Thist's words remained soft, but the false king twitched as if slapped across the face.

"I was born into my position. It was the gods who appointed my family."

"Which gods, I wonder. Most certainly not the ones that I obey."

"See here now..." the king started. His voice fell off when Dowru-Thist looked in his direction.

"It does not matter. They have not come to us. We will

go to them. When we are finished dealing with your slavers we will come back to you and… complete our discussions."

A gesture and the others moved before him, leaving a foolish king on his gilded throne to drink his too sweet wine.

Dowru-Thist heard Frankel break into soft sobs and felt grim satisfaction. The gods were angry. Someone would pay. If the He-Kisshi could avoid the world being destroyed they would, but time was dwindling.

They would act. They had waited long enough.

Once through the gates of Frankel's stronghold and in the streets, they sought out the scent of the slavers and headed for the one called Beron's place.

Dowru-Thist was only moderately surprised by the men who faced off against them. In all cases the desperate tended toward foolishness.

One hundred slavers with weapons and chains. That was the agreed upon number. Twenty from each house of the guild. Those men were seasoned and brave and had been informed that should they succeed they would have their weight in gold. The offer was a very large fortune, but those chosen also understood that no one expected all of them to succeed.

So they moved in fast and hard, determined not to become victims of the Undying.

The eleven figures moved slowly into the road, each looking around, moving their heads or sometimes their whole bodies as they studied their surroundings.

One of them spoke clearly, his voice loud enough for all to hear despite the winds that whipped and howled around the city.

"If you walk away all will be forgiven. If you stay you will be punished."

Lexx was the one who walked forward, his lean arm around the waist of a woman bound with her elbows behind her back and her legs tied at the knees. She was one of those who had been held at Ellis's and was a fighter through and through. She was wearing little beyond a rough cloth dress. He was dressed in armor, his cloak slapping in the sudden winds. Comely as the woman was – pale, but attractive – he'd have never considered being with her or even taking her by force until after she was bathed and perfumed. She stank of her own sweat and piss and waste.

She looked at the Undying across the way from her and sighed.

Lexx regarded them and smiled thinly, doing his very best to hide the way his guts were shivering. These things were nightmares in appearance. Seen from a distant they were cloaked and hooded men. Studied up close as he had seen them they were abominations that should not have existed. Most of the men with him had never seen one up close and the darkness hid the worst of them.

Several of the men held torches. Others stood near the braziers they brought with them for the purpose of handling these He-Kisshi. They were large braziers borrowed from Frankel's stores. Getting them in place had been a harsh task but worth it.

Lexx nudged the woman forward. "Turns out we have a few of your pale-skinned wenches. If you'd like them back you'll have to leave the city peacefully. You can gather them on your way out."

The one that spoke most often tilted its cowled head – if it were truly a head. Lexx could not decide. "There is a misunderstanding. We are not here to negotiate. Give all of our people to us, or suffer."

"Some of them are already gone. Heading away from here to be sold as playthings and good laborers." Lexx shrugged and slid a dagger from the sheath at his hip, placing the blade along the pretty woman's muddied face. "We'll kill the rest if you don't take the offer. Leave here with them or stay and find out how much pain we can cause you."

A long pause and then, "We are Undying. We are He-Kisshi, the Living Word of the Gods. We are their Divine Punishment upon the world."

It made a gesture. Small, insignificant, really, but just large enough for Lexx to notice.

It spoke softly in a tongue that Lexx did not know.

The girl he held onto turned her head slightly then jammed her temple into the tip of his blade. Lexx had learned long ago that the only way to carry a weapon was as if you meant to use it. To that end, he had had a solid grip on his dagger. The tip of his blade drove through her temple and into her brain with surprising ease.

She fell dead, her body shuddering as it crashed to the dirty road.

The thing that had spoken reached out toward him and leather slashed the night. Lexx had not seen the whip, but he felt it. The tip of the creature's whip was a sharpened stone that took Lexx's eye with an audible snap.

Any chance of posturing dropped away. The pain was all that mattered. Lexx fell back, covering the laceration on his face and feeling what was left of his eye bleed from the socket. He dared not try to open it. He could barely stand through the fire that was trying to eat that part of his face.

"There will be no mercy!" The thing hissed the words and as it did the rains began to fall. The winds that had been touching the areas around the city slipped in through the alleys and places where walls did not meet. "Give us our people or die!"

To make its point the thing slashed again and the whip skittered up Lexx's arm and shattered the bones in his hand.

Around him the hundred warriors shifted uncomfortably. The pain was a wave that was drowning him, but if he wanted to survive or even have a chance he needed only give the order.

"Take them! Take them now!" His voice cracked as he gave the command.

A second later the whip came again and shattered his teeth, ripped the side of his face into so much bloodied meat, Lexx fell to the ground in the rain and whimpered. But with his one good eye he saw so very much.

The archers came first. Despite the winds and the rain they were good at their craft. Twenty arrows thrummed down from the rooftops and drove into the dark cloaks. The screams that came from them were proof enough that they were not human. The sounds were closer to howls than anything else.

The Undying reacted, moving into a tight circle, their backs to each other as they looked around. The next volley of arrows came almost as quickly as the first but the Grakhul were not surprised a second time.

The one with the whip turned his attentions to the first man coming closer and despite himself Lexx thanked the gods. The man was dressed in hard leather armor and carried twin blades. He was skilled and came prepared to defend against the weapon. Instead of attacking with the whip the nightmare opened its wings and flapped them in a frenzy. Standing on its toes, the thing directed rainwater and wind at the approaching man until he was obligated to squint and try to block the waters.

The thing moved forward at that moment, wings falling back and whip snapping forward in the same motion. The slashing stone carved through the man's thigh and into his groin. Blood flowed and the first of one hundred men was down.

The archers were not done. More arrows fell and drove into the creatures. Two of them rose into the air, their cloaks opening like the sails of a ship and snapping on the hard breeze.

The weighted nets came down on them and drove them back into the mud, screaming their outrage as they fell.

The one with the whip started to say something before an arrow drove into its shoulder and pierced clean through to the other side.

The whip fell from its hand and it spun toward Lexx. "Call them off before it is too late!"

Lexx managed to shake his head. He did not try to speak again. There was too much ruin where his handsome face had been.

The nets dropped from above and more came from street level, thrown by men who had chased down more than one runaway slave in their time. They were here for a reason, experts at what they did.

That didn't mean the fight was over. The Undying moved despite the nets, grabbing the men who tried to capture them, dragging the nets as if they weighed nothing instead of being enough to drop even a man the size of Beron. Some of them grabbed the nets and swept the heavy weights into the air, slashing them at their enemies and tangling them into the thick mesh.

Once they captured anyone, they dragged them in close enough to tear them limb from limb.

The chaos was too much for the archers. They could not fire without hurting their own, and so they left the heights and came down, bringing their pole arms and bludgeons with them.

The netted men were broken with ease. The He-Kisshi were not so easily broken. Making matters worse the winds came harder and the rains slammed down, extinguishing fires and pelting every form in the street with hard rain and hail as well.

Lexx managed to make it to his knees and then his feet, despite the downpour, and stumbled to the closest wall watching on as the fight continued.

The spears came next. None of the weapons were used to strike fatal injuries. Instead He-Kisshi arms and legs were impaled, and the men wielding the weapons backed away hastily as the Undying continued on. Twenty spearmen learned the hard way that striking did not guarantee victory. Most tried to retreat only to be met with more of the weighted nets. The weights were substantial, they had to be and they were hard. Being hit by them was painful under most circumstances but in the claws of the unholy things the force was enough to break bones.

They had known the damned things would be hard to kill or capture. They were not called Undying for nothing and the stories they'd heard of how brutal the beasts were could only be called plentiful.

That was why five slavers had offered one hundred men a fortune.

Still, inevitably, Lexx was sure the sheer numbers of slavers were bound to overtake the eleven vile creatures.

Lexx nodded his head as fifty men with bludgeons and staffs came out from the shadows and took to beating at the He-Kisshi. Furred flesh was cut and bruised. Bones broke. Inhuman shapes faltered and fell. Slavers were thrown aside or slashed open by deceptively sharp claws.

Still the staffs and clubs did their work. Men panted and grunted and struck again and again as the hellish things curled in on themselves and waited for the beating to finish. In time the Undying were pounded into submission.

Lexx could no longer give orders. His mouth was flayed into bloodied waste. His hand ached. His eye was very likely a loss. He was dizzy with pain. Still, he felt a certain joy.

The damned things were wrapped in their nets, bound with iron manacles and dragged through the torrential rains and sleet. They were Undying, perhaps, but he knew they would suffer. Staggering and half-drunk on his pain Lexx still led the way to Ellis's home and the tender mercies he would offer their unwelcome guests.

Ellis nearly screamed when he saw Lexx. The man was ruined. His face was flayed open, but he came in triumph and brought the Undying with him. The pens under Ellis's house were dry and ran the length of his estate. They'd cost a great fortune to the previous owner, his father. Part training pits, part hiding place, the ceiling was barely six feet in height and the majority of the wall space on both sides was built of hard wood, well-conditioned and meant to endure for generations. His father had never been a man to spare on the expenses of his business. Ellis was grateful for that.

Deeta, the best of his people at fixing wounds, was called upon to do what he could for Lexx. The man went calmly but within ten minutes everyone heard his screams. Sometimes mending took a great deal of stitching. Sometimes wounds had to be cauterized.

By that time Ellis was well into his work. They were called the Undying. He was not there to kill them, but to make sure they could never get free.

The beasts were left chained and netted. To make certain they stayed secured, Ellis added more chains then ordered them placed in one of the pits he often used to let his more obstinate cases contemplate the cost of being too stubborn.

Perhaps they could not die. Perhaps that was a true thing, but he intended to test the notion and test it he did.

Once the bodies were thrown, hissing and struggling,

into the bottom of the pit, his men added rocks. A great numbers of rocks. They formed a line and moved the heavy stones from one person to the next before heaving them into the pit. There was a plan to build a stone wall around his property, but that could wait. In the meantime the stones found a better purpose. They settled against the Undying and pressed them harder and harder into the ground.

The women who were there, the slaves who refused to obey, howled their miseries into the air and the few that could speak the common tongue begged in their hoarse voices for Ellis to free the Undying before it was too late.

Ellis walked to the closest of them and smiled at her tears. "Perhaps if you obeyed. Perhaps then you could have saved your friends." He thought about it. "Perhaps if you obey now I will save them yet."

"We will obey you. Whatever you desire will be yours." Her voice shook, her pale lips trembled. She was a lovely thing in her misery. Ellis always preferred a woman in tears.

Still, he was a businessman. "You are a sweet temptation. Just the same, those things must be stopped."

His men sweated and strained, moving stone after stone until the last was dropped in place.

Damned if he could not hear those hellish things moving down below. Crushed under enough stones to surround his house they continued to make noises.

Still, they'd not be going anywhere.

The rains continued outside.

The thought occurred to Ellis that adding water to the mix might put an end to the things, but that was not the plan. Not yet at least.

When he was certain that the job was finished, Ellis stretched and looked at his bevy of women. The training would start soon enough, especially now that the creatures were pinned. If they were truly still alive they'd be able to hear the sounds of their pale women being trained to accommodate new men. Ellis rather looked forward to that part of the training.

Ori watched the vile man walk away and resisted the urge to spit. Give them a reason, they would surely find a cause for a beating. She had already endured several attempts to make her subservient and had even agreed to one if the slavers would spare the He-Kisshi.

In the pens around her, others stirred and stretched. Like her, they had heard the summons of the Undying.

"What will we do, Ori?" Amira was twelve. She should have been with the children, not penned with adults, but her body looked older and that was enough for the slavers.

Ori looked to the younger girl. "The He-Kisshi have asked us to free them from their prison. That is what we will do."

"But how?"

In answer to the question, Ori braced her back against the wall of the narrow pen and then planted her feet on one of the boards. The wood was solid. It would not break easily. The nails that held the wood together, however, were old and rusted.

Ori pushed as hard as she could, her muscles shaking, her face reddening, splinters trying to cut through the calluses on her feet. Walk a few hundred miles and calluses will build.

She grunted and pushed and strained and finally felt one of the nails loosen and shift. One deep breath, one short pause and she did it again, feeling her spine adjust to the pressure.

The board popped free on one side and Ori dropped to the dirt, panting. The space provided by the loosened board was small, but it was enough. She slithered her thin body through the way and fell into the dirt on the other side of the pen.

The pens were not sealed with locks, but with bars that could not be lifted from the other side. They were well out of reach of groping fingers inside the cage. They were also easily accessible from where Ori now stood.

Perhaps sometimes there were guards here. The men who had carried the heavy stones through the underbelly of the house had strained and sweated enough that it might call for them to rest. Perhaps, as the place where they were being kept was under a house, no one thought they could escape.

Ori slipped the bars from four of the pens and gestured the women out. None of them spoke above a whisper and little Amira was as quiet as a mouse. They knew what they had to do.

They moved to the large pile of stones. Even if they were not malnourished there was little they could have done to move the heavy pieces. They had been raised to serve the gods and some of their kind were indeed fearsome warriors, but not all of them had been trained and while Ori could fight, she could have pushed the stones with her legs but never would she be strong enough to lift them.

Instead she squatted over the rocks and whispered in the proper tongue, "We are here. We wait."

They did not wait long. The thick sheet of fur and muscle pushed slowly past the heavy stones until it could touch her foot and leg.

Ori closed her eyes.

She would not die, not really. As they had been told all their lives, the He-Kisshi remembered every life they took. She would be a part of the Undying.

I am Dowru-Thist. You honor me with your life.

It sang directly into her mind and Ori wept in pleasure, glad to be taken for the gods. Glad to help try to save their people.

Was there pain? Yes, but Dowru-Thist told her not to struggle and that relaxing would ease her suffering. The Undying was right.

She did not die, exactly, but became a part of the song that was Dowru-Thist. There were so many voices, so many notes in the complex song.

Within five minutes they were properly reborn. Weakened by the process, yes, but not without their strength. Freeing the others was a simple matter. A few rocks removed and they could pull the heavy, living cloaks of their brethren from the bodies they had abandoned below.

The pens were full of willing forms to embrace.

Once that was done the He-Kisshi adjusted to their new forms and opened the pens of the Grakhul slaves.

Dowru-Thist looked at the oldest of the remaining women and said, "Find your sisters. Leave this place as quickly as you can. Bogrun-Nisht and Lowra-Plim will go with you."

Bogrun-Nisht agreed. "Leave the city. It is time to end this foolishness."

They did not walk. They ran. The two heavy cloaks that moved with them opened the barred doors and made certain that their charges were unmolested.

Frankel sat up in his bed and gasped, his hands clutching at his chest. The air felt cold and damp and the great doors leading to his balcony were cast open in the darkness. He could make out the high ceilings of the nearby buildings past the courtyard to his estate. The rains hammered the night and occasional blue-white lightning flares teased out the images of the city around him. The woman next to him in the bed – he could not remember her name – moaned in her sleep, whimpered, really, but did not wake up.

A flash of silvery light and a horrific explosion of noise

made him clutch a second time at his chest. The lights showed something wrong with the room and then it vanished.

His eyes started to adjust to the darkness, which was when he saw the cloaks gathered around his bed. Surrounded by them, he could smell the wet, feral scent of the unholy shapes.

"You have deceived us." The words held no anger. That made them more awful to him. There was simply the explanation, as if they were telling him why he would suffer.

"I would never." His voice squeaked a bit. He didn't like that. He was the king. He was supposed to be strong.

"They are no longer here. The Grakhul. Most are gone, taken away. We would have them back."

"Beron is the one who has them. He was supposed to work out everything with you earlier."

"You are the king of this city, of this country. You claim to be the ruler and as such you have let down the gods. They make simple demands. You have allowed your slavers to take the holy people from the gods for your own pleasures."

Frankel's chest hitched and a fine, keening noise came out before he caught himself. His mother had always told him that men did not cry. His father had assured him that even if men did, kings most certainly did not.

"Guards! To me!" He paid very well for the protection of his guards.

There was no response much as he'd hoped for a swift one. "They will not come." That same monotone, soft voice. The woman in his bed did not wake. She merely curled in on herself and shivered. "We are the Undying. Only the foolish would try to face us. Your guards are not fools."

Of course they weren't. The He-Kisshi were the stuff of nightmares. More importantly they were the stuff of nightmares made flesh. No sane being would defy them.

And yet, he had. He'd made promises to Beron, not because he feared the man. Beron was very large and quite capable, no doubt, but he was also greedy enough to behave himself in the presence of a man who could have him killed.

The problem was that he was not here, and he was very likely not behaving.

"Beron. If-if you find him, he can make everything right."

"He has left this town. He has taken the Grakhul with him."

"What will you do?" Frankel suspected he already knew. They would go after him. But before they did that they would make the king of Arthorne – and by extension of Saramond – suffer.

"We will find him. He will be dealt with. Before that happens, we will remove our protections from Saramond."

"What do you mean?"

That black patch in the darkness of the night moved closer. He could feel the terrible heat of the beast. How had he ever believed they were cold?

"We have not brought the storms that surround your city. We have held them at bay. The gods are angry, King Frankel. They seek to destroy the world. We were your one chance at salvation. You might have been spared if you had merely complied with our wishes."

"What? No! Wait!" Frankel rose naked from his bed and rushed at the closest form. His hands sought to grab the cloaked shape and succeeded only in clutching hot flesh and rough fur.

"You dare?" The voice was different now. Still soft, but it hissed.

"Spare me! Spare my people! We've done nothing wrong."

"Had you stated the truth, you might have survived."

Without another word the cloaks shuffled toward the

open doors leading out into the night. Frankel watched as they spread their massive wings and caught the howling winds, rising into the storm. Lightning showed the shapes sailing higher and higher until they were specks.

And then the storms let loose.

The girl finally woke to the sound of thunder shaking the stone walls of the palace. The winds slammed the doors closed, but that was not enough to hide the cacophony. Despite himself, Frankel rose and moved to the closest window, looking out at the sheets of rain lit by the electrical outrages above.

He bore witness to the tongues of white light that drove down like a thousand spears and struck each building he could see, including the one he was in. The window exploded inward, sending slivers of glass and lead frame hurtling toward his naked form. He tried to cover his face and felt blades open his stomach, cut across his privates, and burn into his neck and chest.

Frankel fell back, dying, confused and in pain, but no longer afraid. The girl on the bed moved, arching her body, feeling the deep cuts from the glass that found her in the explosion.

By rights it should have stopped, but the lightning came again, a fury of light and sound and then fire. The walls glowed with heat as the lightning lashed out at the very stones that had built Frankel's family home.

By the time the walls started to fall, Frankel was already dead.

All hail the king.

B'Rath looked back in the direction of Saramond and knew he had done the right thing. Buildings shattered. The very ground looked like it was boiling in the electrical assault.

He'd seen the slavers on the move, taking hundreds of

ghostly white women with them into the plains, heading south, away from the city. He had seen them and thought hard about the Grakhul that had come to the slavers' capitol.

And then he had calmly gathered his family together and stolen all the horses in his stables. He needed them to save his family. That was all the justification he felt necessary. There were wagons. He loaded them with supplies and essentials, with extra barrels of water, then he forced his family out of their beds and took to the roads as soon as the sun was down.

They did not ride in a fury. They did not overtax the horses. Instead they moved slow and steady. That was the secret to fishing, according to his grandfather, and that was the method he used to determine most of his choices in the world.

Slow and steady got them away from Saramond before the gods took their vengeance.

Slow and steady did not work for the horses. They heard the thunder shatter the night, saw the sheets of lightning come crashing across the plains, and they bolted as one unit. And because he valued the idea of living through the ride, B'Rath let them have their way as much as he could, calling out to the others to control, not tame the ride.

Despite his fears they survived the run. The horses scattered a bit, but after they calmed down enough, the family brought them together. There was a stream nearby where they camped for the night. By the time the morning came, it was a river. The waters raged and snatched at the banks, overflowing into the dry earth.

B'Rath gathered his family, his lovely wife and his children and his brother's family and they all worked together to get their caravan back on course. They would head west for the present time, away from the slavers. They would go to the base of the mountains and from there they would travel south until they found a place that suited them. There was enough coin, carefully hidden away, of course, and there were enough supplies if they were careful and they would be. There were three crossbows, and enough arrows to make anyone approaching very uncomfortable or possibly even very dead. He preferred the former, but he would accept the latter. Whatever he had to do to protect his family, B'Rath would do it.

They traveled. They rode. They ate and they rested and at the end of a long day, B'Rath's reward was to see the Grakhul falling from the sky, landing around and near the small caravan. Well and truly, they were surrounded by the cloaked demons.

One of them walked closer, moving with angry, twitching motions.

"We have need of your horses."

"I have none to spare. I have to take care of my family." He was very apologetic. He shrugged his shoulders and did his best not to flinch. When his brother, Uto, reached for one of the crossbows, B'Rath gestured for him to stay his hand.

They were called the Undying. He did not intend to test the name.

"Look back toward your city."

Rather than argue, B'Rath looked back already knowing what he would see. There were hundreds of women heading toward them in the distance. They were underdressed, malnourished and moving in a slow column.

B'Rath sighed. "You must take care of your people. I must take care of mine." He looked at the cowl and saw hints of what lay beneath it. He saw that the cloak was what he had noticed before: a living part of the Grakhul. "I will keep my horses and my wagons. I will share them with you. Is this acceptable? We will travel together, wherever you wish to go. If some among you are too sickly, they can ride the horses or in the wagons. That is the best I can offer you."

He did his best to stay calm, knowing too well that his life was forfeit if the demons did not agree. He would fight to defend his family, even if it meant dying.

"Yes." The shape nodded its head and one thick claw slipped from inside the folds of flesh and pointed toward the mountains. "We go that way, then south."

"As you say then." He nodded his head, surprised that he was alive. Doubly so because Uto was a bit of a moron, really, and he'd half expected his brother to shoot one of the nightmare things surrounding them.

They would be slowed down by the women and by the things that protected them. They would also be safer, he suspected, than most. The storms were not moving as quickly where the women walked. For whatever reason, they seemed to be protected by the gods.

CHAPTER EIGHT
Hunted

"We are being followed, you know." Harper's voice was as calm as ever. Brogan nodded his head.

"That is why we are now descending into the foothills. I thought we might be followed, but now I know it. We need to get away from them. They are very likely trying to get us back to Stennis Brae and I've no intention of being hanged."

"Glad we agree on this. By all rights we'd be dead if they'd found the guards we killed, or decided we weren't merely out to save your family. Why the foothills?"

"Well, it's not for evasion purposes. We're not far from where Desmond makes his home." Desmond Harkness was a friend, he had come to Brogan's aid and had gone his own way back. He would also very likely be among the ones hunted and killed if he was not warned.

"Desmond will not be happy to see us."

"Desmond is never happy, Harper. He smiles and he laughs and he jokes with the best. But he is never happy."

"And yet, of late, you make him seem a man with no worries."

"I've angered the gods and they want me dead, my friends, dead, and the world dead because of my actions."

Brogan wanted to laugh over that. And to cry. And to rage. "Seems I might have reason enough to be grim."

"No one blames you, Brogan."

Laram called out, "I do. Seriously. I was looking forward to retirement. Now I'm running away and the woman I wanted to marry has accused me to the king." He paused a moment while they both looked in his direction. "The first round of ales is on you when we find a pub. It's the very least you owe."

Brogan smiled. His friends were true friends and he loved them like brothers.

The Broken Swords were not gentle mountains; as their name suggested, they were jagged and they had many untrustworthy trails. Brogan and every man with him were used to the challenge. It was his hope that the king's men were not and would manage to get themselves injured or worse. Better that happen before they met with Brogan and his fellow mercenaries.

"Where is Desmond's place from here?" Mosley's voice was weary. The poor lad had lost a good deal when he rode off. He had not had time to go home, to speak with his parents.

It was better that way. His parents didn't need to know his shame, or see him hunted down like a dog.

Brogan shook the thought away. There was a cloud of misery that wanted very much to suffocate him. Instead he focused on his anger. It made a bitter companion and kept him moving.

"We should reach him by sunset with any luck."

Harper countered, "Likely sooner. Desmond has a tendency to meet people before they reach his door."

Brogan nodded. "He is a man who likes his privacy."

"He is a man who doesn't like other men watching his wife, as I understand it."

"Jealousy is an ugly brute to sleep with."

Brogan thought about that. He'd been horribly jealous when he courted Nora, but not after they were together. She had made clear in a hundred ways that they were together and that she would be faithful. He'd reciprocated. Mostly.

That notion pushed at his mind again, wanting him to give into sorrow. Instead he turned to Harper.

"So, they're not called Grakhul?"

Harper shook his head. "The people we fought? The ones we captured and killed? They are the Grakhul. The ones who took your family are not. The ones who take, the ones who deliver the sacrifices and offer the coins are called He-Kisshi."

"Why does everyone call them Grakhul, then? It's the only name I ever heard for them other than Undying."

"Because they don't like to talk about themselves and they don't care what we call them."

"Have you ever actually seen one?"

"No." Harper looked away. "I hope to keep it that way, too."

"Why?"

"As a rule I have no desire to test myself against anything that won't die. I like enemies I can either kill or run from. They are neither."

Brogan looked to the eastern horizon. The veil of black clouds was spreading slowly to the south and even further north. There were silvery trails of water running along the entire area of the plains, where, frankly, aside from the Three Serpents, one was normally lucky to find an occasional stream. Several of the bands of water likely qualified as rivers.

Harper was riding next to him and spoke softly. "The weather is not right. The storms we saw before, the lightning. That was just at Saramond."

"What are you saying?"

"It might well be that Saramond is no more. I've no way of knowing. Not for certain, but it's possible that the He-Kisshi have come for the Grakhul. They might well come for us too."

Brogan nodded. "We need to gather our forces again. We need to reach everyone. If you are right, they'll come for any who helped us. I half expect the slavers to come for us in any event, but if what you're saying is true, we're going to have enemies aplenty for some time to come."

"And if the gods decide to destroy the world, Brogan?" Harper's tone did not change, but for once his face looked stressed and weary.

Brogan did not speak for some time.

When he finally answered, his voice was dark. "Then I suppose I shall have to try to kill a few gods."

"Well now." Harper ruminated on that notion. "That would be a sight to see."

The sun was descending, and they were in the shadows of the Broken Swords before they met up with Desmond. As Harper had predicted, he was not at all happy to see them.

The man sat on his horse, silent and dark, and watched as they came. If they were expecting him to speak first, they were mistaken. His hair was back in a braid and his beard was close cropped. The black hair was shot with silver; more, it seemed, than only a fortnight earlier. He wore leather pants and leather boots and a loose cotton shirt. His hat was large and floppy and currently sagged back across his shoulders, held to his neck by a leather cord. The hat was a prized possession. He kept it behind his back so he could avoid hitting it with either his short axe or his long one.

The horse under him glared menacingly at the lot of

them. The expression matched Desmond's.

"We are pursued."

"Yes I can see that, you damned fool." The words were clipped and angry. "There's a small damned army coming after you and you've decided to come my way, easy as you please. Now give me a reason not to shove my axe down your stupid gullet."

"We were coming this way to warn you." Brogan considered Desmond's axes. They were very impressive as axes went, and he'd seen the bastard cleave more than one person with them. Even from a distance he could see the sheen of oil and the fine edge that said they'd been recently sharpened.

"Well, I'm warned. Get the fuck away from me before I start cutting."

"It's not that easy, Desmond." Harper held up his hands. "There's word going around that we've started a serious problem."

"Do you think I don't know that, you daft bastard?" He was squinting. Desmond had flawless vision. He normally only squinted like that when he was considering which spot to hit first. "The missus, she woke up this morning and said it was time for me to be on my way. Said there would be people coming soon."

"Not this again..." Laram mumbled the words. Desmond heard them anyway.

"I don't much care for your tone, lad. I don't much care if you think my wife has powers or not. I know she does. She sent me to find you damned fools, now didn't she? So this one time, you're invited to my house, but we have to be quick about it, before the fucking soldiers on your trail decide I'm part of your little adventure."

Harper actually stared with his mouth hanging open. No one was ever invited to visit Desmond.

"You mean it?"

"Oh, yes. The missus insisted."

Desmond led the way.

The house wasn't much to look at, but that wasn't surprising. Desmond was a jealous man. He wouldn't want a house that others might covet. He'd been with them on the raid; he had the same cut of the fortune they'd taken in selling off the Grakhul. The small structure, well built and hidden along the side of the mountain, reflected none of that.

Once inside, however, it was clear that Desmond did not live alone and that his wife had different tastes. The walls were adorned with furs to keep away the cold and the rooms were decorated with fine furniture – mostly hand-crafted – and several treasures from abroad. Never anything too large, as Desmond, like the rest of them, tended to travel by horse and not draw a wagon.

The same sort of trinkets that Brogan used to bring home to Nora, small, pretty, valuable.

"Anna! I've brought them as you asked." Desmond's eyes looked around his domicile and then back to each of his road companions. His expression told them not to get any notions about what belonged to whom. Brogan didn't react. Most of the others held up their hands in surrender.

It was a simple situation in Brogan's eyes. The man had ridden with him to try to save Nora. He would understand that Brogan wasn't looking toward his home or his woman with covetous eyes.

And then he saw Anna, and understood the jealousy.

She came into the room wearing a skirt and a blouse. Neither was extraordinary. They were simple wool garments meant to hold the cold at bay. The way they fell on her form, however, was not simple at all. They fell across the most astonishing curves and, despite his mourning, Brogan longed to see what that fabric hid.

Anna had a heart-shaped face, and large gray eyes under a cascade of dark black curls. She could have been twenty years. She could have been forty. She had that sort of timeless quality to her. Her smile was warm and welcoming. Brogan's heart surged again, remembering the many times Nora greeted him after months on the road.

He nodded to the woman and smiled. Then he looked away and tried to rein in his emotions. Foolishness. He was supposed to be a strong man. He should have shoved aside the misery and dread living inside of him and waiting to strike when he least expected. Every time he thought he was past the worst of his family's death it came back at him from another direction.

Harper smiled and nodded. The others joined in.

Desmond spoke up. "This is Anna, my wife. Anna," he pointed to each of them. "This is Brogan, a good man and a good friend. This is Harper. A good friend of dubious character. This is Laram. He tries to be a good man. Mostly he succeeds. And this is Mosely. He's a swine, but only because he doesn't bathe enough." Mosely laughed. Desmond felt little by way of jealousy toward Mosely because Mosely preferred the company of men. His Anna was likely perfectly safe in Mosely's company. "And this is Sallos. He's a good lad with a wandering eye." The look he shot at Sallos was particularly withering because the lad was younger, and sometimes a bit foolish when it came to his attempted seductions. The young heart, as Harper was fond of saying, is often led by the young cock and not by the mind.

Anna shook her head and smiled again. "Sit. I've made tea. We have to talk, all of us, about what is coming."

The room was just large enough to allow a half dozen people to sit comfortably.

"We are pursued," Harper reminded, pointing out what everyone already knew.

Anna shook her head. "They will not find you this day or this night. Tomorrow might well bring a different ending but you are safe tonight."

Harper stared at the woman for a little longer than made Desmond comfortable, but finally he nodded.

Anna continued. "I have certain talents. I've studied the ways of the Galeans."

Such was a polite way of saying she was a witch. Galea was known for sorcery and worse. It was considered too dangerous a place for most people to travel to and was outlawed by most of the Five Kingdoms. Of course, slavery was outlawed too, and that continued on. There were many laws. Remarkably few of them were enforced. Apparently not stopping sacrifices was the exception.

Brogan felt the tendons in his hands creak as he made fists and relaxed them again and again.

Anna saw the looks on their faces and nodded. "I know what most think. I don't care. I had my reasons." There were stories about what a person had to go through to learn from the Galeans. "I did what I had to in order to learn."

Brogan shook his head. "No one here is in a place to judge you. Don't fret it."

That earned him a smile from Anna and Desmond alike.

Anna continued, "I have seen the same things you have, the endless storms, the darkness creeping in from the east. The sun still rises every day, but it takes a damned long spot of time for it to get past the clouds – and that will only get worse. You, all of you, have angered the gods. They intend to destroy the world because you stopped them from getting their sacrifices."

"They got them. They took my family as their sacrifices. They were deprived of nothing." Brogan's voice was low and soft. His rage flared and no one there thought he was talking out of turn.

Anna looked his way and smiled softly. An apology, really. "I know of your loss. I feel for you. But the gods do not care. The sacrifice was tainted in their eyes. You threw bodies into the Wells of the Souls that were not prepared properly."

Brogan took several deep breaths, his chest hitching. His eyes burned but he said nothing. Ranting at the woman because of what some sort of deities believed would solve no issues.

Anna said, "The gods have declared that the only way to cleanse the sins of the world and save it is if you, and I mean all of you who raided their keep, are gathered together and sacrificed at the other place where they will accept purified bodies."

All but Brogan looked around at each other. He saw them all with his peripheral vision, but he did not stop staring at Anna.

"They want all of us as sacrifices? As an apology?" His voice was still soft.

Anna nodded.

"That will not happen. I owe no god an apology. I owe no god fealty. They have offered me nothing that I wanted and I have never made a prayer for them to answer."

Anna nodded again. "They do not care. The gods do not answer prayers. They demand sacrifices. They are not the same thing."

"So what do we do?" Laram looked directly at Brogan.

"We find a way to fight the gods."

Harper chuckled.

Mosely said, "We can't fight gods."

"Why not?" countered Brogan.

Mosely spread his arms and shook his head, nearly laughing at the very notion. "Because they are *gods*, Brogan.

They are too big to fight!"

Brogan stared hard at him. "Watch me try."

Mosely stopped laughing.

Brogan turned back to Anna. "How are the gods ending the world? What can I do to stop them?" He did not assume that the others would go with him. Whatever he chose to do, he could guess it would look like madness to most.

Anna shook her head. "I don't know." She shrugged. "How does one stop gods?"

"It must be possible." Brogan waved toward the mountains they'd just left. "According to every legend the Broken Swords are where gods fought and at least one of them broke a sword. The fight isn't going on anymore, so there must be way to end them."

"I will try to discover the truth of that." She shook her head again, but she smiled.

Later, after they had eaten a meal around the small kitchen, Desmond gestured everyone to silence and they heard the sounds of the soldiers passing by. The men were silent, but the horses were horses and made noises, stomped and whinnied and doubtless crapped wherever they walked. There was no doubt they could spot the droppings from Brogan and company's horses. They should have been able to see the damned animals outside in the pen near the front door, but they kept on going, fifty men moving past as if there were no house to see, no horses to observe.

They sat in silence for some time, until the horses had moved on and their noises stopped. Sallos stared at Anna with wide, frightened eyes.

She looked back and shook her head. "I'll not steal your soul, if that's what you're worried about."

He blushed and looked away, scowling. No one mocked him. Not even Desmond, who looked like he wanted to say something.

"Stay the night." Anna gestured around the room. "It'll be a snug fit, but warmer than the outside and you'll have time to rest before you have to make your way past the soldiers."

"Like as not we'll go a different way." Brogan looked around at the others and they nodded.

"No. You won't. Whatever it is you're looking for, it's to the south of us. And likely on the other side of the mountains."

"You don't know what it is, but you can guess where?" Harper looked at her as if she'd grown a second nose.

"I'll be studying portents and trying to understand that through the night, Harper." She looked at the man and smiled. He actually blushed. He was smitten. It was possible they all were. Except, of course, for Mosely. Though that, too, was something Brogan could not have said with certainty.

Brogan kept his peace as Desmond and Anna moved to their own room and left the men alone in the shadows of the mountain. He could not say whether true night had fallen as yet, but he knew that he was tired.

Mosely sighed and Laram and Sallos made noncommittal noises.

Harper spoke up. "Are you worried about fighting the soldiers if we run across them, Brogan?"

"Of course I am."

That was the last spoken for some time, but Brogan knew what his friend was aiming at. If he was worried about fifty men, why was he so calm when it came to the notion of killing gods?

The day after Myridia met Garien and his troupe, the grasses rose overnight in the vast area around them, changing the landscape completely. Where before there had been sand

and rocks, now there was a field of green that varied in height from a few inches to over a foot. The green fields undulated in the wind and sighed and snapped. Most people might have found comfort, but Myridia had never seen such a thing before and it was unsettling.

"You look nervous." Garien spoke while deftly cutting away the bruised parts of an apple. It was starting to wither, but one didn't throw away food in the desert if one wanted to live. That was a lesson he'd already taught her and her sisters.

The entertainers had been generous with their clothing. Myridia wore a shirt that was large enough for three of her and had belted it with a sash. She suspected it belonged to Garien, as it was of similar style to the one he wore, but had been mended more often and washed enough to lose most color. She also wore boots made of soft leather. They were deliciously comfortable. Most of the rest had managed tops and skirts out of various cloths. The two groups still stayed apart mostly, but they were civil to each other, even if Garien and his troupe looked at the weapons the women carried with unsettled expressions.

"I'm nervous." She pointed out across the fields. "I have a very long way to go and not much time. And I do not like the way the ground here has changed. I can't see the places where I might fall. I can't see the stones, or the spots where animals have made burrows."

Garien nodded and offered her half of the apple. She gratefully accepted. "First, trust your horses. They'll be on the lookout for pitfalls. Second, the grass will keep your horses fed. They don't die as often if they're fed, I've noticed." He smiled as he spoke.

"You still intend to go east?" She looked at the storms, which were closer now. Not much, but enough.

Garien turned to the east and studied the land. His brow

knitted in concentration lending him a brooding quality that Myridia found pleasantly distracting. "I'm not certain. The weather there looks… unkind."

She nodded her head. "The weather will not get better unless the gods are appeased."

"Tell me about these gods."

"What is to tell? They demand sacrifices. Denying them only makes them angry. You have seen this already." She pointed to the ground and to the river not far away that had only been a stream, before.

He turned to face her. "Yes, but why are they so demanding?"

She frowned. "I do not know."

"What do they do with their sacrifices?"

"I do not know."

Garien looked to the east again. The sun was up enough to see past the clouds, but they were towering affairs and had hidden the dawn away completely.

"I think we will go west," said Garien.

"I think that is best." Myridia didn't want to try to find her way past the vast plains without help. She hated admitting it, but there it was, a simple fact.

"Should we travel together for a while?"

"I would like that."

"Still, you must tell me about these gods of yours."

"What makes you say they are mine?" There was ice in her belly at the comment.

"You are not known to me and I have been most places, Myridia. I have never been very far north, however. There are rules against it. Still, I've known a few travelers who said the people in the north were very pale."

"You are not angry with me? With us?"

He leaned back a bit and smiled as he appraised her face. His eyes were so very blue, pale and unsettling. Despite the situation she wanted to know him better. To know his embrace, and his kiss and…

"You've never done me any harm," he said, disturbing her thoughts. "Why would I be angry?"

"Because we serve the gods that demand sacrifices."

Garien chewed at his apple for a moment, then asked, "Do you have a choice?"

"No. We are trained and raised in the way of the Grakhul. It is the life we live. What we have always done."

"And if you did otherwise. What would happen?"

"The gods would punish us."

"Then it would be silly to be angry with you. You are only doing as you are told."

Myridia stared at him for a long time. She was prepared for anger. Acceptance had never been a consideration.

"So you will ride with us to the Mirrored Lake?" she asked.

"Probably not. But we will ride with you to the mountains."

She nodded. It was enough.

The winds changed and Garien frowned. His body grew tense and he tilted his head, eyes squinting as if he strained to hear something she could not. "We should leave very soon."

"What is wrong?"

"The night people are closer than I would like."

"What are they that they scare you so much?"

Garien finished his apple and wiped the juices on his hand.

His eyes looked at the distant horizon and then across the fields and finally back at Myridia. The wind ruffled through his short hair and made him squint. "Hungry. They are very, very hungry."

Instead of continuing the conversation he let out a shrill whistle and called his companions together. Em arrived first. She was a compact woman. Short and muscular and incapable of standing still, she moved constantly, often stopping whatever she was doing to stretch her limbs in uncomfortable positions. Her hair was dark and thick, pulled into a tight bun. Every time Em let her tresses loose and Myridia noticed, she was stunned that so much hair could be so tightly tucked away.

The rest showed up soon enough. The one who stood out the most was Ian, who looked big enough to carry a horse on his shoulders like a shawl.

"I think we should turn back," Garien said. "Those clouds... I don't like them. I don't want to run into the weather under them."

Ian nodded his head. "Nor do I." He shrugged and the muscles under his flesh moved in ways that were nearly mesmerizing. Myridia had never seen a man that large. "I think it wisest to head away from that sort of storm."

Em looked her way and then at Garien. "The night people? Will they be a problem?"

"Not if we leave now. Our friends have fed us fish and we've more than enough for a good meal, caught just this morning. If we leave after we eat we can make many a mile before the sun sets."

Noral, the minstrel, looked around and smiled. He did not much care where they went, according to Garien, so long as there was an audience to hear him sing.

Just that quickly it was decided.

The fish was cooked and seasoned with herbs that Myridia had never heard of before meeting the troupe. The flavors were wonderful and in her mind she compared them to a rainbow, each flavor distinct and bright after mostly consuming fish raw her whole life. When they were done, they moved on, heading south and west, toward the distant mountains.

The ground was exactly as treacherous as she'd feared, but the troupe handled that by having a lookout walking before the horses and checking for pitfalls. Though there were a few occasions where the wagons rocked back and forth and the horses pulling them looked ready to fall over, they managed.

Despite her trepidations, the group moved away from the river. There would be more water, surely, but after suffering her first true bout of dehydration, Myridia never wanted to experience it again.

Lyraal walked next to her as they traveled, her sword wrapped in fabric and carried across her shoulders, much as Myridia carried her own weapon. The two of them did not speak often. They did not have to. They both understood very well what was at stake.

Lyraal said, "This joining with strangers? It's a mistake."

"It is temporary." Myridia waved the idea aside, though in truth she felt a flutter in her stomach at the idea.

"What are these night people who are supposed to hunt us?" Lyraal asked the question as easily as she might ask about the weather. If she were afraid she hid it well.

"I don't know. But we need to be prepared if they show themselves."

Lyraal was easily half a foot taller than her and heavily muscled. She looked askance at Myridia and her hand tapped the blade of the sword over her shoulders. "I will manage something, I suppose."

"How are the others?" Myridia stepped past a steaming pile of dung. Horses, she was learning, did not care where they crapped. They walked at the present simply because the horses needed to recover from their arduous trek. At least she felt they did. She'd only ever ridden a horse once before this entire affair started.

"They are nervous. We are far from home, amongst

strangers, and heading for a place none of us has ever seen in the hopes that we can appease the gods before it is too late."

"Yes, but aside from that?"

Lyraal smiled. "Well, not getting burned on my shoulders and breasts is nice."

"Gods, I thought it was just me." Myridia laughed. It was nice to laugh, even if she knew she would feel guilty about it later. The men were dead, the women of their people were probably enslaved. She could not go after revenge and she could not go after the women.

Much as it stung, she had to have faith in her gods to protect the others. Garien had previously asked what the gods did in return for the sacrifices made in their name. The honest answer was nothing, that she had ever seen. There were no miracles from the gods, though she had heard of such things. Her people were still enslaved or dead. Her brothers, her father, weak as they had been, were all she'd had and she missed them. Her mother had died giving birth to Len, her youngest brother. While she had many memories of the woman, she had not seen her in almost fifteen years and she wished she could depend on her mother's wisdom now.

Instead it seemed that everyone was depending on her, and she was not at all certain she was up to the task.

"You are worrying again."

"What? No, I'm not."

"You are." Lyraal always sounded so smug when she knew she was right.

"And if I am?"

"Don't. I'll tell you if you get it wrong."

"Why are you not in charge of this?"

"I have no desire to be in charge. This way I get to blame you if everything goes wrong."

"You are wise beyond your years."

"Also, I am horrible with decisions. Most cases I think cutting off their heads is a good solution."

"That, too." They walked in silence for a good five minutes before Myridia spoke again. "Do you think the rains will reach us soon?"

"I hope not. We have too far to travel and I do not like all of that lightning."

"Yes, well, one would hope the gods take that into consideration."

"Our traveling companions seem genuinely scared of these 'night people'," Lyraal said, scanning the the fields.

Myridia frowned. "I do not think they are fighters."

"There is that." While fighting was not the first principle the Grakhul women learned, it was considered very important. A few years of training took place with every woman. How else to defend the children? The notion that men did not fight was not that unusual to them, but to have females who could not defend a tribe was puzzling. "How long will we wander with them?"

"Until we reach the edge of the mountains. After that they will go their way and we will go ours. Should our paths continue on the same course, that is just as well, but we have only a short time to reach the Sessanoh."

"So what about these night people?"

"They are an obstacle. We must be prepared to deal with them. I will try to get more information from Garien, but so far he seems determined not to tell me what we need to know."

"Why?" Lyraal looked her way and frowned.

"I'll try to find out." It was all she could do.

"Why did they do it? The men who came to Nugonghappalur?"

That one Myridia could answer. "Because we took from

one of them. The He-Kisshi chose to take four from the same family and the man who claimed them as blood was not happy."

"That is something that should be discussed with the gods." Lyraal shook her head.

"The gods do not discuss. They command."

Lyraal nodded. "And we obey."

They walked in silence for a time, both of them thinking their own thoughts about gods and duty. Finally Lyraal spoke up. "I might have done the same."

"Truly?"

"I mean, I have no children, but if I did. I might have."

"Even if it meant the end of the world?"

"Unwynn always said that her children meant more to her than her life." Lyraal chose her words carefully, which was rare. She needed to make her declaration clear enough, Myridia supposed. "What else is there to lose after that?"

Myridia frowned and gestured with one arm. "Everything."

Lyraal nodded again and sighed. The last sliver of the sun was sinking behind the distant mountains. They were close enough that the crystalline forms that rose throughout the rocky surface were nearly blinding as the sun passed through them.

"Have you ever seen such a thing?"

"The Blade of Sepsumannahun. That's what is left of it after he fought Walthanadurn."

"Truly?"

"Who can say but the gods? And they are not talking to us."

To the north and west something let out an unholy shriek that warbled higher and higher in octaves, even as it grew louder and louder in volume. Both of the women took the time to check their weapons were in order.

The horses made nervous sounds, and the troupe did their best to calm them. Garien looked back from where he was sitting at the lead wagon and his long face drew down in a nervous frown.

Lyraal asked, "Do you suppose that is the night people?"

"If so, I am not sure I want to meet them."

"What do you suppose they are?"

"It is said that the gods have opened gateways to other places, other worlds, on ten occasions as punishment for being disobeyed. Whatever made that noise, I think it came from another realm."

Lyraal frowned. "What are those things called again?"

"Demons. They are the things that eat the world the gods have made for us."

"Why did they let them in?"

"To remind us to obey, I suppose."

Lyraal shook her head. "They should have just asked. When have we ever failed to obey?"

For that, Myridia had no answer.

They buried Doug one day after they left the lodge. Despite all that they tried, the young man died in his sleep. As he'd been blinded and maimed, Niall felt it might well have been for the best. He didn't say that of course. The man's family was in mourning.

Niall dug the hole himself, while huddled in a thick shawl and shivering. Temmi wept and Scodd lay burning and feverish, the wounds in his arm and hand deeply infected. Niall had cauterized the injuries, and the bleeding had stopped, but deep red lines ran from the burn marks and showed where infection was growing. He did not like the man's odds of surviving.

Tully would have helped, but someone had to keep an eye out for the He-Kisshi. They had only seen the one, but one was enough.

The rains had not stopped. If anything they were worse than before, and when Niall had finished burying Doug he found several very heavy stones to lay atop the man's grave in an effort to keep the waters from washing him back to the surface.

All of which seemed like fine enough ideas in civilized times, but part of him wanted to be done with the entire affair. That demon was still out there, likely watching them and readying to strike. It felt wrong and ungrateful to have thoughts like those, but ultimately he was a gardener and not a brave warrior. He wanted to be home.

As soon as Doug was buried it was time to move on. The beast would certainly be back and the waters were rising around them. Stay any longer and the wagon could not avoid being washed away.

Besides, no one wanted to be near the lodge any longer.

The whole of Scodd's family lay in the wagon as they moved. Tully kept watch and Niall sometimes drove the wagon and other times urged the horses on through areas where the road was simply gone, washed away by the rising waters.

The skies above them were nearly as black as night. Occasionally, in the far distant west, they could see spears of light fall down and cut holes in the clouds, but not often.

"Where will we go?" Tully had asked that question even as they'd started packing the family and their supplies into the wagon.

Niall had considered that while making the poultices for Scodd and wrapping Doug in a shroud of canvas. "We cannot go north. We cannot go west. South and east are our only choices." They agreed that Saramond was not the right place. Stuck as it was on the plains, the rain would surely cause disasters there soon enough. "We could make for Giddenland, but it's a long journey and like as not we'll have to head for Hollum first."

"Hollum I know well enough." Tully looked down at the ground as she spoke. "I can get us there, I reckon. A map would make life easier, but I haven't found any on the wagon as yet."

"Get us to Hollum and I wager we can find someone to sell us a map if we need it." He sniffed and looked up at the clouds. "We get to Edinrun in Giddenland and I have enough family to guarantee us safety and a place to stay."

"I've never been that far south."

"First time for everything. I've never been this far north."

She forced a smile. "Are you liking your first trip north?"

He smiled back. Looking at her made that easier. "I've found some of the company exceptional."

Three days they moved through the slog of half-formed streams and mud, before they finally got ahead of the storm. The clouds were still there, just behind them and towering like black mountains. Sometimes, when Niall looked back at the storms, he could almost swear there were titanic faces looking back. He had never seen a storm that so fired his imagination when it came to the shape of the clouds.

He wondered if the faces he saw were the faces of the gods and hoped not. Though they were surely only his fears painting his imagination, the visages he saw were fearsome and angry.

On the fourth day, Temmi slipped free from the wagon and walked with them as they strode on through the still, humid air. The storm was not touching them, but it was close enough to feel the world holding its breath and gathering for a proper blow.

Tully looked at the other woman and offered a weak smile. "How is your father?"

"Better, I think. He's not burning up any more. His wounds aren't so angry looking."

"Good to hear." Niall nodded his head.

"Where do we go?"

"Hollum first. We need to find news of what is happening and we need to get a good map."

Temmi nodded. "Dad always said the best map is in his head."

"A lovely notion, but I wouldn't know where to look to find it." Niall kept his tone light and Temmi managed a very small smile in response to his jest.

"Thank you. For burying…" Her voice hitched and she looked at her feet for a moment, then closed her eyes. "For burying Doug."

"You and yours, Temmi, have been beyond kind to us. We only offer a small return of your kindness."

"You offer more and you know it."

"Temmi, what do you know of the gods? What can you tell us of the He-Kisshi?"

"Never actually met one of the Undying before the other night." She shook her head. "We dealt with the Grakhul. The cloaked ones were normally out gathering the next sacrifices."

Tully shrugged. "How about the gods? Do you know their names? The number of them?"

"My grandfather always said the best way to avoid the attention of gods is to not think of them. No one in the family ever wanted to get their attention. Least not that I knew of anyways. Mum might know." She looked down at her feet again. "I'll ask her."

Niall shook his head. The notion of disturbing Doria bothered him. She was in mourning. "It's just an idle thought. I'm trying to understand what might have happened."

"I'll check just the same. She could use the sunlight on her skin."

The young woman walked to the wagon and came back a few moments later with her mother in tow. Doria had shrunken in on herself. Her grief was like a physical ailment eating her away.

Doria did not smile, but she nodded a greeting. "You've questions about the gods?"

"If you could. We're just trying to understand what happened. What is happening."

"I was told some of it, before Ohdra-Hun showed itself."

"Ohdra-Hun?"

"The He-Kisshi. That is its name. Means something like the Divine Anger of the Gods."

"Lovely." Tully shook her head and spat.

"The gods demand their sacrifices. There were men who interfered with the last sacrifice. And then there were some who escaped from the group meant to be sacrificed next. Of the four who should have been sacrificed, none even made it to the Nameless Keep."

"The place where you were going?"

"Yes."

"I thought it had a name."

"It does. No one can ever pronounce it. It's just called Nameless."

"So the gods are angry?"

Doria nodded. "They are angry and they are hungry. If they do not receive their sacrifices soon, they will destroy the world."

"Seems a bit excessive to me," Niall said. "I mean, I understand being angry, but how is destroying the world going to make it better?"

"There are legends and stories, of course. You've likely heard some of them. This is not the first time the gods have been disappointed. In the past they opened holes in the sky and let demons rain down as punishment, but there have been promises that the world would suffer greater losses with each punishment offered."

"So our ancestors got off easily and we get the beating they had coming?" Tully scowled at the thought. "How about a little warning?"

"Do not expect me to have the answers, child. I only know what the gods have told me in the past. If I still followed the ways of the scryers, I would not be able to tell you any of this."

Niall worried his lower lip with his teeth. If she followed the ways of the scryers she'd have likely turned him and Tully over to the He-Kisshi. "Is there anything to be done about it?"

"The gods have spoken. The men who stopped the sacrifices must be taken to another place where they will stand in for the failed sacrifices. If that happens, the world is spared. If it does not, the world will end before the next season comes to us."

"The next season?"

Doria shook her head. "The seasons change. Winter is here now. When the spring comes, if the men are not sacrificed, the gods will eat the world. In the meantime they'll damage it to make their point known."

"Couldn't they give a warning?" Tully shook her head again.

"Tully. This *is* their warning." Doria looked hard at the short woman. "They are giving us time to save most of the world if the right people can find a way to fix this."

"Who are the right people?"

"The pale ones. The Grakhul. The He-Kisshi."

"The very thing that wants us dead is what is supposed to save the world?"

"The He-Kisshi have many names. They are supposed to be the most devout followers of the gods. They were created by the gods to obey and to serve. I do not know what has happened to Ohdra-Hun to send him after you, but I do not think he is obeying the gods any longer. He is so very angry."

Niall thought back to the fight on the wagon. The Undying had died. He knew that in his heart. The damn thing was beaten and still and dead. Water filled its vile mouth in a puddle. But he saw the scars from where he'd injured it, from where the chains had slashed and cut. He knew it was the same beast and he shuddered at the thought.

Niall carefully moved the horses from the path they were on. The land was starting to slough away ahead of them and the higher grounds to the right would hopefully survive a while longer. "So where can we go to get away from this?"

"South and west." Doria shook her head. "I do not know, if I'm truthful." The woman looked toward him and frowned, her angular face seemed sharper than before.

"So, about these demons?"

"Most are long gone. They don't like the light and so they hid themselves away."

"Well, there's that at least."

Doria looked back the way they'd come. "I am not so sure. They don't like the light, but those clouds are as dark as any night I have ever survived."

"So, on to Hollum then?" Tully did not sound enthusiastic. Then again, she seldom did.

"We need a map. We need to get to higher ground. Hollum offers both."

Tully nodded and said no more.

While Niall was considering why Hollum might bother his friend, Ohdra-Hun came out of the skies, dropping like a stone until the last second, and drove both of its feet into Doria's spine. The older woman didn't even have time to make a noise before she was slammed into the mud and waters, her back bent into a shape that made clear she was already dead.

Ohdra-Hun was injured. Scars showed where fire had tried to consume it and bald patches of blistered skin marked where it had suffered the most. The beast looked torn down and waterlogged. It also hissed and took a step off Doria's shattered form as it regardedd Niall.

Niall looked at the poor, dead woman and the beast standing on her remains, his eyes wide. He was guiding the horses. The wagon was close enough to crush him if the animals panicked.

Ohdra-Hun was coming closer and the horses snorted and rolled their eyes.

Tully hurled a short spear at the thing. In the time it took Niall to understand what was happening, the younger girl had already moved to the wagon and grabbed one of the weapons she'd set up for when the thing came back.

Temmi let out a sound like a cat being skinned alive, and hurled herself at the He-Kisshi.

The thing was pulling the short spear from its stomach when the girl rammed her body weight into the end of the weapon and drove it in deeper. Temmi was round and sweet and had a face that normally looked like it belonged on a toddler, but there was nothing kind or innocent about her expression as she impaled the monster. It fell back, shrieking, both clawed hands trying to pull the spear free even as Temmi held to the end of the spear and shoved it backward with all her weight and strength.

The sound that came from it made Niall's skin crawl. It also made the horses try to bolt. The great beasts reared and whinnied and looked around wildly and Niall found himself in the uncomfortable position of trying to calm the brutes down before they could flee.

"Nicely does it. Nicely, gently." The horses did not rise completely onto their rear hooves a second time, but their eyes rolled with fear.

Tully crawled out of the wagon with another spear in her hand. This one was longer and the tip was barbed.

Ohdra-Hun threw itself at Temmi, and in return she slammed her hands into the throat of the thing, under the vast, drooling mouth. The blunt end of the spear was pressed into her belly, and the pointed end was driven deeper into the bleeding guts of the thing she struggled with every time either of them moved. She was likely going to suffer a massive bruise, but the point of the spear was deep inside the He-Kisshi and it let out a strange warbling noise as it pushed even further toward her.

Her fingers hooked into that throat and drove in hard. Temmi was half-roaring as she continued to push.

Tully's spear cut deep into one of the Undying's wings, carving a red trench through fur and burned flesh alike.

Ohdra-Hun shoved back, bleeding freely from the stomach and from the opened wing. It did not attack again but instead rose on a sudden, savage gust of wind, spiraling high into the air before vanishing back into the black clouds.

Temmi screamed after it, her words made incoherent by anger and grief. She stared after the thing that fled, eyes wide and tearstained.

Tully watched on, her own eyes looking toward the skies and watching for another attack.

Niall moved over to Doria and confirmed what he already knew. She was dead. Her spine was broken and her face was buried in the mud.

There was no question of it, of course. He found the shovel and while Temmi lost a piece of her mind and Tully watched the heavens, he started digging Doria's grave.

•••

Ohdra-Hun settled on a large rock and pulled in on itself until it looked like a ragged cloak abandoned and draped over a large pumpkin. Unless one knew what to look for, one would never guess what the thing was that shivered and panted in the rains.

This was not the way the world was supposed to work. The He-Kisshi were formidable and terrifying. They were the enemy of all who opposed the gods and as such they were to be feared.

Yet here it was, bleeding, injured and running.

And so very angry.

"Why does this happen?" It spat the words, coughed as the wound on its side healed slowly. The itch was familiar and infuriating. Currently everything made Ohdra-Hun angry.

The shape rose from the waters nearby, a stream that was quickly adding to the flooding tide running toward the plains. It had mass, it seemed solid, but the body was formed out of the mud and waters, held together by the will of the gods.

Ohdra-Hun fell prostrate before the shape, ignoring the pain of wounds that still bled and the mud that spilled across them.

"You have not answered the calls, Ohdra-Hun." The words rippled through Ohdra-Hun, felt more than merely heard.

Long claws dragged through the muck and then pulled into fists. "Their existence offends me!" The He-Kisshi did not look up from the waters, but instead stared at its own rippling reflection.

A voice like a week-old drowned copse replied, "They have defied the gods. That they offend you is only natural. You have served faithfully for centuries and your goal is a just one. The gods accept this. Still, time is limited. You may pursue your vendetta, but you must also serve the gods in other ways. Do not forget this."

Ohdra-Hun lowered its face closer still to the running waters, opened its hands and once more dragged them through the cold muck and debris.

"The gods offer you one boon to aid you in your tasks. Find the children stolen from the Grakhul. Do not let them fall to the slavers. Kill the slavers if you choose, but do not fail in this or you will find the gods can easily forget to be merciful."

"One boon?"

The shape moved forward, wavering with every step it took as the waters moved and changed.

"Rise, Ohdra-Hun."

The Undying did not question but rose, still looking down.

A hand touched the hooded face. The hand was made of the elements that washed across the area, but it felt comforting just the same. The wounds the He-Kisshi felt on its body were healed. A chain was draped down over the hood, thin and shining and weighted down with a bauble – a teardrop-shaped red gem, half-hidden beneath a thin filigree of silver. The red color shifted and swirled.

"It will aid you only the once, and you will know when to use it. The children are nearing Hollum. Your prey goes to the same place. Do not disappoint."

Ohdra-Hun dared look up even as the shape was collapsing. In that instant it saw a hint of the glory of the gods and felt infused once again with holy purpose.

It settled itself once more against the rock and drew in on itself. The rains offered cold comfort, but it needed rest and it needed to plan for what would happen next.

Harper lit a pipe and smoked something that was sweet and left Brogan's eyes burning and his skin tingling pleasantly. Harper did not smoke often, but when he did he tended toward potent combinations.

They'd eaten, and soon they would be on their way, but first Anna wanted to give them a few warnings from her search.

What was slowing them down was the muffled but very heartfelt argument coming from the bedroom of Desmond and Anna. No one was eavesdropping, exactly, but everyone knew the gist of the problem. Desmond had to come with them to avoid having his house burned down when he barricaded himself inside. Anna had no intention of letting him leave indefinitely. To that end, she planned to come along. The very notion was driving Desmond into a lather. Anna? With other men? Nonsense!

It was almost enough to make Brogan smile. He'd never had to worry about that. Nora was his. Except possibly when he'd been away and in those cases if anything ever happened, she'd been discreet. But he doubted that. He doubted she had ever strayed. She had been a better person than he.

Now she was gone. The thought filled him with anger again and with hatred. The two should never be confused. Anger fades. Hatred is often eternal.

Something very heavy slammed into the wall of the bedroom then clattered to the floor. Brogan and Harper both winced at the thought that it might well be Desmond.

A minute or so later Desmond left his room and entered the common area where everyone was gathered. "Anna will be joining us," he announced.

"Seems a fair idea," Brogan commented. "If she has gifts that can aid us, we can surely make use of them."

Harper looked at Desmond and nodded, saying nothing. That seemed enough for the man. He smiled, nodded his own head, then went back to find Anna and whatever supplies they planned to take along.

Once he was away, Harper and Brogan looked to each other and held back the laughter that wanted to sneak out. Desmond would take it poorly and the man was very good with his axes.

The weather outside was colder, if the breeze through the doorway was an indicator, and so Brogan unpacked his tartan and swept the layers into place. Winter was creeping in and baring teeth of ice. He half-expected snow.

The rest followed suit, except for Harper, who preferred a proper cloak.

Most of their gear was still with the horses. Desmond and Anna had more supplies, though only enough to accommodate riding on horseback. Like Harper, Desmond wore a cloak. Anna wore two cloaks, several shawls and enough cloth to make a few tents besides. Brogan stared only because it seemed impossible for so slight a woman to haul so much with ease. Besides her numerous layers she also carried the largest bag he'd ever seen. She made it look easy. Even as he contemplated her, she headed back into her house one more time, moving against the flow of riders ready to leave.

When they had gathered all they needed, Anna delayed, looking around one last time.

The sun was bright and just peering past the clouds. For a moment they were nearly blinded. Still, there was something, a sound, perhaps, or a smell. Whatever it was, Brogan paid attention. "We've company."

The others listened, moving quickly and staying lowered in crouches as they made for the horse pens. In moments they were on the horses and ready to go.

The soldiers of King Bron were sporting about it. – they didn't shoot when they very well could have.

Brogan had never met Ulster Dunnaly, but he recognized him just the same. There were tales aplenty about the man.

He had served with King Bron and was, according to all of those stories, a nightmare to his enemies.

He was not handsome. His face showed a dozen scars, including where a well-placed mace had flattened his nose and shattered one cheek. Still, he had recovered from those wounds and had killed the man who administered them. He was not overly large, a little smaller than Brogan himself, but he was hard. There was no part of him that looked capable of being soft.

He stared directly at Brogan as he spoke. "Regrettably, King Bron must retract his previous judgment. You are found guilty of murdering the king's guardsmen and angering the gods. You must be made to pay for your sins." He looked around. "You and the rest of your crew."

"There were more than six of us."

"Indeed there were." He gestured to a slight girl who looked very unhappy to be there. She kept staring at Laram and it wasn't hard to guess her name or position. "The scryer says that she can find all of your associates."

Brogan took the time to look around and felt his spirits falter. There were a great number of them. Worse, there were dogs. Dogs came in low enough to maim horses. They could tear the belly from a man with ease, especially if they were trained well, and if he knew one thing without having to consider it, it was that the Dog of Kinnett would know how to do so. The king allegedly had a love of training the damned beasts.

"We cannot go with you." Brogan held his arms wide and then settled them at his sides, where his weapons were waiting. "We will not go willingly to our deaths."

Ulster nodded.

"Take them. Bring them in alive."

"Alive?" Harper smiled.

Ulster smiled back, a reptilian grin if ever there had been

one. "Alive does not mean intact. I will sacrifice as much of you as I need to in order to bring you to King Bron."

"It was a nice thought, at least."

Anna stepped from her house and glared at the men outside. "We're leaving here. You will not stop us this day."

"Won't we though?" Ulster shook his head, amused more than angered by her claim.

"Not in the least."

"And what would you do to stop us?" He leaned over his saddle as he stared at her.

"Oh, not me." She shook her head. "Them." Anna pointed to a spot behind the soldiers and they looked. Almost everyone looked, but Brogan kept his eyes on the woman. She was up to something.

Sure enough, the powder she pulled from under her shawl and cast into the air gave her away. No one else noticed, they were looking for whatever she'd pointed to.

The black powder defied the winds and whipped toward each of the soldiers. The dust struck the closest ones, started them blinking and in the case of one horse sneezing. Then, as the stuff made contact, it changed form. From small granules each piece transformed, grew larger and angular and buzzed violently. The sound was one Brogan knew well from his more curious adventures as a child. Wasps. They were the very image of hell on earth as far as he was concerned. For a moment Brogan felt pity for his enemies.

Only a moment.

He tapped the sides of his horse and called, "Ride, lads!"

The soldiers of King Bron might have tried to stop them, but they were far too busy with the wasps attacking them, their dogs and their horses alike. Brogan had no notion of how Anna had summoned or created the wasps, but he was delighted.

Somewhere in that mix, Laram's woman was screaming

just as loudly. Brogan felt no pity for the creature that had shown the soldiers how to find them.

He rode hard from the corral and the others followed, heading south as fast as they could, while all around them horses and men and hounds let out screams of pain and thrashed, trying to escape the wasps.

Men were thrown from their saddles. Horses kicked and bucked and bolted. Dogs ran.

Brogan smiled and rode harder still, taking full advantage of the chaos. Harper rode near him, laughing so hard Brogan thought he might fall. The others were not far behind.

The soldiers did not pursue.

When Harper had finished laughing he looked over his shoulder at Anna and shook his head. "They're going to be very, very angry."

"I find I can live with that notion better than with a sword through my heart."

"Aye. True enough."

After twenty minutes of hard riding they slowed down and came to a halt. The horses needed a moment to rest and they needed, as a group, to assess their situation.

Brogan smiled at Anna. "Thank you. I've no idea how you did that, but it was all that saved us, I think."

Anna nodded her head.

"There is a scryer among them. Can you hide us from her eyes?"

Laram looked back, frowning. "I should have gone after her."

Anna shook her head and frowned. "No. She gets her visions from the gods. They have a bit more power than me. A very large bit, actually. Nearly infinite. But I might have a few more tactics to keep them from getting too close."

"Where are we heading, Brogan?" Laram looked down at his saddle, his face was stormy. Brogan understood why.

"You'd have gotten yourself stung senseless if you'd gone after her, Laram. Besides which, she is where she wants to be and I'm done with hostages and prisoners." He sighed and continued. "We're heading south. We need the warmer temperatures, because that's where most of our lot has headed. Most if not all of the sad bastards we run with are down in Torema, if I had to guess."

"Why Torema?" Anna's brows knitted as she spoke.

Desmond said, "Because that's where a lot of people traveling are going to need guards, and that's what we've been doing on the road. Guarding."

"Aye," Harper agreed.

Brogan shook his head. "No. Mostly because the damned fools have more money than they've ever had in their lifetimes and a number of them will be determined to satisfy their curiosities on things they could never afford before."

"Aye," Harper said again. "That too."

They started moving again and Brogan stared to the east, where the wall of black storm clouds was still crawling forward. They were high enough from the ground that they could see the silvery streams and rivers building along the plains.

"Have any of you ever heard of 'Marked Men?'" Anna's tone was soft.

Mosely answered, "Yes. I've heard they work for the Mentath. Dangerous men, hard to kill."

Anna nodded. "While I was talking to others last night, the name came up several times. They might well be on the lookout for the lot of you."

Harper slid his eyes her way. "Marked Men? Are you certain of that?"

"My talents aren't like those of scryers. The words I hear come directly from the sources and those sources are people I know and have met. I'm certain."

"Well then. We should ride faster."

Brogan looked toward Harper and shook his head. "And what have you heard that you're not sharing this time, my friend?"

Harper shrugged. "Not much to hear, really. The Marked Men are supposed to be the best the king has and made stronger by sorcery."

Brogan almost said he didn't believe in sorcery, but he'd just seen it happen. That sank in as he contemplated Harper's words.

"Where did you hide the wasps?"

Anna brushed her hair back with her hands, her body swaying with the horse's movements. Brogan made himself look away. "You liked that, did you? Took three nests to perfect that trick and one gesture later they are all gone. I won't be doing that one again any time soon."

Brogan nodded. "Well, we'll need to find more tricks. I don't think this is going to get easier."

"Absolutely not, Brogan McTyre. You are the most wanted man in the world right now. And any that follow you will be wanted, too."

"Then why are you here, Anna?"

She did not speak with harsh tones, but her words cut just the same. "I have my magic. They have a scryer. My best spells only delayed the girl finding us. Anyone other than a scryer would have spent years looking and never found us. The gods favor that girl. Because of you, my Desmond is in danger, too. So is the world. So where else would I be but making sure my husband lives through what you started?"

"It wasn't my intention." Brogan's voice was hoarse. "I only wanted–"

"Aye. I know." Anna looked to the southern horizon. There were mountains on one side and plains on the other, and between them the distant hints of other things. Cities, and places where people lived.

Places where the people living were doomed, unless Brogan either found a way to fight the gods or surrendered himself to their desires.

He would not be surrendering.

"So find it, Anna."

"Find what?" When he looked her way her eyes were wide and guileless.

"Whatever it takes to help me stop the gods from ending the world. I'll not lie down for them and I'll not sacrifice my friends. The fuckers have taken enough from me."

Anna rode on, her eyes toward the south. "I'll see what I can do."

CHAPTER NINE
In Dark Places

Scodd died in his sleep four days after his wife was buried. Doria was not forgotten. Scodd and Doug were not forgotten. Still, they were dead and that left Temmi on her own. The girl who laughed and smiled and made bawdy jokes at Niall's expense was as good as dead. In her place was a young woman who stared too often at her hands, and who scowled deeply in thought when she was not crying.

Niall and Tully took care of driving the wagon. The rains kept hammering down and the waters cut trenches wherever they could and rushed around whatever obstacles refused to get out of their way. The horses were wet and cold and Niall knew exactly how they felt.

He wore a cloak made of oilcloth – likely it once belonged to Scodd – and a large floppy hat with it, but they were necessary in order to travel. They were almost to Hollum, but it was still too far for comfort.

As far as stormy moods went, Niall had them all. He wavered between pouty at his unfortunate position in life to angry that everything seemed to have gone sour.

Almost everything. Tully, though silent a lot of the time, still managed an occasional smile for him. He returned the favor whenever he saw her lost in her own brooding thoughts.

The rains were relentless and there was little time for talking. When they did find safe places, they stopped long enough to let the horses rest and Niall for that matter. He led the horses through the rough areas and seldom had a chance to rest his legs. The only saving grace was that they were moving slightly downhill most times and so the waters crept past instead of rising.

The seventh day was black and bleak. There was no other way to put it. The skies behind them cracked and roared and cast lights that left them half-blinded when they were foolish enough to look directly at them. The horses were not at all happy about being where they were and keeping them calm became a challenge. More than once Niall had to throw himself in front of them and calm them as best he could while they threatened to rear up and make a run for it.

The horses seemed to calm, but there was always the chance they'd take it personally and stomp him into paste.

When they finally found a spot with a large enough collection of stones, they stopped for the evening and Niall hitched the horses and the wagon both to the heavy outcroppings.

Tully had kept a lantern burning. It was the only reason they managed to start a small fire.

"This will never end. I'm certain of it." Niall shook his head. He meant the words to come out as a jest, but he failed and he knew it.

Tully carefully set a pot above the fire and started the water inside it to boiling. There was no fresh meat, but they had plenty of dried rations and with a little work it would make a fine stew.

Temmi did not join them. She remained in the depths

of the wagon. He knew Tully would coax her out in time. Tully was good at that sort of thing.

Another barrage to the north of them made night into day for a moment and left them both blinking. The horses made noises, but seemed to know they weren't going to get anywhere with the extra ropes Niall had lashed in place.

"I don't know about this." Tully squatted near the small fire, moving her legs a little to keep them from settling into sleep.

"Know about what?"

"Going to Hollum. It's not a good city."

"You know it well, do you?"

"It's where I've lived all my life before those things took me."

"Then you have a home there?"

"No. I have a place where I stayed. I didn't like it and I don't want to go back." The winds shifted and water slipped past the rocks, wetting the side of Tully's face, but she barely blinked the droplets aside or noticed them. She was focused on something that Niall couldn't see.

"Listen. We'll go in, and we'll get out, quick as you please. If you can tell me where to buy a map, I'll go in and leave you with the wagon. Might take a little longer that way, but I understand it. There's a few places I would rather not revisit from my earlier days."

She smiled her gratitude. "I appreciate that more than you know. I have a history there and I've no desire to ever return to it."

Did he want to know more? Of course. Did she sound like she wanted to tell him? No. So he left it be.

"This is all madness. I just wanted to be a gardener. I like trees." He looked toward Tully as he spoke. "What about you? Any big plans?"

"No. Surviving, I suppose."

"No, I meant before we were taken."

She stared at him and shook her head. "So did I."

The stew was starting to boil and Niall's stomach to rumble when the waters came down the hillside with enough force to wash over the top of their stone barrier. The sudden cascade of cold waters was shocking to say the least and it extinguished the fire and knocked the stew pot aside as well.

"The bloody hell?" Niall stood, half expecting to see someone standing above them on the outcropping with a bucket. Instead he saw more water coming. Somewhere above them the storm must have raged harder than ever and broken through a natural dam.

To prove that point the lightning flashed again and let him clearly see that the ground above them was dissolving, collapsing under the constant barrage of rain.

"We've got to move!" His voice was almost lost in the sounds from above. The mud came hard and fast and he grabbed Tully, pulling her closer to him in what little shelter the rocks provided. They'd hardly held off the wind and he doubted they'd stop the mud, but perhaps they'd part the wave coming.

The lightning left and the thunder came shattering down along with a sea of muck and debris. Rocks and mud and plants and even a few small critters came hammering down and Niall leaned close to the wall and waited as best he could.

He did not wait long before the mud hit, flopping over the rock and slapping down on the both of them with enough force to drive Niall to his knees. He kept his death grip on Tully, refusing to let her go, though the torrent did its best to pull her away. Niall felt her hands clinging to his shirt and neck, nails clawing desperately for purchase.

How long did the wave last? He couldn't say. He only

dared breathe in three times for fear of inhaling the filth. It did not stop, but eventually it slowed to a trickle.

When he looked up the wagon was farther down the hill, on its side and spilling everything it had previously held.

There was nothing for it. He let go of Tully and charged down the slope, looking for Temmi amidst the remaining slough.

"Temmi!"

She stood up as he came along, and he reached for her, to pull her to him.

She shook her head and pointed back the way he'd come.

It wasn't mud this time. It was something else. The very ground shook above the rock outcropping they'd tried to use for shelter. The debris and water and mud there danced and shimmied and ran faster down the hill.

"Tully!" His voice broke. "Hold on to something!"

When the wave hit this time it wasn't mud. It was vibration. The ground split itself to their left and to their right, ripping apart and opening like fresh wounds. Muck slipped into the newly forming gashes in the ground and surged back out, vomited forth by the force of the world trying to shatter itself.

The ground under Niall's feet shivered itself apart and he felt himself falling backward. There was no time to breathe.

The world fell away.

He would have died right then, but Temmi was faster and stronger than she looked. He'd thought her soft when he first met her, but her arms were powerful and caught him at his waist even as he started to fall. Her feet were wide apart, braced on the shaking earth, and she spun at her hips and threw him away from the opening chasm. Niall landed badly and grunted, but even as he hit, he was trying to stand, to make sure that Temmi did not meet the fate she'd just saved him from.

He needn't have bothered. She stepped back from the edge and shook her head, looking uphill toward Tully.

Tully moved down the hill, her feet barely seeming to touch the ground. "Run! There's more coming!"

They listened.

They ran.

Still the rains came and the ground roared and split itself asunder.

Ulster Dunnaly looked across the plains and shook his head.

"They've a proper head start." The words came from his second, Owen Wortham. Owen was a hard man. He was thick with muscle, solid around the middle, and tended to keep his tongue. He looked little enough like a competent man but that never stopped him from being a cold-blooded killer when the need arose.

Currently, Owen's face was still swollen in a dozen places because of the wasps. None of them fully understood how that'd happened, but it had and the bastard McTyre had taken full advantage to escape.

"We've dogs. We've also got Mearhan Slattery to keep us informed." Ulster's left eye was swollen half shut. He could feel the lump where the insect had stung him every time he blinked. His left ear was swollen. Most of his exposed skin felt like it had been run through by thorns. He supposed in a way it had.

Owen scratched at his thick red hair then winced when his fingernail caught one of the stings on his forehead.

Ulster said, "We'll find them, Owen. And when we do, we'll bring them back to Bron as he ordered."

He let his gaze move to the north and the clouds coming closer. They did not look like clouds. They looked like a great funeral shroud stretching along the horizon.

"I hope you're right."

Ulster looked back to Owen. "No choice, my friend. We get them or we die."

Owen nodded.

"Me?" Ulster climbed into the saddle on his horse. "I've plans that don't involve dying."

He slipped two fingers into his mouth and gave a shrill whistle. The soldiers of King Bron looked toward him and nodded, none of them questioning his authority. They obeyed despite the painful stings they were all dealing with. They'd spent half the previous night rubbing poultices of mud and herbs into their stings.

Then they'd burned down the house where McTyre had spent the previous night. Whoever had given the bastard shelter would never offer it again.

Owen said, "How large a lead do you think they have?"

"Enough. They have us by a day. We'll find them."

Owen spat. "I've a plan to discuss with them how much I like wasps."

"The next time the bastards try to run I might have something special for them as well." Ulster watched the last of his people get settled then started moving forward. They followed, each and every one of them, regardless of the painful stings and the bruises from falling. They were among the best soldiers in Stennis Brae and they wouldn't be caught off guard a second time.

"They'll not run again after I've cut their feet off."

Owen said nothing to that. He knew Ulster meant it.

Garien grew paler the longer they rode. Not overnight, but over the course of days. He fidgeted and he looked back over his shoulder almost constantly. At first Myridia thought the man was looking at the clouds, but eventually she realized he was looking for the night people.

Lorae and Memni sat at the same fire as she and the

troupe leader. Both of them stared at him with the sort of rapt attention that only young girls who are smitten can ever truly manage. He was good enough to smile for them, but Myridia knew he was not interested in them in that way. He kept looking toward her, casting his eyes in her direction.

Truth be told, she was tempted. He was a handsome man, and kind. But Lyraal was not as easily distracted and reminded her every day that they were making a mistake. The mountains grew closer, and they would part company soon enough.

They had made camp for the night. The river was nearby and that was a blessing. Storm clouds hid away most of the world, but she knew that these were natural formations, not caused by the gods. They were still safe, for now.

Still, it was nearly impossible to travel after the sun vanished behind the mountains even on clear nights. The darkness was too complete and the paths were too treacherous. She wanted to move faster. There was so far to go.

"Garien, these night people, do you think they are close?"

"Closer than I'd like. I think they've almost caught us up."

"We ride hard every day. How is that possible?"

"They do not ride in the daylight, Myridia. They ride at night. They have eyes meant to see in the darkness." He paused a moment and looked around, a weary half-smile on his face. "This close to the mountains, the nights are longer. They have an advantage on those of us who travel by day."

"Tell me about them. Tell me why they follow you."

He sighed and leaned back, his long body casting an even longer shadow in the light of the closest fire. Garien's hair slipped and moved in the wind and his eyes were lost in shadows.

"There was a time when we rode together. We were a very large troupe, you see. There were nearly a hundred of us, all told. It was the best way to make sure we weren't attacked. No one is traveling this far north right now, not many at least, but the plains here are an open invitation to brigands and they often raid and take as they would.

"You see us now, and there're only twenty of us. But back then it was magnificent."

He smiled, but there was no joy in the expression, only a memory of it. He had damnably expressive eyes and she liked looking into them.

"On the other side of these mountains, in Mentath, there are stories that tell of places where a bold man can walk between worlds. When I was younger I thought that was a wondrous notion. Can you imagine it? To step into another place, to be where no one has ever been, and to explore lands where no one has ever met your like. I thought it a grand idea."

She was taken by his voice when he spoke, drawn into the tale as easily as the younger women with her. He had a sense of wonder that carried in his words, and that was something rare among her people.

"I thought it the very finest of notions until we ran across one of those spots."

Again he shifted, either the ground or the tale making him uncomfortable to the point of wincing.

"We had never gone past the mountains before. Mentath was new territory for us. Still, we were a hundred strong and none of us foolish enough to believe we didn't need to defend ourselves. It was always our way to sit and discuss what had to happen. Everyone had a voice, even if only a few of us ever truly spoke up. Chief among the talkers were myself, Evelyn, who told fortunes and sold potions, Seryn, who seldom lost an argument and Garth, who made the most glorious pastries I ever did taste."

The darkness grew stronger and he leaned closer to the fire. The angles of his face took on a slightly sinister edge. That should have made him less attractive, but it did not.

"We didn't plan to find a place that was not there, but that is exactly what happened. Remember, we had no maps. We didn't think they were necessary. We spoke to people in one place, dealt with them fairly, and then we asked directions to the next. That had always been the way and we were fine with that. Not like we didn't remember most of the places, mind. We'd made circuits of all of Arthorne over the years, and points north and south. Any town of decent size had seen us many times. But Mentath was different. We had only just begun our travels there. We'd not even hit the palaces in Gaarsen, which are said to be places of wonder and joy.

"No. We ran across the city when the day was ending. There are rough patches over in Mentath. Places where the ground rises into high foothills then settles back. We had the pleasure of exploring new areas and almost never knowing what was around the next bend and I liked that, and so did Seryn, who was, if not my betrothed, then at least a good companion. We spent more than a few nights keeping each other warm."

That smile again, nearly tragic, marred by a desire for happiness that did not blossom.

"It was a large city. The gates were open and the city itself was lit with a thousand torches, or so it seemed, after days of nothing but dales and hills. We only spotted it as we came around another bend in the pathway and we thought it best to move a little further to reach the town instead of spending another night in the cold."

He paused and shook his head. "Listen, I love my wagon, it's my home, but now and then a fresh bed and a meal in a tavern are lovely things.

"The gates of the city were open. That's a rare enough thing in some places, but Mentath was new to us and we'd heard nothing of anyone being at war with anyone else.

"I've heard some of the most dangerous plants are some of the prettiest. I've no certainty that adage is true, but I can tell you the city we saw was lovely. Clean streets, smiling people, shops set up offering a thousand delights and inns large enough to accommodate a dozen or more. A lot of us took to the taverns and inns. The idea was to spend two or three days there, and while some of us would watch our wares and supplies, others would relax. Then, if all went as we hoped, we might do a dozen shows there to make back what we spent.

"I was one of the leaders, I chose to stay with the wagons. It was my duty, wasn't it?"

Garien finally looked at Myridia. His eyes were wide, dark, and lost.

"I went to bed that night with a good thought in my heart. Our coffers were full, our troupe was happy. I was happy. Garth, my brother, was happy. Garth was a fine baker, but not always happy. That night, he went to sleep in a fine bed after having a fine meal and eating pastries that someone else cooked for a change. The plan was, he'd take my place on the wagon the following night and I would sleep in that lovely bed and have a bath besides."

He shed exactly one tear and wiped it away, not angry but certainly annoyed by the presence of the moisture. His chin dimpled and his lower lip trembled, but only for a moment. It was grief, but it felt like an old grief, fresh enough to hurt, but not really to cut any deeper.

"I woke early, to the sounds of Evelyn screaming. It wasn't an angry sound. It wasn't a happy sound. It was complete despair I heard in her voice.

"I climbed from my wagon fast enough to catch my foot and fall to the sandy ground. That was my first thought that something might be wrong. Not Evelyn's screams, but the fact that my hands landed in sand instead of getting battered on cobblestones."

His face was pale. His eyes stayed dark, and his hair fluttered in the breeze. A knot of wood popped in the flames and Lorae and Memni jumped.

"They were gone. Not just the people, but all of the buildings as well. The entire city had vanished overnight. I looked around and screamed myself, because that sort of thing, it isn't possible. I know how it sounds, but I could not believe it. Sun's up and bright, the people who were in the wagons with me are all there. The town and most of our troupe had just gone.

"We headed back the way we'd come and made it back to the town we'd last visited the same day, getting there before sunset. The baron of the area, a man named Quinn, gave us a safe place to stay that night and fed us. He listened to our story and then told us that there had been tales of a town in that direction, but no one believed them. No one had ever seen any evidence.

"We'd no reason to go out there again. Before we left, the baron sent a few of his men to investigate the area and they found nothing other than our tracks.

"Quinn had his men mark the way to that area and had them place signs warning of danger. It was all he could do. As for us, we left. There was nothing to be done of it. Ghost towns should not come and go. We wanted nothing more to do with the wonders of Mentath, or anything else on the wrong side of the Broken Swords. We headed back here as quickly as we could.

"We make a route, you see. Only this time, because of that," he gestured to the north, where they knew darker storms were raging relentlessly across the land, "we must change course. But mostly we follow the same routes each time. There are small towns and there are big towns and there are cities and in each where we stop we stay a few days, until we have almost worn out our welcome, and we go on. That's the way we've always managed.

"That only changes when winter comes. We head north through the autumn then turn east for a while and meander down to the south. By the time the worst of winter is here, we're normally traveled through Saramond, and Hollum, then down as far as Torema and finally Giddenland, where we stay until the worst of the cold is gone again." The names were only words to Myridia. She had never even seen them on a proper map. There had been no reason when she knew her entire upbringing would be at the keep. Still, she nodded because he seemed to want recognition of the distances.

"There's plenty that head for Torema. Plenty make their way to Edinrun. We'd stayed in both on occasion, but because we needed more recruits, we kept to Torema. There are more people there with interesting talents, and more who are willing to take a life on the road over living in the rundown parts of town.

"I mention this because if we'd chosen Edinrun with its colleges and universities and the scholarly ways, we might never have noticed the disappearances.

"People in Edinrun tend to be at home and in bed after the sun goes to sleep. Some parts, maybe there's a concert or player putting on a performance, but the city is spread far and wide, and most folk stay inside. They wouldn't have seen the night people. They wouldn't have recognized them."

By the light of the flames Garien looked older. "They came a week after we reached Torema. It's an old city, you see. And there are too many people there by far. The docks are overrun by people from other lands. The lost and the desperate live in the alleys and find places where no one with any sense would stay. Rotting buildings, broken structures. Torema lives on that. The more people, the better the chances that what happens at night isn't seen or talked about. They say you can have any pleasure known to man there and I believe it. But you must first have the coin to pay. We never stayed in Torema because we enjoyed it. We stayed when times were bad and it was all we could afford.

"Still, we were known and we were fair. People still paid us for our little shows and bought our wares and they were wise enough to know not to try to steal from us. Troupes like ours have teeth, you know.

"A week after we settled, the first of the bodies was found in the river. It was stuck against a bridge pillar and the folks that saw it were properly scared. Take no offense, but that body was as pale as yours, and the look on that lad's face said he died afraid.

"There were some thought a plague had come. Every night the sun set and in the morning there was another body or two, normally near the water, but sometimes in the oddest places. One of them, as I recall, was found on the roof of the closest watchtower to the palace. That was when people started getting nervous. Torema's like any other place, really: you expect there's trouble where the lowest people rest, but not where the richest feast.

"A man named Hitchins told me he'd seen my brother, Garth, in the Gilded Goose. A wretched establishment if ever there was one. They had bare-fisted fighters and the sort of whores a man would have to be very drunk to consider. Having never been that desperate I tended to stay away, but I went there after hearing from Hitchins.

"I told Hitchins my brother was dead, you see, but he

insisted that he remembered Garth for his pastries and that was enough to make me believe him.

"Hitchins was a nervous sort. I should have thought that through. Why would he approach me and tell me my brother was in town when they'd only met a few times? I was too excited by the thought that Garth might be alive to pay any attention to those tiny voices in my head advising caution.

"The Gilded Goose was in worse repair than I'd remembered. The wooden walls were weathered and rotting, the paint long peeled away. The place was still busy, however. I could hear the noises of people celebrating and talking as I drew closer. I was so excited that I barely noticed Hitchins skulking away from me. He didn't matter anymore. I nodded my thanks and moved on.

"Inside the sounds I'd heard were different. The braziers lighting the place were damped down, little more than coals, and the tavern was darker than I wanted to think about. There were fires burning, but I felt a chill run through me."

Garien was paler still now, nearly as pale as Myridia and her kin. His skin was sweating despite the breeze and his eyes had a lost look to them.

"Garth was sitting at a table in the center of the room. He was not alone. I saw several of my old friends there, all with goblets in front of them. I could not see Garth's face, or his hands. I should have seen them, even in the muted light, but I could not. Still I knew him. There are a hundred little signs, aren't there? The way a person moves their hands, or holds their body or tilts their head. I knew all of them the second I saw my brother and I wept right then and there. I had abandoned him. I had lost him almost a year earlier and now, finally we were reunited.

"I wanted to go to him. I almost did, but there was that chill in the room, and there was the way he looked at me under his hood. I felt his anger.

"'You left us, Garien. Wherever did you go?'

"Those words were spoken with Garth's tongue. But to this day I do not believe he spoke them. As he spoke the folk in that room stood up and I recognized them. They were the troupe, of course. I knew them all. But they weren't. I can't explain it better. All I can say is that they felt *wrong*. Even standing where I should have seen their faces, closer to the fires, I saw only shadows and night.

"I was trying to find the words to answer my brother when I saw the bodies. All around the room, in corners, draped over tables, as if they were too drunk to move, I saw the pasty white skin of the plague folk. They were dead, or they were dying. I'm not sure. I saw no wounds, but I knew that Garth and the others had killed them.

"'Come here, Garien, and all is forgiven.' I heard the words and knew they were a lie. I felt they were a lie, I could feel how much he wanted me to suffer, though I had no understanding of why.

"'What happened to you, Garth? What happened to all of you?' I should have run. I knew they meant to do me harm. Still, I stayed and looked at them, trying to understand what had happened to my friends and all the family I had left in the world."

Garien shook his head again, and she could almost see that room full of shadows and corpses.

"'Only come closer, brother, and I will show you.' He raised one hand and gestured to me and I saw that his flesh was not in shadows, but had been changed. I could see the seat behind him through his hand. His hand, the color of a shadow itself, was transparent.

"Four of them came toward me, moving in ways that made little sense. They seemed to flicker between steps, as a candle flame flutters. I saw them, but they did not move smoothly as a person should. They jumped and twitched even as they took simple steps."

Garien took the time to look at each of the women around him. He met their eyes and spoke slowly and softly. "I'm an entertainer. I'm not a warrior. I can fight if I must, but that is never my first choice. My first desire is to flee rather than risk hurting another or being hurt. If that makes me a coward I accept it.

"It was Seryn who managed to touch me. Like Garth she seemed made of shadows, but her flesh was solid and cold to the touch. Her fingers caressed the top of my hand and it burned with cold where the tips of her fingers met my flesh. It burned, but I liked it. I wanted more.

"'But come with us, Garien, and all is forgiven.'

"I was never with Seryn, but I always wanted to be. She was Garth's lady, you see. Sweet and kind and warm, in all the same ways as my brother. Was she beautiful? Maybe not to others, but she always was to my eyes, you see, and she touched me and I felt that old desire again, not just to hold her, but to be held, to be possessed, to be wanted by so wondrous a woman.

"And I felt my flesh burn. I saw it wither the slightest amount and grow pale.

"I am a coward. I backed away from the promises in her voice and the blessed contact with my brother's lover.

"And she laughed at me. It was a sound of pure contempt. It was a sound that Seryn, the Seryn I had known and loved, could never have made. It was a sound she was *incapable* of making. She had not a drop of venom in her soul, you see. Neither she nor my brother. Oh, I know my beliefs are colored by my heart, but the fact is, that was not Seryn any more than the thing that spoke with Garth's tongue was my brother.

"I looked at my hand where she'd touched me, and I

looked at that room full of things that were supposed to be my troupe, my family, and I ran.

"Seryn came for me. She flickered and shuddered as she approached and her hands reached out to me with long shadowy nails that looked like claws. I did not panic. I knew what I was doing. I'd seen the plague-dead and I'd seen the shadows and I wanted no more of either, so I shoved over the brazier closest to the door and watched a wave of ashes and coals scatter across well-seasoned wood."

He stopped and gulped air, struggling to find his breath as he sorted through memories he did not want to recall. Myridia almost told him to stop, but she could not. She needed to know all that she could about the night people if she and hers were to survive.

"I did not stay around to see what happened next, but I heard screams of anger and I saw the night light up with flames as I moved toward the camp where the troupe was resting.

"By dawn the Gilded Goose had burned down. We left the town not long after that. That's all there is to tell, really. We've heard stories from time to time about the plague-dead. They tend to show up in town after we've left, because we never stay more than a few days.

"I hear of them and what they've done. I don't dare stay long enough to know that they are following, us, but I know it. I *know* they are. They've been following for a long time now."

Garien looked at each of the women, focusing at last on Myridia. "Does that answer your questions?"

"Yes." Myridia could not lie to herself. She felt differently about him after his tale. She was not yet certain how it was that she felt differently, only that her perceptions of him had changed. She would ruminate on that before responding to any of the signals he offered her with his quiet gestures.

"Wonderful." He smiled again and it was a genuine smile. "I've told you, now you tell me. What are you running from? What are you running to?"

"We are running from what was. Our home was destroyed and our people were captured." Myridia looked him in the eyes as she spoke. "We are running to a place that is supposed to be exactly like our home. It is called the Mirrored Lake. There, if we can manage it, we will appease the gods and do all that we can to prevent the end of the world."

"Who is ending the world again?"

"The gods."

"Your gods?"

"There are only gods. They do not belong to anyone. If anything, we belong to them."

"Why?"

"Because they are angry, Garien. Because they have been offended by the man who came to stop a sacrifice, and who, when he failed that, killed our men and enslaved our people."

"What sort of madness is that?"

Lorae answered. It was not her place, truly, but she wanted to impress the man. "The gods chose to kill his family. They were chosen by the He-Kisshi, the Undying, to be the sacrifices, and..." The younger woman's voice broke for a moment and her lip trembled but she made herself be strong. "He was so angry. He came with others and they tried to stop the sacrifices, to deny the gods their right. And when he failed, he started killing everyone he saw, even the men who were always so devout and so gentle."

Garien did not laugh at the notion of gentle men. He had traveled most of the Five Kingdoms, it seemed. Likely he had met many men who were not warriors.

"So what must you do now?"

Lorae answered again. "We must prepare the way for the next sacrifice. The He-Kisshi will come. They will bring us what we need. But the Sessanoh, the Mirrored Lake, it must be made ready, it must be sanctified in the ways of the gods."

"And you say the world will die if you fail?"

"Yes."

"Why would the gods do this?"

Lorae looked to Myridia, suddenly silent in the face of his question.

"Because they are gods," Myridia answered. "They created the world and they make the rules for what lives in their creation." It was a lie. They had not created the world, she knew, but taken it from the creators. Still, it simplified the tale and she felt a growing fear that there simply was not enough time.

"The first time the gods are defied they destroy the world?" Garien leaned forward, his face inscrutable, and stared at Myridia.

"Well, no. Of course not. We are taught that they have been defied ten times in the past and that each time they offered a larger punishment." She shook her head. "They do not tell us why they do things. They do not speak to us at all. They speak only to the He-Kisshi and to the scryers."

"Scryers?"

"They are the voices of the gods. They are chosen at birth and prepared. Many can be scryers but only a few at a time."

"Really?" He frowned. "How are they chosen?"

"Only the gods could say, and they do not."

"Rather elusive for beings of ultimate power, aren't they?" Garien spoke lightly but his face was serious. "It would make more sense if they simply said what they wanted."

"They did. They want four sacrifices every month, to be delivered to my people for purification and execution.

Those four are chosen by the Undying, who serve the gods as messengers and as personal servants. They are granted great power and eternal life in exchange for their service."

"And what do you get out of it?" Garien raised an eyebrow as he asked, and Myridia could not decide if he was challenging her or if he were merely curious. She did not know his expressions well enough.

Myridia frowned. "What do you mean?"

"If these Undying get eternal life, what do you get?"

"Nothing. We are told to serve the gods and we do."

"Hardly seems fair. I mean, honestly, you do the work and you get nothing."

"We are gifted by the gods. We are blessed to them. Even now they will find the ones who took our people and bring them to justice."

"How?"

"The He-Kisshi will stalk and kill the people who have our children and sisters. They will find the right people to sacrifice. We will save the world. That is all that matters." Despite herself, she was getting agitated. The questions should have been easy to answer and yet they were not.

"I am making you angry." Garien leaned back. "I apologize. That was not my intention. I just thought, well, Evelyn could sometimes see what has not happened and what should happen. I thought she might be able to help."

"Evelyn is a scryer?"

"She can sometimes see things. I suppose that means she is. Would you like to talk to her about what's going to happen?"

She could not put a face to Evelyn. "Yes. If I could. I think that would help us."

Garien smiled. "I'm sure we can work something out."

Before she could respond, the same sounds they'd heard before came again, ululating noises that echoed from the mountains and seemed to dance around the thick veil of evergreens to their west.

Garien's smile faded. "They are closer." He shivered. "Much closer."

"Then we should talk to Evelyn all the sooner."

"Tomorrow," said Garien. "Tonight I think she will be busy trying to find the best way to escape the night people."

CHAPTER TEN
The Slave Trade

"Shut it!" Argus smashed his club against the bars of the cage, expecting the boy who was jabbering on to flinch. Instead the boy looked his way and stared with his large, dark eyes. If he was at all intimidated, he hid it well.

Argus stared back, furious with the whelp. He was tired of the pale folk.

The pale people were a creepy lot, to be sure, but they would earn a good price. That was what mattered.

Beron had sent riders to offer up the news of all that happened in Saramond. They would not be meeting in the slavers' city after all. They'd be meeting in Edinrun.

Edinrun was as fine a choice as any. More banks and businesses there and it seemed, with Saramond likely destroyed, they'd need a new place to call home and a new business besides.

Aside from Argus there were fifteen men on the trek. They'd been picked by hand and they knew their duties. They were leading the very finest of the crop to Torema, there to sell them at the bidding houses owned by the slavers.

They'd paid a fortune to have the pale ones and now they needed to make as much as they could in short order.

The thing about children was, even if they were savages and liked to fight back, the clients didn't mind. Pure were preferred and paid better, but at the end of the day the sorts that liked children didn't mind if they struggled. Some of them even preferred it. Argus preferred the little shits behave. They apparently couldn't even speak the common tongue, which meant they were annoying and disobedient. He couldn't beat them, however, as they tended to bruise easily and heal slowly.

The pale skin and general looks of this lot would make them a prize, but they were a prize he'd be glad to be done with.

For that reason it was eight men at a time riding with longbows. They wore the slavers' colors and bore the flag of Arthorne. Whether or not Saramond still existed, the country did. Whether Frankel was in charge or one of his siblings was also irrelevant. They represented the king in any event. People would stay their distance, but just in case, eight marksmen kept any possible raiders at bay.

The sun was setting. The crew followed orders and as the sun descended, the flag was lowered and the red adornments were peeled from their garments. Raiders would not be warned off. They would be killed.

Some might have worried about the children. Argus did not. They were fed and given water. There were two rivers before one reached Torema and at the closest they would be bathed. Until then they could stink as much as they pleased. So far none of them were foolish enough to avoid eating. Some seemed to try it on every trip, but not this lot. They ate their food, they watched the areas around them and they were mostly quiet. Argus was feeling positively spoiled by them.

The screaming boy was still quiet, but he was looking at Argus with that contemptuous expression again. Argus resisted the urge to beat him senseless. It wasn't worth the effort of pulling him from the cage.

If any of the children spoke the common tongue they hid it away. When they did speak it was in a subdued babble that sounded wrong to Argus's ears.

Off to the west, behind him, he heard a horse let out a whinny and a moment later heard the sound of a man – was it Allan? He couldn't be certain – calling out an alarm. There was a powerful desire to go and investigate, but he knew better.

"Daren?"

"Aye, Argus?" Daren was resting. He could spare a few minutes.

"Go find Allan. He's screaming about something."

Daren nodded, looked annoyed and got up. He was paid well to obey. That was the thing about the slavers, they paid a good wage.

Four, perhaps five minutes. Long enough for the sun to finish descending and the herd master to call it a night. The task of feeding the little shits would start up soon.

Long enough for Argus to wonder what the hell was going on with Daren.

Call the name and the troubles come. That was what his mother had always said. He thought of Daren and sure enough the man came trotting back toward him his bow unslung and an arrow half-notched.

"No sign of Allan. His horse is there. He's gone."

"Horse looked scared?" There was always the chance Allan was foolish enough to try to find a place to relieve himself. If so he'd answer to Argus for abandoning his post.

"Not scared so much as extra alert."

"Rouse Beck and Morris. Look for the damned fool and check with the others if you see them."

"Beck'll be pleased."

"If Beck finds Allan first, he can take out his anger as he sees fit."

Daren smiled. Beck liked little as much as beating the breath out of anyone foolish enough to make him lose rest.

It was too easy to assume innocent actions. Someone needing to empty his bowels wasn't the only option. That was why three extra men were out looking. Just the same, Argus took a look around the landscape. The stars were bright above them and Emila, the first moon, was already in the sky. Harlea wouldn't be far behind. The night was darker than the day, but not as black as pitch. The winds picked up and Argus felt the fingers of breeze teasing through his blond hair.

The area around them was low and level. They'd chosen their routes a long time ago to ensure that no one could easily surprise them. Every attempt in the past had been rebuffed, but there weren't many as thought it was a good idea to attack them in the first place.

Fine drops of rain fell across his arm and Argus frowned. The sky was clear. The rain was dark and warm.

Allan's body crashed to the earth only fifteen feet away. Allan was a big man. He was a skilled fighter and one of the bravest men Argus had ever met. He hit the ground with such a force that most of the meat on his body exploded away like a melon dropped from a tower.

Argus was not a coward. Just the same, he backed away, his eyes looking to the heavens.

And there he saw the shape, moving high in the sky, well above where an arrow could reach. It had wings of a sort, which rippled and moved with the air.

Not twenty feet away, a second body fell from the sky and broke as it struck the earth. He thought it might be Orton, but could not be certain; the face was buried in the ground.

"Get off your asses! We're attacked!" His voice broke like

an adolescent's but he barely noticed. He could worry about appearances after he'd killed the invaders.

"You are warned." The voice was soft and seemed to come from directly behind him, but when he turned to look, no one was there. He glanced up, but saw nothing aside from the stars. The shape he'd seen before was gone. "You have offended the gods and taken their children. Set them free. Now. Or suffer for your choices."

"Come speak to me face to face!"

"As you wish." There was an unsettling level of glee in that voice.

Before he could say he had changed his mind, the heavy claws punched into his shoulders and sent blood and pain soaring down his arms. Argus closed his eyes against the agony and then wished he had not.

His stomach lurched and a sickening feeling moved through his body. The ground fell away and he rose into the air.

"Open your eyes and look at me." He felt the warm breath of the speaker against his face and shivered. Despite his dread he opened his eyes and stared into the face of his captor.

The face made no sense. There was a large hood of flesh, dark and lightly furred, and inside that hood there was a surface like the inside of a mouth. That surface fell inward to an array of teeth, each as long as a finger and as sharp as a good cutting blade, but there seemed hundreds of them moving down toward a throat that bellowed out the smell of a slaughterhouse with each breath. Around that hood of flesh, were glossy black spots. It only took him a second to realize that they were eyes, like the eyes of the spiders he used to kill and examine as a child.

Did he scream? Of course he did, and pissed himself too.

"I am Ellish-Loa. I serve the gods. You have angered

them. Do you understand me?"

Argus could not make himself speak. Instead he nodded his head and trembled. Part of him wanted to look down, to see how far from the ground he was. He couldn't. He was far too busy looking into the face of a nightmare and trying not to faint. Argus was not a man who believed in anything he could not see and until that moment he had never seen one of the Undying.

"You will free the children. I will take them with me. If you agree, nod your head. If you do not agree, I will kill you."

The pain in his shoulders was potent. He looked first at the thick claws that sank deep into his arms, then downward. The heavy hide of the Grakhul snapped and moved in the powerful winds, and below them, far away, the black earth stretched on and on.

"Only don't drop me! Don't let me fall!"

They dropped together toward the ground, leaving most of Argus's courage above them. Just before they could be have smashed into the earth, they halted. Argus moved his feet and felt the tips of his boots scrape at grass and dirt.

Deep inside that hood several dark shapes moved; tongues he supposed, though they moved more like snakes.

"Free the children. Take your remaining men and move away from the wagons."

Argus closed his eyes for a moment and considered. He was paid well to deliver merchandise. His men were paid well. They would not be paid if they were dead.

"Take them."

Argus lifted his hands and backed away. Not far away another of his men let out a scream as he descended at the speed of falling fruit and was saved at the last possible moment. Another scream from a distance. There were at least three of the monsters. That was three too many.

"Take them!" He stepped farther back, his body shivering with adrenaline. He would not run. He could not fight.

An arrow drove into the shoulder of Ellish-Loa. The thing grunted then moved. The winds tore at Argus hard enough to stagger him and then the living cloak was in the air, moving like an arrow itself.

Argus could only watch as the creature slashed out with the same claws that had dug into his shoulders and disemboweled Daren in one strike. The blow was massive and Daren's body flew backward, leaving a heavy trail of guts and blood. Daren's bow never left his hand.

"Stand down!" Argus bellowed the words and looked around, making sure that he was obeyed. The next fool that tried to be brave would taste his steel. He had no intention of dying for someone else's profits.

Let Beron come for him. He was bigger than Beron and he had a few secrets of his own. In any event he had no desire to die this night.

The rains kept coming and Beron trudged through them, disgusted by the mud, the cold and the wet.

To the side of the trail and their small caravan a gully had become a stream and then a creek, and was now a river. They adjusted accordingly.

The women they held as captives were silent, though some of them tended to smile at the strangest times. They were not normal people. He knew that now and he cared not at all. They were his. He'd paid for them. He would sell them for a profit. He would keep his earnings, and he would spend a small part of his fortune making certain that Brogan McTyre died slowly.

To that end he had spent the last day of his travels talking with a courier who would take his offer to Hollum. He'd planned to stop there himself, but had changed his mind when he heard that great numbers of people were already heading in that direction from Saramond. Best not to be seen with the refugees. The He-Kisshi were probably already headed there and looking for him and his. He did not doubt they had escaped his trap for them. They were Undying, after all.

Now his courier had done well and his prize was before him. There was real business to attend to.

"These 'Undying' you speak of, they are the ones who offer coins and take sacrifices?"

"Yes," Beron replied to the woman walking next to him. She was scarcely half his size. He knew without thinking about it that she could kill him easily. She and her brethren were considered the most dangerous fighters alive.

"You should avoid them."

"I intend to, but they are not why I've asked for your services."

"You want us to find Brogan McTyre?"

"Precisely. I want him found, captured, brought to me. Him and all of the men who worked with him. I imagine he can tell you their names."

"I would say that we don't work cheaply, but in your case we can't work for you at all." She looked toward him and shrugged.

"Why so?" He felt the scowl on his face deepen. He was not a man used to being denied.

"We work as mercenaries from time to time, but King Parrish is our lord and he has claimed the lot of them."

He could offer a lot, he could not offer as much as a king. "I don't suppose I could pay you to geld them for me? Bring me their cocks?"

She smiled. "They've made you very angry."

"They sold me a bill of goods that has already cost me a city. The Undying want me because of the slaves I travel with. I would have my satisfaction."

"If I find them first, perhaps something can be arranged. King Parrish never said I had to bring them in complete, only alive."

"Excellent. Of course, if I find them first I'll kill the bastards."

She looked at him again and he wished he knew a name to go with her. "As I understand it, the gods themselves want them. They are to be sacrificed in order to save the world."

Beron shrugged. "I need to find someone who can talk to the gods for me. Can you do that?"

She laughed and shook her head. "No. Me and the rest of the Marked Men tend toward the other side of the equation."

"What do you mean?"

"I mean the gods did not solve our problems, so we bartered with something else instead."

"I still don't understand."

"You don't need to. I will make you a counter offer, Beron. Find the men you seek, capture them, torture them if you want, but leave them alive. Whatever price you paid them, we will triple it as your reward."

Beron stopped walking and looked hard at the woman. She stopped and matched his gaze.

"You're actually serious, aren't you?"

"King Parrish wants them. He needs them alive. He will pay you dearly."

"Done."

"*Alive*, Beron. If they are dead, they are useless to us. They must be alive."

"Done." Beron smiled.

"Excellent." The rains continued and painted her hair to her scalp. She looked like a half-drowned urchin. Just the same he listened when she continued and he nodded solemnly. "Beron, do not try to offer them to anyone else. Do not try to get a higher bid. You will not and your profit will already be high. You know what the Marked Men are capable of. If you betray us, you earn our wrath."

"Why would I betray you?"

"You are a slaver, Beron. You're practically the high lord of all slavers. Your reputation precedes you, as well. You are a skilled fighter. You are a strong man, and you are a brave man. Make certain you are a *wise* man when it comes to this."

Her body was cloaked against the cold, just the same she took the time to peel off one glove and show him the markings on her flesh. He could not tell if they were tattoos or something else completely, but when she showed him her palm the marking there, a serpentine spiral with a slash from the very center to the very end of the mark, writhed and shimmered on her flesh.

"My word to you, Beron of Saramond: deliver them alive and your reward will be wealth. Cheat me and the reward will be everything you would have done to Brogan McTyre."

"My word to you, servant of King Parrish. If I find them they will be delivered alive, provided you pay what you have promised. Disappoint me, and I'll see to it that you and yours are locked in irons and sold to the highest bidder. Do you doubt me?"

She smiled. "Not in the least."

"I have always enjoyed coin more than revenge. I find it spends better."

"On this we are in agreement."

He nodded as she strode away from him. Wherever her horse was, it remained out of his sight.

He was cold and he was wet and he ached from the travel, but Beron smiled.

Brogan McTyre was a dead man any way you looked at it, but now he could profit from that death.

Beron strode on, his mind already working the necessary angles.

"You've changed, Parrish." King Bron McNar sat upon his throne, looked upon his closest neighbor and tried to hide the feeling of dread that clawed at his guts. In the past King Parrish of Mentath had been a hard man, yes, but he'd been a man. Now Bron had his doubts.

He was the same size as before, true enough, and his face was still his face, but everything else about him seemed off-kilter. He was confident where before he had been unsure. He stood as if he had no worries in the world. Not like he had lost to Bron in their last battle.

It was the markings, of course. He'd heard of the Marked Men but seeing that the king of Mentath had done to himself whatever it was he'd had done to his finest soldiers left him doubting his abilities to fight the bastard a second time, should it come to that.

His arms and his neck, where they were bared, were covered in the markings. They seemed inked across his flesh, but they couldn't have been as they also shimmered and changed even as Bron looked at them. The changes were subtle. They were small, but they were not his imagination and he was certain of that.

Parrish had brought a dozen fighters with him, but hardly seemed concerned about whether or not they were there. He exuded a preposterous level of confidence and the odd air that he was onto a joke no one else understood. He had that in common with Harper Ruttket, actually. That was probably why Bron so disliked Brogan McTyre's second.

Parrish was not a large man. He was slender and he was tall, bordering on too thin to take seriously, but having met the man in close combat, Bron knew better. His hair was long and coiled into curls and adorned with stones and ringlets. The entire mass was drawn back into multiple smaller braids in the style of his people. The Mentath never cut their hair deliberately. When they had short hair it was either because they had offended their king and he demanded their honor or because someone had cut it for them when they lost a duel. Even asking why a Mentath had short hair was considered an offense, as Bron understood it.

"You have changed, too, Bron. You're actually bigger than you were before." There was a genial enough tone to the words, but the smile on the man's face was cold and thin. "We are another year from a formal Gathering of Kings, but this seemed an important enough issue."

Bron nodded and poured them both a heavy goblet of red wine that was thick and sweet. "Emissaries are on their way from Arthorne, Giddenland and Kaer-ru."

Parrish took the wine and sipped it with a nod of thanks. He knew well enough that Bron wasn't the sort to resort to poison. Besides which, these days they were supposed to be allies. He'd married Parrish's sister, after all. "Even the islanders are coming this far?" Parrish nodded his approval. "I suppose the gods are serious about ending the world, after all."

"Why wouldn't they be?"

"'Ten times before they have made their threats. Ten times before they have merely punished.' Isn't that the line the bards most often sing about the gods?"

Bron sighed. "I never really wanted to listen to the tales. I just followed the instructions and called it done."

"What do you suppose they are, the gods? Have you ever known anyone who could say?"

Bron shook his head. "I'm not even sure what their punishments were. We've the Broken Swords to consider, where gods supposedly fought. No proof of course. And if those are swords, where are the hilts?"

"Maybe the hilts were crystal as well?"

"Well, that would certainly explain why they broke, I suppose."

"The punishments I can explain. Ten times the kingdoms sinned and ten times the gods let demons into our world."

"And what are demons, then, Parrish?"

"Bad things, one supposes."

"Well, that explains it all then."

"Don't look at me, Bron. I've no notion what a demon is." The worst part of the conversation? Bron knew at that moment that the other king was lying. He thought about the odd markings that moved and shimmered and closed his eyes for a moment. He didn't know what a demon was himself, but he intended to find out.

Bron took a small sip of the potent wine. "In any event, we know we must deal with what Brogan McTyre has done."

Parrish nodded. "Aye, or face the end of the world."

"You seem very calm about this."

"As I've already said, ten times we've supposedly been warned. No reason to think the gods will destroy the world. If they did, who would sacrifice to them?"

Bron stared at the far wall for a moment then nodded his head. He had news that Parrish apparently did not. "Saramond is gone."

"How's that?"

"The city of Saramond is gone. Completely. The very land where it was has been destroyed, washed into the sea."

Parrish shook his head as if to deny it, the calm arrogance knocked away from his face by the news. Bron felt a certain satisfaction in that knowledge. "That's madness. Saramond is fifty miles from the sea."

Bron bit back a harsh note of laughter. He didn't want to laugh. It wasn't the sort of thing that even made a good joke. "Oh yes, I know. Frankel will not be joining us. He's dead. Died when the city was torn apart by lightning strikes. I doubt you could see them from where you live, but up here we had a good view from our towers. I haven't advertised the knowledge to everyone in Stennis Brae, but I took the time to climb one of the towers and look myself. I can take you to see the view if you'd like."

Parrish, who had been looking very confident until that moment, shook his head and wandered to the closest chair to sit.

"Gone? Completely gone?"

"Ruined. Lost. Washed into the ocean, which is now fifty or more miles closer than before." He rather enjoyed making Parrish nervous. It was a sad little victory, but he would take what he could from the man he knew could take him in a battle. "I daresay I'll be fine up here in the mountains, at least for a while, but the plains of Arthorne are looking very different these days. Waters flooding everything out there, a little at a time. It'd be faster, but most of the plains are lower than the area closer to this end. The waters can only get so far before they'll have to form a lake instead of rivers."

"We've got to find those bastards." Parrish looked up. He didn't quite accuse, but he didn't ask, either. "You had them. You let them go."

"Aye. He offered me a valid argument."

"How so?"

"The Undying took his entire family as a sacrifice."

"Impossible. They've never done that before."

"They did it just the same. He showed me the coins. Four of them. His wife, all three children. He asked me what I would have done."

Parrish nodded.

"Would you have done differently, Parrish?"

"Possibly. Then again, I have four wives…"

"I can't say I'm happy about the situation. I intend to do my part to see him and his men recaptured. Sent fifty of my best after them. Good soldiers, good hunters, and twenty dogs. He'll be found and likely soon." He did not mention the first twenty killed by Brogan. Why offer any sign that his soldiers might be weak?

Parrish nodded. "How long until the rest arrive?"

"Who can say? I've no idea where their emissaries are coming from."

"Troubling times, Bron."

"It was easier when we were younger," Bron agreed. "Then all we had to worry about was whether or not we were going to kill each other on the battlefield."

Parrish snorted laughter and raised his goblet in salute.

Brogan looked at the rolling hillside and the small hut on it, and shook his head. "Hut" was a generous word. The structure was made of rocks that had been slathered together with mud once upon a time, but now most of what seemed to hold it together were the creeping vines that covered the hill. The sort of vines, in his experience, that hid snakes and the like. He did not much like snakes.

Harper, who knew very well of his dislike, was smiling ear to ear and had one hand over the lower half of his face to try to hide that fact. A small army on their asses and Harper found something to laugh about. He always did.

"Why are we here, Anna?"

Desmond scowled at the question. His wife answered it.

Anna placed her hands on her hips and shook her head. "Because I was trained by the Galeans, and Darwa is a

Galean. I can't answer the questions you want answered. She can."

"Can you have her come out here?"

"No. You have to go to her."

"That's a rule of some sort?"

"Darwa doesn't like to leave her home. She has invested it with a great deal of her power. Leaving it would make her vulnerable."

He stared at the woman and contemplated that. Had she left her powers behind when she left her house? Were they powers that could be stolen and used against them? He had no way of knowing and wasn't sure he wanted to ask. Better to hope she had a few more defenses in place for the next time an army came knocking.

"Will you at least introduce us then?"

"No need." Anna waved him toward the front of the dubious dwelling. "She's expecting you."

Harper's body shook with suppressed laughter and when Brogan looked his way he shook all the harder, one hand waving frantically as if warding off a swarm of flies. His eyes streamed with tears.

Brogan jammed a finger in Harper's direction. "Shut it!"

Harper leaned over his horse nearly braying laughter. No one else got it and Brogan wanted it to stay that way. He liked his dread of snakes left between him and no one else.

There were stones buried in the thick ivy. Brogan could see them if he squinted just so. Carefully planting his feet he moved across the lichen crusted steps, making certain not to slip. He had a powerful suspicion that falling into that heavy veil of ivy would be very bad for his health.

Once past the seventeen stepping stones he knocked at the door.

The woman who opened it was the very definition of average. She was middling in height, middling in weight, had mousy brown hair and a face that was utterly unremarkable. The good news was, she wasn't quite the horrid hag he'd been expecting. Galeans were rare, but had reputations for looking much as they had lived. That is to say, a truly evil Galean was supposed to bear the marks of every sin upon her body. That was all just rumor of course. He'd never met one until just that moment.

She looked up at him, and squinted a bit as she took his measure. "You are Brogan McTyre of Stennis Brae."

"I... Yes I am." He hadn't really thought she wouldd know his name. They had traveled several hours to meet her. At no point had Anna left them or ridden ahead.

"Come inside, then, and let's have done with this."

She moved back. Her simple dress was a functional thing, and like her, seemed designed to be as nondescript as possible.

Brogan followed, ducking through the door and into the structure itself. It was bigger than he expected, and bore the sign of the Lodges on the beams of the ceiling. A low fire burned in a stone fireplace. The walls were stone and unadorned, save for where water had run along and stained them over the years. There was a smell of burned herbs about the place that was cloying and oddly sweet. It made his senses ring.

She moved over to a small table with a seat on either side. All of them made of stone and designed for function instead of comfort. Still he sat when she gestured.

"Tell me what you want to know."

"I want to know how to stop the gods. They want to end me and mine or end the world. I don't like those choices."

"You act as if that's as easy as brewing a love potion or a curse."

"I don't care if it's easy. I want to know if it's possible."

"In my experience anything is possible. But what you

ask? That'll take a great deal of work."

"I'm not afraid to work for what I need."

Darwa looked at him with her unremarkable eyes and reached out to grab his wrist. With surprising strength she turned his arm so that his palm and wrist faced the ceiling.

"You want what, exactly?"

"I want the gods to ignore us, to forget us. I want them to leave us alone."

"That will not happen."

"Why not?"

"Because they are *gods*, Brogan McTyre. Even the weakest of them can change the shape of the world. Have you not seen the rains? Have you not noticed the floods, or the way the earth splits and shakes where their great keep used to be? That is a warning, nothing more. That is the mildest of the powers that gods have."

"Well then I want to make them go away, or at least spare my companions."

"Not possible. For the same reason. They are gods. Their minds cannot be fooled; their senses will not accept lies. In the past one of the gods tricked the others. They killed him. That is what happened to your mountains."

"Honestly? I thought that was a myth."

"No. It happened. Probably not as we tell ourselves but there are still elements of the divine to find there if one looks."

"Well then, what can be done to gods?"

"Some say they can be captured, but I suspect it's harder than it sounds and it sounds nearly impossible. Gods have power. Before they can be captured that power must be used up. The gods have demanded sacrifices for thousands of years. They have their power. That is why they demanded the sacrifices. So that they would never go hungry again."

Oh, how his rage swelled. Food for the gods and nothing

more. A meal that the gods might not be peckish. All of his loved ones.

"What then? What else is there?"

Darwa leaned back in her seat but held onto his hand. She shook her head for a moment and then asked, "Do you truly want to know?"

"It's why I'm here."

"The four coins. I need them. I will not give them back."

He stared hard at her and finally nodded. His free hand went to the satchel in his belt and slowly pulled them out. All that remained to hold them by. Brogan handed them over one by one and she accepted them.

Next she lifted a very large needle. "I need your blood." She paused and looked at his expression. "Not all of it. A few drops will suffice."

He nodded and the needle punched into the palm of his hand, near the wrist. The pain was brighter than the room and Brogan bit off a yelp.

A thin stream of his blood fell across the stone table and pooled. When the trickle faded, she let go of his hand and looked at the puddle of crimson. Her fingers deftly tapped a black powder into the blood and then several others besides. In short order, she had a blackish paste that she lifted between two fingers.

Darwa moved over to the fire, carrying her prize. The flames cast a long shadow of her that was distorted, and matched neither her actions nor her form. Brogan did not move, but he watched, observing every action she made – and every action her warped shadows made too.

She spoke and placed the paste into a small metal dish. The dish went over the flames and the Galean whispered words that he could not hear, but that made the air cold nonetheless. That doughy blob of blood and other things swelled and danced and hissed on the metal, as surely as a lump of cold lard will do in the same situation. Cooking fat, however, did not scream.

After almost a minute of watching the globule dance and simmer and shrink, it faded completely away, leaving not even a trace of powder that Brogan could see.

"There. We have your answers..." As she stepped away from the fire her shadows converged into one. It still made no sense with the rest of her body. Despite the unsettling aspects, he kept calm and looked at her face.

"Truly?" He leaned back in his seat. "How then, do I stop the gods from following through on their threats?"

"There's only one way that I can see, and that's to actually kill them."

"Kill the gods?"

Brogan stared at the fire, the flames that flickered and rippled over the remaining wood. His lips felt oddly numb, but he thought that was the smoke in the air.

"Aye, Brogan McTyre. They must be killed if you are to be free of them."

"How many gods are there?"

"Five."

"Where do they live?"

"There is a great stone bridge called the Gateway. It is near their nameless keep, which now lies abandoned. One must pass through that place to find the gods in their home. Even then, one must know the proper way and the only people who know the way are far to the south in Kaer-ru."

Brogan nodded, remembering seeing the place before. "The land near it is tainted."

"No. The land near it is gone, shattered by the gods in their anger. The ancient keep is gone, too. There is no way to the Gateway by land."

"Then how do I get near it?"

"Hire a boat. Hire several. Steal one if you must for I can't imagine too many would help you. They risk death."

"I've never been on a boat."

"There are plenty. You will also need one of the Louron with you."

"The Louron? What are the Louron?"

"A people who seldom speak to strangers. There are stories that they can navigate the waters between the worlds. They reside amongst the Kaer-ru islands."

"You did get answers, didn't you?"

"Oh, yes."

"So then, Darwa of the Galeans, how does one kill a god?" He looked from the fire to the Galean and stared at her face. Her features seemed to reshape for a moment, but when he blinked she was once again an average woman.

"That would be the challenging part." She leaned closer in until her fingers touched his hands. "Listen carefully..."

An hour later he walked out of Darwa's hut and strode carefully over the stepping stones.

There were three too many men outside waiting, and he recognized all of them.

Jon Lonson, Davers Hillway and Bump were among the men who'd helped him in the unholy place then made a fortune alongside him only a short time ago. Though he counted them as friends, none of them looked happy to see him.

Jon was from the southlands and wore their clothing, which meant baggy pants, baggy shirt and boots that ran to his calves. Dark skin, dark hair, dark eyes and sadly, his usual easy smile was missing. Most of that was hidden under a cloak as the weather here was colder than he'd ever liked. Davers was from Hollum, which meant he tended to leathers. Most Hollumites did, as you never knew when someone was going to try to steal from you assisted by a dagger in the side. A little leather armor went a long way. Bump? No one knew where Bump was from. Every time someone asked him, Bump had a different answer. Bump was thin, short and as bald as could be. He was also one of the fastest men Brogan had ever seen in combat.

It was Bump who spoke up, just as Brogan cleared the last of the stepping-stones. "What the fuck have you gotten us into, you bastard? There's a bounty on each and every one of us!"

Brogan nodded and offered a weary smile. "Aye. I know that. I'm working on fixing that very matter."

"Work faster! I had to run from a brothel with my pants and boots over my shoulder when the fucking soldiers came looking for me!" Bump was deadly serious, which only made Harper's explosion of laughter more enjoyable. Bump's eyes bulged with righteous indignation.

"The gods did not appreciate us ending their sacrifices." Brogan's voice was as serious as Bump's. He liked the man, but he never much cared to have anyone yelling at him and he felt no remorse for the actions he'd taken. "They've decided we must be the replacement sacrifices, apparently. And so I intend to discuss the matter with the gods."

Bump's jaw dropped open for a moment as he processed that concept. "You plan to have a little chat with the gods of all creation, is that it?"

"Aye. That's the idea."

"And where are you going to have this chat? Going to just yell at a scryer and hope the gods hear it?"

Brogan stared hard. "Do you suppose that might work, Bump?" He walked closer to the man while his blood sang in his ears and his vision tinged crimson. "I was thinking I might travel to see a Galean and ask her how it might be done, but if you happen to have a scryer around, I'm willing to have a go at your way."

Jon leaned in and said, "Easy, Brogan. We just came to offer our services. Bump can be a bit on the mouthy side."

"I've just been having a talk. Learning what I have to do in order to make this stop. I'm grateful to each and every one of you. You know that. I've been driven from my home, exiled from my country, and sent out to find a way to stop the gods because of what I did to save my family."

Bump nodded his head. "Of course, mate. Of course. No harm us having a talk. Just saying my piece is all."

Davers shook his head. "The others are coming, Brogan. We heard of the hunt for us and figured there could only be one reason. Can't trust everyone, true enough, but you can find a few allies if you look in the right places. We started for your home. Just found you sooner than expected."

Jon added, "Aye, especially you'll find allies if you happen to have enough coin to pay more than any bounties offered." He grinned as he said it, which helped a great deal.

Brogan nodded his head and felt his blood calm a bit. "Let's talk then, lads. We've much to discuss."

CHAPTER ELEVEN
The Night People

B'Rath leaned over the pale woman and wished he could do more for her. She moaned in her feverish sleep; he looked away from her and back to his mother.

"You feeling better?"

His mother nodded and smiled, but it was a lie. She was not feeling better and he knew it. She would be dead soon and there was nothing he or anyone could do for her unless the gods themselves intervened.

As a whole the caravan moved on at a decent clip. As decent as it could, considering that almost everyone in the group was on foot.

They did not speak to him and they barely tolerated his existence, but all seemed perfectly willing to wear his clothes and eat his food. There had been a great deal of food stored away. Most of it was gone now. The cowled thing said they would be provided for on the journey. He was not so certain. Still, the weather was calm enough around them, and the women did not actually throw rocks at him. One found small blessings where one could.

Uto approached, his mouth set in a frown of concentration. Uto, being not very smart, often had that frown in place. When he was younger, B'Rath thought his brother angry.

In truth, he was merely confused.

"Where are we going?"

"With the Undying to their new home."

"Why?"

"Because they could kill us with ease and we do not want to die. Once they are where they need to be we will move on."

B'Rath looked past his brother to the pale women. Most of them now had clothing of some sort, provided by B'Rath's family. They were lean and they looked lost, but they were healthier than they had been. That was something at least. He had been raised to help where he could, as long as helping did not cause his family harm. So far they had not been harmed. It would have to be enough.

"We should move on, B'Rath."

"We cannot. They can't be left on their own and the Undying would not permit it in any event."

Even as he spoke, however, the shapes of the Undying rose into the air. All of them. A few had left at a time over the last few days but never all at once as they did now, rising into the air on a wind that came from nowhere to lift them as high as the clouds.

"We can leave now." Uto stared at the dwindling shapes of the He-Kisshi and smiled.

"You may leave. You may even take our families, but I will continue on this path because to do otherwise is to offend the gods."

Uto scowled in thought again. It was less than an hour later that he took his family and their parents with him and headed directly south.

B'Rath did not stop them from going. He knew what he had to do, but that did not mean he expected the rest of his family to suffer with him.

The family went south, heading for Edinrun. He would

follow when he could. In the meantime there was a very large collection of women who needed food and shelter and he would make certain that they had it whenever he could. The gods would expect no less from the faithful.

Once the others moved on, B'Rath climbed back into the wagon where the pale woman still moaned and fought in her sleep, and tended to her as best he could. There was so much that could be wrong, and he was not a healer. They would ride on soon, but first he needed to make certain his charges were still alive, even the weakest among them.

Lyraal said, "This is a mistake."

"That is all you ever say, Lyraal." Myridia shook her head, irritated.

"It bears repeating."

"Look, we can't go alone. We need to have as many as we can to make this work."

"You are wrong." Lyraal's words held no malice. They were simply the opinion of a woman she respected and admired and believed would probably be a better leader than she was.

"This is why you should be leading."

Lyraal shook her head. "No. You should be leading. But you should actually lead." The other woman's brow was knitted with stress. "He is a handsome man, this Garien, and I know you feel the same urges we all do, but he is not going to abandon his people to be your mate and even if he were, we do not have the time right now. We must move on, Myridia."

Myridia flinched. The troupe was not far away. She did not want Garien hearing the conversation, and Lyraal didn't care in the least if he heard every word.

"That's not what this is about."

"That's exactly what this is about. You want him. Fine, want him. As far as I'm concerned, have him. But then move on. We need to reach the Sessanoh and we are not going fast enough."

"You think we should take to the waters?"

"I know we should."

Myridia had nothing to say to that. "We'll discuss this later. The night comes."

The sun set behind the mountains again and the darkness swept across the area almost as swiftly as the water overflowed the banks of the river.

Myridia clenched her sword a little tighter, careful not to cut herself on the scaled blade. Beside her, around her, the others did likewise.

The steel gave her comfort. When she looked back at how she killed the blacksmith she felt no guilt. She needed a weapon and he had it. She needed to get to where the gods wanted her, and for that reason whatever happened next was a requirement. If the troupe died she would accept that. She had no choice, no matter how much the notion might hurt.

The screaming noises of the night people had grown stronger and closer the last time the sun set, and Myridia suspected in her heart that they would be attacking soon. There was no choice in the matter: they could flee, or they could fight. Fleeing meant leaving with little or nothing. Fighting meant having the strength of the troupe with them when the night people came.

The rains were constant now. That worked to the advantage of the Grakhul. They had not manifested their other shapes around the humans. That would be a mistake and she knew it, but when the time came, if they had to eliminate the night people, they would do so with the blessings that the gods had provided.

Time was still running too quickly for her satisfaction and the night people would only slow them down.

Lyraal looked back the way they had come and frowned. "There is something back there. I can see it, but I cannot see it clearly."

Myridia looked. There was a darkness there, deeper than the night and darker than mere shadows. She did not like the way that odd stain moved or the way it made her feel. She did not like the off-kilter, distorted music she heard coming from that direction. It sounded to her like the music one might hear while drowning in the ocean. This was the time then. The night people were coming and, one way or the other, someone would be bled and stopped before the night was through.

"Tell Garien to move his people forward." The command was for Lorae, who was nervous enough to nearly twitch at every noise.

The girl nodded and bolted toward the train of wagons.

They had prepared for this moment as best they could. According to Garien and his troupe the night people could not stand light. So they set a few surprises between the wagons and the coming darkness.

The wagons moved on into the gathering night and rain. Myridia and her sisters stayed behind and let the change come. Scales shivered through flesh, eyes bulged, teeth and claws grew and muscles became harder.

The darkness sounded of wagon wheels and light, cheerful music, but it radiated a cold as deep as the sea. There was an undertone, a barely heard clicking noise that made her feel uncomfortable. She had to focus to notice it, but once heard it would not go away.

"We are not here for you." The voice came from the leading shapes in the darkness. They were not shadows, nor silhouettes, but seemed a bit of both. The voice itself was as distorted as the music, warbling and broken, but understandable despite that. The clicking sounds were actually amplified when the voice spoke.

"Yet you have followed us for days, and we are on a mission from the gods themselves."

"You have merely traveled with our prey. Move aside and you will be unharmed."

The darkness broke apart. In the center the shapes remained the same, like shadows of wagons cast into the air instead of across the ground, and just as distorted, but from those shapes humanoid forms moved, also as stretched and malformed as long shadows thrown by a light source that none could see.

"We have business with the wagons ahead of you. We will handle that business even if you stand in our way." The voice was familiar, the inflection and the accent.

"You are Garth?"

The shadow that spoke tilted its head then nodded. "I am."

"Your brother says he lost you in Mentath and that you and yours never returned quite the same."

"We are changed. We would be with our families just the same. They are our kin, our people."

"You move only at night. They move only by day. How can you ever be together again?" Myridia looked at the form and saw that there were features on the shadowy shape. They were faint and as distorted and stretched as everything else, but she recognized those features. They belonged to Garien.

"We tire of this conversation. They will be ours again as they were before the Sundering."

Myridia shook her head. "The what?"

"We did not leave them. They abandoned us. We will have them back again. That is all you need to know."

There was no menace from the shadowy people. That was the part Myridia found most puzzling. Garien had made them seem as if they might well eat the souls of whatever they came across. He made them seem like a plague that could not be stopped.

Lyraal spoke up. "Garien claims that you seek to hurt the troupe. They are our companions. We cannot permit you to do this thing." The words surprised Myridia, but warmed her, as well.

"Your world is ending. We can feel that. We can taste the anger of the gods in the breeze. Yet you worry about your 'companions' and let them distract you from what you must do."

"We must reach the Sessanoh. We ride in that direction."

"Do you indeed?" Garth stepped closer. His body moved and flickered as a shadow moves along a dozen surfaces. Each step he took showed different distortions. His head warped as if he were walking past a wall and a window and perhaps furniture and the shadow ran across those separate surfaces on the way to Myridia.

Others moved the same way, flickering across the air and the land as they moved. It took only a moment to understand that there was one shadow for each of them.

"We are attacked!" Lyraal swept her sword around and dropped into a defensive stance, but she was too slow. The fingers of her personal shadow touched her face and covered her eyes. Lyraal, surely the strongest of them, fell backward, her body seizing and her weapon falling from twitching fingers.

Myridia did not have time to respond before daggers of ice sank into her brain, her eyes, and laid her back in a stupor. Garth's voice spoke to her. "Watch and learn what Garien and his friends did to us."

•••

When Myridia awoke, both the night and the night people had gone. The wagons were gone as well. The rains came down in sheets, the ground was waterlogged and the plants she had seen grow from nothing were drowning in waters deep enough to kill a human. Humans did not have gills.

Her sword lay under a foot of water but finding it was easy enough. She gathered it to her and shook her head. Better a wet weapon than no weapon, but she was glad she'd oiled the blade before the encounter with the night people.

Myridia stood up and looked around the area. The waters were coming faster now, the river well past its banks. The river that had not been there only days before.

In the distance, a mile or more away, she saw the earth tremble and the waters spray upward as if something vast shoved through the earth, pumping and thrusting through the water-soaked but otherwise solid ground.

The movement was fast and violent – and actively veered away from them. That was the part that unsettled her the most. Whatever it was, it likely came from the gods and softened the land for proper destruction.

The others were up and moving. None of them seemed worse for what they'd experienced, though all of them bore the same shocked expressions she imagined she had on her own face.

"What do we do now?" Lyraal asked the question and deferred to her. As if she had any desire whatsoever to lead.

"We leave here. Wrap your weapons in your clothes and tie them to your bodies. We will not be caught without them again. We leave and we swim as far as we can. There is little enough time left to us."

The preparations had to start.

She looked around again, hoping in vain to find some sign of the troupe, but it was a wasted effort. If the wagons had traveled in any direction their markings upon the ground had been lost to the waters.

Around her the others obeyed her orders and Myridia closed her eyes, felt the pull of the Sessanoh upon her guts and nodded.

Garien. The name echoed through her like a distant memory. She wanted him, yes, but he was gone and they had so far to go. Enough. She had been foolish and Lyraal had let her be foolish. But enough. They had to go.

Garien and his troupe had been helpful, but they had also been a distraction. It was time to move on now. It was time to obey the gods and their decisions.

She felt oddly unburdened. Traveling with the troupe had been pleasant, but she knew in every fiber of her being that she should not have been with them beyond the time it took to gain the clothes needed to survive the cold and to regain the strength needed to travel. They had been an interruption that neither she nor her fellow Grakhul needed.

For several hours they traveled along the river, riding through the waters and making good progress. They came to a passage through the mountains, a place where great crystalline shapes crashed against each other and made a natural opening. The waters of the river moved through that passage and they let the waters take them along. That pulling sensation in her guts told her she was going in the right direction.

On this side of the mountains the day was longer. The sun was not hidden behind stone and crystal, but rather fell slowly. The night was held at bay for several additional hours.

Though they made up for many lost miles in that first day's journey, they eventually grew tired and needed to rest. That was easier done on the river's bank than in the currents that would drag them away from any place where they sought to rest, and so they climbed free of the waters and let the change take place, pulling them back to their more human forms.

Both Lorae and Memni flopped themselves dramatically into the mud and gasped at the chilling rain falling from above to wash over them. Myridia smiled indulgently. She had been just as bad in her youth.

When the screaming, ululating noises came cutting across the river and the night, Myridia felt a shiver crawl across her damp body; it made her scalp crawl.

Lyraal glanced in her direction and she looked back, nodding at the unspoken question. There could be no doubt.

The night people were following them.

"I can't just point a finger and make it magically happen. It's not something I control, but something the gods let me do." The scryer was pretty enough, Ulster supposed, but he rather wanted to sew her mouth shut. Whenever he asked for updates she whined and complained.

"Yes, well, pray or something. This is getting us nowhere."

A score of hounds and one scryer and they couldn't find any sign of Brogan McTyre or his people.

It was the damned rains, of course. They weren't constant, not yet at least, like he heard they were in some places, but they were bad enough to throw off the hounds, and the woman who was supposed to guide them was no better.

She glared at him, her earlier docile disposition lost, apparently forever, more the pity. "It's not like they draw me a bloody map. They just tell me landmarks. I've never left Stennis Brae in my entire life and landmarks don't mean much out here. I could point you to a bloody tree, but which one should I point to? They're everywhere and they come in all kinds of shapes and sizes. Honestly, the land here is mad with trees."

"Did the gods say anything about a tree?"

"Well, no, it's just an example."

"Then unless they do, let's leave off the fucking trees and you try to find Brogan McTyre."

"You've a foul mouth."

"And you've a useless fucking talent, scryer."

She shot him a look that would have withered many men, but he was not impressed. He'd promised to bring McTyre and his lot back alive. He could forgive himself if the whining peasant girl failed to make it home intact.

Without another word, she stomped off to the tent that his men set up for her every night. He had overheard a few of the boys making comments about what they'd like to do with her, and right now he was half-tempted to let them.

No. No, he wasn't. But she was frustrating him to the ends of his wits.

Three days lost looking for any sign of the bastard McTyre, and that was after losing most of a day to recover from the stings they'd all received. Bron would not be pleased if he failed. An unhappy king was never something to aspire to.

The sun had set. They had moved away from the mountains and started south on a proper trail, not because they were certain where to go but because, in Brogan's situation, there were worse places to aim for than Torema, and Owen was willing to bet five gold coins on the bastards going that way.

Unless and until either the hounds did their work or the scryer managed something, it would have to do. Besides which, out of the shadow of the mountains they could travel longer each day.

Owen came his way, looking tired. They all looked tired. They were riding hard to make up for lost time.

"You've got to stop making that one angry."

"What?"

"The girl, Mearhan. You've got to stop making her angry."

"Why?"

"Because she has better luck hearing from the gods when she's relaxed and not considering hacking your manhood off while you sleep."

"Did she say she was going to do that?"

"Not in as many words, Ulster, but she's not happy with you and she's angry enough to do it."

"Owen, I'm not here to watch over her. I'm here to find McTyre."

"Aye, and you'll have an easier time of it if you stop infuriating the help. Does it do any good to whip a horse that's being testy?"

"Well, if you're going to talk good sense to me…" Ulster shook his head. Life was easier when it was just the troops. They actually did as they were told.

"So might I suggest you go apologize and make nice? All the hounds and hard soldiers in the world won't do you a damned bit of good if you can't find the bloody targets of King Bron's wrath."

"Life is easier when you deal with soldiers."

"Aye. But I like a good looking woman better as a tent mate."

"Let me know if that ever happens."

Owen laughed and shook his head as he ambled back toward his tent.

The guards were set, the fires were burning. They'd find the bastards soon enough. In the meantime, he had to make nice with the shrieking woman who was supposed to find their enemies or face Bron's wrath.

With a reluctant sigh he wandered over to Mearhan Slattery's tent and called out, "I'm coming in."

She was sitting in a chair, sorting through several bags of herbs. He had no idea if she planned to cook them, smoke them or make a tea. He also did not care.

"I'm sorry for being harsh. You know why I'm being so demanding. You're the one that warned us, and believe me, I'm grateful. I just... I don't want to miss the men we seek and risk the world."

The girl blinked angrily and he understood the expression. She was trying not to tear up. She had an interest in one of the men riding with McTyre. Whatever the case, the man was as good as dead if they were captured.

"I'm trying," she said finally. "I've a few things that might make me more receptive, but it's a risk. I need silence and I need to be alone. If I can find anything, I'll let you know." She did not look at him. He understood the reasons.

Ulster nodded. "I appreciate your efforts, milady."

He left before he could look at her as more than a servant. She was fair enough on the eye and he was looking for pleasant distractions. Neither of them could afford the time or the potential conflicts that would arise later.

Harper nodded and breathed the order to attack: "Now."

The seven archers with him did their part and fired at Ulster's guards. Bowstrings thrummed and in the distance men dropped. Harper had picked carefully when he chose the archers and it had paid off.

"Walter? Where are you, ye damned fool?" Whoever was calling out was going to ruin everything. Still, one adjusted.

Across their enemy's campsite he knew that Brogan was working on the horses and Anna was handling the dogs. He had no idea what the witch was doing, but Brogan had likely already opened the pen for the animals. Now it would be up to a quick and painful method of startling a few into action and then–

Whatever his companion had chosen to do, it happened. Two of the horses let out panicked screams and then Harper could hear the sounds of horses stomping and charging. More of them made sounds and the ground fairly shook with the thunder of fifty or so animals trying to escape.

They had been riding hard for two days when the crew that had raided the Grakhul found them. Apparently it was now common knowledge that Brogan McTyre was a wanted man, and several of them had been on the list of hunted men. They came looking for Brogan to explain it all.

He was direct. "Either we all surrender and are killed, or we find a different way. I've no intention of being killed to appease gods that took my family from me. I'll kill them first."

The argument had gone on, but no one had a better idea. They were all dead if they got captured, and they knew it. There would have to be another way found, and so far Brogan's was the only option that gave them a chance. Four of the most seasoned mercenaries had gone off on a mission for Brogan. The rest of them were here, trying to break an army.

"What the bloody hell! We're under attack!" Harper recognized the voice. Same bastard that had been calling for Walter.

One more arrow, then. He targeted, sighed, released and watched the screamer fall backward with an arrow through his face. He was certainly screaming now, but it no longer mattered. The damage was done.

"Try for one more each, lads. Then it's time to get personal."

Harper sighted and fired, saw his target start dancing around in pain. The arrow had likely caught on a rib. The man was alive, but very unhappy. Harper let the bow fall to the ground. He'd retrieve it later if he needed but for now he wanted his arms free and his swords in his hands.

The others followed his example. By the time they were done, most of the men in the camp were out of their tents and looking for their attackers.

They were easy to find. Brogan came charging into the camp on horseback and once again Harper was struck by the figure his friend presented. He seemed larger than life in his fury, his braided hair slapping, his face set in a demon's mask of rage, a sword in one hand and an axe in the other as he rode hard into the middle of the camp, delivering death blows to anyone too slow to respond.

His horse trampled one soldier. Brogan swept his sword at a man with a spear who didn't realize Brogan was already upon him until it was too late. The axe in his other hand chopped through another man's neck. The first three men to face him died quickly. The others had a chance to fight back and they were among the king's finest. They struck well and they struck hard.

Brogan dropped from his saddle and into the fray, screaming his challenge at the enemy.

Harper lost sight of him in the crush of bodies. He'd find him again soon enough.

The soldiers were mostly facing toward Brogan and the men who rode in with him, another six, which meant that they had their backs turned to Harper and his companions. Even as he charged, more men appeared from a third direction, leaving few options for the king's guard.

There was no attempt at mercy.

Most of the men with them had shields and were glad of it. They bashed at their enemies with them, and did their best to run them through or cut them open. The guards were doing the same in return and judging by the screams some were successful.

Harper caught the first man unawares and drove his

sword into the soldier's kidney. He knew the pain on the man's face. He'd seen it a hundred times on the battlefield and felt it nearly as many times himself.

A sidestep and a turn, and his hooked sword was blocking a strike from a spear. The man wielding it did not throw the weapon but held it in his hands and drove the long blade at the end toward Harper's chest. He blocked but grunted and stepped back as the force of the blow staggered him. The hook was there for a reason. Harper wrenched the sword to the side with familiar ease and caught the spear's head in the barb. While the man was struggling to pull free, Harper cut open his thigh just below his manhood and stepped back. Blood erupted from the opened artery and the man staggered back, halfway to dead and quickly moving to finish his journey. There was no saving a man from a cut like that, not in the middle of a battle.

The press of bodies was everywhere. Far less than a hundred people, but they all wanted to get through their fighting alive.

And there was the thing of it. The soldiers were fighting, yes, but they weren't aiming to kill. They were trying to keep their enemies alive, because they'd been told to. The poor bastards. They were at a very severe disadvantage.

So, naturally, Harper took full advantage.

Brogan planted his heel in the knee of a man lunging for him and felt the joint break the wrong way. The man started to scream and Brogan's axe ended his pain.

The fellow on his left came in hard, swinging his shield up to bash Brogan in the face and all he could do was raise his sword arm and take the blow along his side and along his arm. From the elbow down his hand went numb. The axe came up under the shield and the point at the top of each blade cut into the man's belly. When he dropped the shield, gasping in pain, Brogan headbutted him and shoved him backward. He might live, but he'd hurt.

Brogan didn't care if the bastards lived or died, so long as they stopped hunting him. Numb arm or no, he held tight to the sword and blocked a blow with it. The axe did the bloody work, hacking clean through the soldier's arm just below the shoulder.

The winds were rising furiously, and his hair snapped like a whip. Most of the enemy's horses were gone now, running off to avoid the pain of another slap to the ass. The soldiers would be hard pressed to follow them, assuming any of the bastards lived long enough to offer pursuit. A long time ago Brogan had worn a uniform like theirs. It won them no loyalty. They were hunting him. They were the enemy. That was all there was to it.

He'd learned that from a sergeant in Bron's army. No mercy could be offered to a man fighting against you. It would only get you killed. You could offer mercy to survivors of the conflict, but not to the ones engaged in it.

A bastard with an axe came for him and he barely managed to block the blow with his sword. Metal screamed along metal then cut into wood, and while the axe was occupied with his blade he shouldered the man back and then chopped into his stomach and side. Flesh parted around blade and the man fell back howling. Someone hit him hard in the back and Brogan stumbled. Whatever hit him was bladed but did not cut horribly deep. Lucky, lucky fool.

Before his attacker could try a second time, Harper's sword opened his throat to the night air. Brogan took advantage to move on to the next enemy.

The enemy were retreating, backing away, most of them bearing frightened expressions. He had no idea why. It made no sense. There were more of them and the ground was level. Even with the element of surprise they shouldn't have been able to push the bastards back.

The wind roared in his ears and the force of it made his eyes sting.

Around him several of the soldiers were running. A few of his own joined them.

Ah. So they weren't afraid of him or running from him. That made more sense in his mind.

Brogan squinted against the howling winds and looked around. Left, nothing. Right, nothing. Behind him – a snap of thick leather.

No. He felt his own fear rise and quickly suppressed it.

"Of course." His voice was a dry croak.

Harper was looking at him from thirty feet away, shaking his head.

Harper would know, of course. He'd met the things before.

The Undying hovered above him, cloak filled with air, edges snapping. The hood full of darkness seemed to stare directly at him.

The Undying.

Brogan looked around again, and saw two more of the things in the air. They were surrounding him. They knew him.

That was all right. He knew them, too.

"You're the fuckers that stole my family from me!" He shook his head and felt the winds carrying the bastard things blast against his face.

"You have committed sins against the gods, and you and yours must now be punished."

"You've committed sins against *me*! I'll gut you like a rabbit, you disgusting beast!"

On both sides of the battle, the men who had been fighting now stood still. Even Harper, who had dealt with the followers of these things before, did not move.

"Insolentblasphemer!"

"Come on then! Come get me!" Brogan spat.

The nightmare dropped to the ground five feet from him and reached into the leathery wings that made its cloak. Brogan had no idea what it might be reaching for and he didn't care. His axe sailed across the short distance and chopped a divot of meat from the arm and wing of the He-Kisshi.

The sound it let loose was cringeworthy, but Brogan didn't have time for such matters. The unwounded arm of the thing pulled out a whip with a weighted tip, and Brogan charged. Whips were fine weapons at a distance. Up close they were nearly useless. Truly, the beast was unsettled. It flinched back as if utterly surprised by the notion that someone would attack.

Brogan snarled as he smashed his shoulder into its bulk and sent it backward. The thing wobbled, tried to right itself and fell on its backside in the dirt. Brogan drove his elbow into what he guessed would be the throat, the area directly under the false cowl of the Undying's face. Up close he could see the small eyes around that cavernous mouth. He could see the teeth and the serpentine tongues. Part of him was terrified, repulsed. Most of him was furious. This thing and its ilk had chosen his family, had taken them away, had stolen from him all that mattered, all that he loved.

It gagged and choked as he rammed his elbow into the hot, furred flesh beneath that monstrous maw and forced his weight down on its body.

Claws. The fucking thing had claws! It scraped at him so Brogan shifted his body mass, driving his knee into the nightmare's bloated belly. The sword was cast aside. No good this close in, so Brogan sought and found the dagger sheathed in his boot.

Hot red pain dragged down his other calf and scraped at his ankle, and Brogan let out his own gasp of pain. Still, his elbow pinned the creature's throat. It gagged and wheezed even as the dagger drove through the flesh of the ribs and was hauled down the length of that furry grotesquery.

The sound it made might have been the squeal of a pig if not for the elbow crushing down. Cartilage broke under Brogan's weight but still he did not relent.

The claw that had hooked his calf before tried again and only caught his boot this time, but that was luck and only luck. The third time that clawed foot could go higher and rip his leg open. Brogan stabbed again and again with the dagger, forcing his arm harder against the thing's throat until blood vomited from the shadows of the mouth.

"Enough!" One of the other things screeched the word, commanded Brogan to stop.

He looked to Harper and felt a savage smile pull at his mouth.

The spear Harper hurled struck true, driving into the cowl of the screaming nightmare. It fell from the sky and collapsed like a tent as it landed. The soldiers of King Bron backed away, as any sane person would, but they were not hunted. They had not been demanded as sacrifices. They had less to lose.

Harper and three others charged the thing, weapons drawn. It was still strying to dislodge the spear that had pierced its cowl when the first sword came down and slashed another opening.

The third of the Undying rose further into the air, crooning out a mournful noise as it went higher and higher.

Brogan looked down at his victim and smiled. He was still disgusted by the thing, even as it shuddered and died.

Harper stepped back from the other one, pale and shaking. He was panting as if he'd run a dozen miles and sweated nearly as much.

Brogan didn't take the time to find out why. He rose from his grisly task and grabbed his axe and sword. Bron's men were not all dead. There were still plenty that would try to take them, and that needed killing. He was sneering as he looked around.

"Which of you bastards is next?"

The answer came from Ulster Dunnaly. "Surrender. You're as good as dead and you know it."

"Right then. Come get me!" He started toward the man and saw the briefest moment of panic cross his enemy's face. Brogan's smile grew. "That's right. I nearly forgot. You can't kill us, can you?"

Ulster did not answer.

"You need us alive. We're to be sacrificed to the gods." Brogan shifted the axe and the sword, staring at Ulster. "We do not have that disadvantage.

"All right, lads! Time for us to end this!" Brogan charged at Ulster.

The man was an excellent swordsman. He was, if Brogan was honest, plainly more skilled than Brogan. He was also working with a severe disadvantage and they both knew it.

Ulster blocked the sword blow that Brogan dealt him and stepped back. A flick of his wrist and Brogan's blade sailed away. Undeterred, Brogan got a better grip on his axe.

Ulster spat and shook his head. "Retreat! Retreat and regroup!"

A fine soldier, a good soldier and, from all he'd ever heard a good man, turned and fled. He had no choice. Neither did his men.

Brogan called off his mercenaries. Not necessarily as a sign of respect, but because he'd made a promise to the Undying.

The one he'd killed was still dead. He had no idea why they

were called Undying. He also had no desire to investigate the claims. His skinning knife started at the broken throat and cut deep into dead, furry flesh. The stench of the thing was hidden by a smell of spices until he sliced deep enough, and then the charnel odors were nearly overwhelming. He pulled flesh away from the seam he'd created. If he could, he'd take the damned hide and use it as a flag to rally his troops.

He peeled the flesh away only to find a different body underneath. There were arterial lines running from the pale, naked body of a dead woman – he suspected one of the slave women he'd sold, by the color – and Brogan cut those apart as he encountered each of them. The furred exterior hide of the thing twitched as each line was severed. That was enough to keep him going.

To his side, Harper watched on, his eyes wide and his breath coming in sharp, harsh pants.

When he'd finished with the first, Brogan walked to the other and repeated his actions, peeling the two parts of the thing, like separating a seed from a fruit.

When he was done skinning the things, he laid them out in the dirt and took coals from the fire left behind by Ulster and his men, and spread those coals across the body of one of them. It should have been dead, but it shrieked as the coals struck and it smoldered then caught fire, the flesh burning and hissing as a thick black smoke rose.

The men backed away, horrified, and Brogan almost joined them. He would have, but he remembered Nora's death all too well.

As he prepared to do the same to the other one, Anna approached and shook her head. "You should not." She had two men with her. Between those men was a lovely lass who was struggling until she saw the carnage. Then she shivered and slumped in their arms. Mearhan Slattery.

Laram moved closer to the small group and said something to the girl that calmed her a bit.

"I must," Brogan said.

"They could tell us secrets from the gods."

"Well, we now have a scryer to do that for us, don't we?"

Anna's eyes grew wide and she turned to look at the woman held by men she'd walked over with. "Her?"

"Aye."

"That could be even deadlier than I want to think about."

"What do you mean?"

Anna stared hard and spoke slowly, as if to an addled child. "The gods speak to her? Then ask yourself this, can they see through her eyes to know where she is? Do they follow her ears and hear what she hears?"

Brogan smiled thinly. "Let them. I'd rather have her with us than telling others where to find us. If the gods only speak to scryers and these things," he kicked the hide at his feet, "then I'd rather her be here. Maybe she can warn us the next time one of the Undying is coming to hunt me down."

"And maybe she can listen for what you plan to do and tell the gods how you will kill them?"

Without hesitating Brogan reached to his boot and unsheathed the same dagger he'd killed the nightmare with.

He offered the blade to Anna. "You feel the need to see her dead, I'll not stop you. She means nothing at all to me."

Anna shook her head and refused to touch the offered weapon. "You take foolish risks, Brogan McTyre, and you risk more than yourself. Consider that. You've risked a great deal already, and my man and your friends are slated to pay for those decisions."

"Where are the hounds? I'd have thought sure I'd hear them by now."

"Unlike you, I prefer to see problems ended completely

and not sent off to find reinforcements."

That was all she'd say on the matter.

Still, she had her wisdoms. Instead of burning the second hide, he rolled it tightly in on itself, then wrapped it in the belt and whip that he had pulled from the thing's body. As an added measure, the whole, mostly bloodless hide was tucked into a saddlebag. It was deceptively heavy.

CHAPTER TWELVE
Hollum

One thing to know a place exists. Another to see it.

Niall looked down the hillside at the sprawling city of Hollum and frowned. The whole of the place rested under a miasma of smoke, as if the winds and the rain were not enough to remove the stain of the city's decadence.

He had never been to Hollum, but he'd heard many tales. In his homeland of Giddenland, they called Hollum "the Torema of the poor and wretched". Giddenland had many wealthy citizens; Torema was a pleasure palace of a city, with every possible vice. He'd once tried coming here when he was younger but his father caught wind of his intentions and beat the notion out of him with a heavy fist. His father, who almost never even raised his voice. When the man was angry, Niall listened. From time to time he had wondered what he'd missed.

Now, he was looking down at Hollum and suspecting he could have anything at all in the town for a price – ad that he'd ignore most of what was offered.

Tully spoke, her voice soft. "We should wait until morning."

"What? Half a mile more and we can be sleeping in beds tonight."

"First, we've no money. Second, you seem a good man, Niall, but you and Temmi ain't prepared for Hollum after dark."

"And I suppose you are?" His pride stung at the thought that she found him too frail to defend himself after all they'd been through.

"I'm *from* here." Tully looked over the city. It was mostly made of stone and thatched roofs, near as Niall could tell. He had no idea what she saw when she looked, but her face was knotted with stress and her eyes were hooded at the thought of going there.

"That's reasonable. Morning is soon enough. Not likely to find a decent map in the night time anyway."

Temmi sat behind them, cross-legged on the ground. Over the past few days she had taken a small knife and every time they stopped had carved away at a heavy reed she'd found. Now she took it out and played on the homemade flute as she looked down on Hollum. The notes ran together to make a soft, mournful melody. The girl barely spoke at all, but she didn't need to. Niall didn't need to know what she thought, it was written clearly on her face. She wanted to find the beast that had killed her family and destroy it. She wanted to stop thinking or feeling. Mostly though, she wanted revenge.

It wouldn't last, that feeling. That sort of anger could never sustain itself for overly long. Just yesterday he'd caught the girl in a rare moment when she allowed herself a smile. He had to hope that Temmi, the one he had met first, managed to survive all the anger.

"Have we money for a map?" The thought hadn't really mattered before. They'd had supplies they could have bartered with. Those were long gone along with the horses and the wagon.

Tully shook her head. "I'll find the money. Not to worry."

With that, she curled in on herself and did her best to stay dry in the constant drizzle.

A short time later, exhausted from a day of walking and half wishing he'd gone down to Hollum anyway, Niall drifted into an uncomfortable sleep. In his dreams Ligel accused him of letting the boy die. There was little he could say against that. Even when he was awake he saw the look on the boy's face as he went over the cliff.

Niall woke to the sound of flute music. Tully was already up and coming back from washing herself at the nearby creek. He was struck by her looks every time he saw her freshly cleaned and so very different from the night that he watched her escape her chains in the mud and rain.

There were a hundred different stories about how Hollum had come to be, but the most logical was probably right. There was a river and there was land enough for people to move around without obstruction. Also, sometimes people need a place to rest.

Hollum spread along both sides of a very wide river. The buildings nearest the water were built on stilts for when it rained, and currently it had been raining a great deal. Though the houses and shops were still safe from any flooding, Niall doubted it would stay that way much longer if the rains continued.

Tully looked around and scowled. "Fucking river's overflowing and so are the people."

Temmi cleared her throat. "So it's not always this way?"

"No. Something's happened. The entire city is full of people, but not like this." She pointed to the wider roads, where desperate folk had built tents and set up wagons in alleyways, adding to the already considerable clutter. Niall was used to large cities, but he had never seen anything remotely like Hollum. It was an enormous, chaotic, ramshackle structure that seemed to overflow onto itself at nearly every corner. Wooden buildings that were easily twice or more his age leaned against brick and stone structures that were close to ancient if one looked at the dirt that had crusted into the walls. On top of the usual chaos it was impossible to miss the new collections of people and items.

Gods, but the air stank. There was a heavy stench of people, unclean and reeking of body odor. There was the smell of wood fires, some for warmth and others for cooking. The latter made Niall's stomach rumble loudly despite the fact that most of the meats were likely dubious in a place like Hollum.

The noise of the place was overwhelming after so long in the wilds. They'd heard storms and nature, but this was different, this was the din of people calling out names, hawking their wares, or just talking to each other in the patois of the street people.

A dozen feet from where they entered the city, a man lay in the road, either dead or sleeping off a drunken night judging by his appearance. He didn't seem to be breathing.

Tully walked right past him and called out to a young man around her age. The man was thin and twitchy. He made Niall think of a starving rat, the sort that would bite if cornered.

Whatever she said, Niall couldn't understand her question or the rat man's answer. Neither chatted in the common tongue.

The exchange was fast paced and the rat man came closer, smiling, his eyes narrowed to a squint and his rotting teeth easily seen. Rat man's skin was pale and had several sores from bug bites. Niall reached for his pouches but grunted when he realized that they were gone. Rat man seemed friendly enough and he could have given him a poultice that would have kept most insects away.

Tully's eyes grew wide and she actually screamed at the man, not out of anger, but likely out of shock. There was a part of Niall that wanted to see if he could help but he restrained himself. She was still talking and the man had not attacked. Whatever she'd heard was news of some sort and she would tell him if it pertained to their quest.

Temmi looked around with horror. "Is there nothing here that isn't dark and diseased?"

"Hollum has a reputation. It's not a very good reputation, I'm afraid."

She looked down at the river. "A reputation for what? Drowned things?"

"You have money, it can be a paradise. If you don't, it can kill you. It's a place where people travel and only the desperate stay. I was warned away from here by my father when I was younger."

They might have continued talking but the spectacle of a hundred half-naked women being marched through the streets was enough to distract them both. They were in chains and all of them pale as a winter frost. Niall saw them and shook his head. His father had slaves, but these were not the sort that his mother would have tolerated. Like as not they'd be sold to whorehouses and used most poorly.

"Those are Grakhul!" Temmi's voice carried across the road and all the way to the chained women and the folk who were moving them along. What had to be the very largest woman Niall had ever seen looked toward them and came their way. She was muscular. Her arms were as thick as his thighs. She was big, taller than him and easily capable of throwing him across a room.

He held his staff a little tighter and wondered if he could use it to knock her down if he had to. He had his doubts.

She did not look to him. She looked down at Temmi, from a full foot or more above the girl. "You speak their language? The tongue of the pale ones?"

"Aye, the Grakhul. My family traded with them for years."

"Where are they from?"

"From?" Temmi frowned at her. "They're from Nugonghappalur. The great citadel of the Grakhul."

The large woman gave no sign that she understood the words.

Temmi shook her head. "You know how people are taken for the gods by the Undying?"

"Yes. I lost my mother many years ago." The way she said it, enough time had passed that there was no longer any grief, just acceptance.

"The Grakhul are the folk that make the actual sacrifices. They prepare them for the gods and then kill them."

"And how do you know this?"

"My family's had dealings for generations. It's what we've always done."

"So they're not from the north? From beyond Trant's Peak?"

"Nowhere near it."

The woman cursed and spat and made a few gestures that meant nothing to Niall but were plainly obscene.

"The fucker lied to us." The large woman was upset. As she had several weapons on her in addition to being incredibly muscular and rather angry, Niall once again considered whether or not he could stop her if she decided to attack.

"Who lied to you?" Temmi seemed not at all worried. Then again, she had recently seen her family murdered and was probably not in her right mind.

"We had westerners, like as not from Stennis Brae, sell us all of these women and they told us they were from past Trant's Peak."

"Having been to Trant's Peak and back, they've lied to you. The people from those parts are nowhere near as kind."

"Trust me, this lot isn't kind."

"Well, no, the women are rather like you."

The giant woman scowled. "How do you mean?"

"They're trained to fight. Their men aren't. Their men are softer, timid even." Temmi's eyes moved to Niall and he felt himself flush. Was he timid? He didn't think he was. Then again, he was staring at a woman who was bigger than him and he'd felt nothing but a need to not attract her attention. He watched the exchange without saying a word. He wasn't invited into the conversation, but he hoped to learn something.

"So what's happening here? Why are there so many people in Hollum? I mean, they've built their tents in alleys where people piss. Doesn't make much sense."

"You've not heard?"

"Been lost in the wilds a while. Attacked and had my family killed." Temmi blinked back tears but continued on. "Haven't heard any news in a month or so."

"Sorry to hear about the family, love."

Temmi nodded and the huge woman continued. "Whatever has happened, great storms came and took Saramond."

"How do you mean, 'took'?"

"Destroyed. Swallowed by the sea. And the storms are heading this way, they say."

"So all these people?"

"From Saramond. We're selling our stock and moving on, which is why I wondered if I could hire you to talk to the Grackle people and tell them to calm themselves. None of them speak any languages we've tried."

"Grakhul."

"Not as it matters to me. Just want to tell them to be calm

before somebody takes a whip to them."

"I..." Temmi sighed and lowered her head, fighting with her emotions. "I can speak to them, but I expect you'll not want to sell them. The He-Kisshi will come looking."

"Big fellas? Faces that are always hidden?"

"Those are the ones. The Undying."

"The *Undying*?" The big woman actually paled.

"Aye. They watch over the Grakhul. They need each other, you see. The He-Kisshi gather the harvest for the gods. The Grakhul make the prayers then offer the harvest. Been that way for a thousand years or more."

"My mum was taken by them." The woman's face softened with fear and for a moment Niall could see the ghost of that girl child who'd seen her mother snatched away.

Niall said, "They won't stop." He nearly surprised himself. He'd had no intention of getting involved in the conversation.

The woman looked his way. "What say?" Damn, but she was a big woman. Solid as a rock, handsome more than pretty and oddly appealing though he knew she could throw him over her shoulder like a cloak.

"The He-Kisshi. I was taken as a sacrifice. I got away. One of them has come for me twice now and they won't stop. I think if they discover you've sold their people, they'll come for you, no matter what."

"I'm to sell this lot and move on. If these hooded bastards want to pay for them that's fine by me."

Niall shut his mouth. He'd offered his warning.

The woman turned back to Temmi. "I'm Stanna. With the slavers, obviously. We're taking them to the auction house now. I just need someone to tell them to stay calm. I'll pay you."

"I'm Temmi. I'll talk to them."

Stanna smiled and slapped Temmi on the shoulder. To the latter's credit she did not fall on her side in the mud, but she was staggered just the same.

Niall stayed where he was as Temmi walked away and Tully returned.

"Where is she going?"

"Apparently she's been hired by slavers to tell their new stock to behave while they're being sold."

Tully shook her head. "Only here. I mean that."

"Aye."

"Saramond is gone. Destroyed by the gods."

"Truly?" Niall frowned. He'd almost convinced himself that the woman's story of the city being gone, actually destroyed, might have been an exaggeration. "Do you suppose they'll stop there?"

"We can hope. There's a bounty on a large group of men. They're supposed to take the place of the failed sacrifices."

"Maybe that means we're safe?"

Tully shook her head. "I've my doubts."

"Aye. Me too." He frowned. "Friend of yours? That one you were talking with?"

"Business acquaintance. He was catching me up on what's happening here."

"Refugees and the like. Yeah. Did he say where you could get a map?"

"He did." Tully's eyes wandered around the area and she called out harshly as she looked past him. Niall turned to see a child dressed in rags backing away from him, a sour look on her face.

Niall frowned. "What was that about?"

Tully flicked a hand toward the girl. "She planned to rob you."

"Nothing really to steal." He felt oddly accomplished in that moment.

Tully nodded. "Aye, but if she'd found nothing she'd like as not have stabbed you for the inconvenience."

Tully's ability to sour a mood was potent. "Lovely town. Glad we're leaving soon."

The blonde woman looked around briefly, her eyes barely even noticing the corpse. The dead man had continued to not breathe and that was enough for Niall. "Yes, well, sooner is better. I need you to wait here. We can't lose Temmi and I need to get your map."

He blinked in surprise. "So I'm just to wait here for the two of you?"

"Did you have any other plans?" She shot him one of her looks. She could wither a tree with her expressions.

"Well, no, of course not." He looked toward where Temmi was talking with Stanna and the pale women.

"Then we're all in agreement. I'll be back before midday."

He looked back to where Tully had been but saw no sign of her. "I should hope! The morning's only started!"

So far his day had been rather eventful and he'd barely moved from his location. He spotted the street girl coming toward him from the corner of his eye and glared. "I'll knock your teeth out as soon as look at you. Move on."

She made a gesture that matched one of Stanna's from earlier and ran off down an alley.

It was going to be an interesting day.

Temmi liked Stanna the second she saw her. Stanna was what her father called a no-nonsense soul. She was direct and honest. If she liked you, she liked you. If she didn't, you were probably going to die.

Temmi wanted to be no-nonsense. Tully was full of secrets. She tried to hide them, but they followed her.

Niall was too cautious for his own good. He was quick to defend another, a trait he did not see in himself, but when it came to making decisions, the man was slow and meticulous. He wanted to study every possibility. Still, he was pretty enough with his light hair and his blue eyes and his nervous smile. He made her losses more tolerable, as did Tully.

The Grakhul looked at her and a few of the women recognized her.

She could place some of them, though she couldn't have told a single name if her life depended on it.

It wasn't her life hanging on the edge.

Stanna looked at her expectantly and the Grakhul looked on as well.

Temmi nodded her head, thought of how her father would have handled matters, and started the conversation going.

"You're to be sold at market. This one, Stanna, wants you to behave."

The closest of the women looked at her and shook her head. "The He-Kisshi come. They are directed by the gods. If we are not freed, everyone in the city dies."

Temmi nodded again. It was going to be a long conversation.

Lexx groaned, his body racked with fever chills. The beast that had ruined him was long gone, but in his half-conscious dreams it lashed out again and again, shredding his hand and face.

He'd never imagined a whip could hurt so much. It was almost enough to make him regret the times he'd used one on slaves who refused to listen. Mind you, he'd only ever torn a little flesh, never broken bones or stolen an eye.

They'd traveled a great distance, the slaves walking and he carried in a wagon, thanks to the loyalty of Stanna. Had she not done so, he would have died, along with everyone else in Saramond. He tried to speak but his mouth was too dry, his tongue too torn and the inside of his mouth was swollen with infection. The gums around his shattered teeth throbbed with every heartbeat.

Sans opened the door to his room and stepped inside. "The healer will be here soon, Lexx." There had been a time when Sans looked at Lexx and he knew she wanted him with a near desperation that was flattering and amusing. Now she looked on him with little more than pity.

He nodded his head. It was easier than trying to speak past the bandages covering most of his face. Even nodding hurt. It sent an ache through his skull and neck.

There were claims that the healers in the city were among the best in the world. They were not afraid to use sorcery to finish a task that required it. Lexx was not afraid to pay them a great deal if they could restore what was left of him. He had the money. Like everyone else in the guild, he kept his monies spread through several guilds and even stashed in hidden areas, though some of those were likely under water by now.

Sans stopped staring and then nodded herself before leaving the room.

Lexx's hand thrummed with agonies he didn't want to think about. The swelling was nearly overwhelming and the pain came in waves. He closed his eyes in an effort to hide from the constant aches and unwillingly drifted into a fitful slumber.

When he woke up a man he'd never seen was staring at him. He was quite the sight. His body was not heavy, it was just grossly fat. His skin was pale and discolored and his hair was patchy. His eyes were a disastrous mess, with several ruptured vessels and whites that were as yellowed as old parchment.

"You are awake. That is excellent."

Lexx stared at the man, horrified. He looked *diseased*.

"I shall say this simply: when I heal people, I take their sickness into myself. Through the magics the Galeans taught me, I pull your illness away then, well, to say it simply, I eat the illness until it is gone from you. I have been busy of late. There are a lot of people who came to town injured. I am a bit overfull right now."

Lexx nodded.

"Your business partner, Stanna, has already paid me. We can begin whenever you'd like."

Lexx nodded again, desperate to be cured of his ruination. He gestured with his uninjured hand for the swollen nightmare to get on with it.

The healer licked his lips. Those horrid, bloated hands reached for him and carefully started peeling away his bandages. As much as his flesh hurt where infection was having its way, the thought of that pale, mottled skin touching him seemed almost worse.

The healer touched his face with a caress that was as soft as a feather and nearly burned with feverish heat. Lexx stiffened, his entire body going rigid with a desire to get away.

"This will hurt quite a bit. Scream if you must. It makes no difference."

Did Lexx scream as the pain roared through his body? He did not know. He might have, but all he remembered afterward was the pain as large as a castle that fell on him and crushed him into darkness.

When he awoke again, the healer was in the corner of the room, so bloated that his clothes strained and seams had split. His body looked bruised, as if he'd fallen from the top of a building and somehow managed to survive it. He stank of illness and disease. Even from this distance his body radiated as much heat as an open fire pit.

"I have done all I can." The voice was strained and weak. There was no pain.

Lexx closed his good eye and looked out of the ruin that had bled across his face. His vision was a little off, softer in focus, but he could see again. His tongue ran across the inside of his mouth, and felt teeth that were mostly complete and gums that were no longer shredded. The inside of his mouth was intact. He clenched his hand and felt the fist he made as tendons and bones moved the way they were supposed to. Though there were scars on his hand, they were faded as if they were twenty years old.

The healer wheezed with each breath and said, "I must stay here for now. I cannot walk."

There was a time when Lexx would have had the man removed from his room. Instead he merely nodded and walked past the wretch in search of a mirror.

His fingers already told the story. His skin was almost smooth and his teeth were almost repaired. He had been broken and now he was mostly intact.

It would have to do.

There was a mirror of polished glass in the room. The slavers paid handsomely for good accommodations. The mirror gave a better report than he'd expected. His eyelid was a bit lazy on the ruined side and his eye's iris was distorted. Considering that the eye had literally been torn to shreds, he could accept that. The scarring on his once handsome face was excessive, but it could be argued that it lent a certain air of menace. The scars spoke of a survivor, not of a weak man.

Stanna had been good enough to leave his weapons wrapped in a cloak. Lexx ignored the man whimpering in the corner and changed into fresh clothes after washing himself as best he could with a bowl of cold water.

Sword and dagger went in place. He found a small

collection of coins in one boot and smiled. He owed his friend so very much.

Once dressed and presentable, Lexx headed for the door, wondering if he could find someone selling a proper weighted whip. Time would tell.

The sky was a strange mixture of gray and green that he had never seen before. Still, it was bright enough that Lexx squinted in the daylight.

He had been to Hollum before. Moving toward the auction blocks was easy enough once he oriented himself. The pain was gone. That was the part that mattered. Scars? Fine. The pain that had crushed him under its weight was missing.

A wretched little thing in tattered street clothes tried to sneak in close to him. He'd met her type before. Without wasting a breath he unsheathed his dagger and buried it in her neck as she reached surreptitiously for his purse.

She fell back coughing, drowning in her own blood.

The day was already getting better.

"They'll do as you say." Temmi shrugged and looked at Stanna. "You should let them go. The He-Kisshi are coming for them. They destroyed Saramond, and if they don't get their way they'll destroy this area, too."

Stanna looked back. The girl had been hurt by life. Stanna understood that sort of ache. "The He-Kisshi? They're the Undying?"

Temmi nodded vigorously. "Oh, yes."

Stanna looked at her carefully, appraising her words and their merit. "How do the women know that?"

"Because they are all servants of the gods and the gods tell them things."

"Let them go!" Stanna ordered.

Rhinen, a large man who served her and very nearly always obeyed looked her way and scowled. "There's not much of a profit in that, is there?"

Stanna shook her head. "We keep them, we die. We let them go, we have a chance."

"That direct then?"

"That direct, Rhinen. I've no desire to die for a profit I don't need. It was Beron who took all the risk on this one."

Rhinen arched an eyebrow. "I'm getting paid the same either way?"

"Aye. You signed on with me and I honor my debts."

The man nodded his head and promptly started unshackling the chains of the women he had been cleaning for the auction.

He said, "I get paid, I do the work you ask. It's just that easy."

"I knew I liked you for a reason."

Stanna looked back to Temmi and nodded. "Would you tell them they're free then?"

Temmi called out, and the woman she'd been speaking to looked at Stanna and signaled her agreement. Within ten minutes the last of the women had been released from the shackles.

They did not stick around to see if anyone would change their minds. One of them called out to the rest, then they were all running toward the river in the distance.

She handed Temmi ten silver crowns, more than sufficient for her translation fees. "You did me a good service, lass."

"I'd advise you to move on from here and soon. The gods are likely going to seek out judgment on someone. I'll be leaving with my friends. We have plans for Edinrun."

"Torema is more my sort of city, but aye, we'll be moving on soon enough."

The girl did not count the money Stanna gave her, but waved once and headed back to where she'd left her companions.

Beron would be furious. Stanna found she did not care. Fight an army? Certainly. Fight the Undying? She could not spend if she was dead. That was the end of the discussion. And if Beron didn't like it, he was welcome to settle the argument any way he liked. She had seen him fight and watched his style. She could take him.

In the shadows, not far from where she stood, she thought she saw a cloaked figure standing watching. She shivered. When she turned to face the form spotted from the corner of her eye, it was gone.

On a whim more than anything else, she followed Temmi. The girl was interesting, and she found she wanted to know more of her and more of what she had learned about the pale people and the demons they served.

The human child stumbled into the alley with both hands clutching at her savaged throat.

Ohdra-Hun caught the squirming girl-child in its claws and lifted her until its mouth clamped on the back of her skull. Teeth set to work, thick lips suctioned to her head and the He-Kisshi's tongues pulled the sweet gray substance from her skull.

It was wounded, but the wounds were minor. The worst of them already healed. Still, it ate the flesh of the little girl, the better to speed up the healing process.

Anger was a tool. Now and then Ohdra-Hun forgot that fact and let the anger hold the reins. It had lost its way when the humans escaped and killed it. It had grown sullen and angry because the gods were also sullen and angry, and sometimes the He-Kisshi felt the needs of their masters too keenly.

Still, Ohdra-Hun would find those that got away and punish them, because the gods also understood that sometimes honor must be defended. That was why they wanted the interlopers. That was why they wanted the men who killed their Grakhul. It was not because they needed those particular people sacrificed. It was because they were offended that anyone would interfere with them.

The gods understood Ohdra-Hun's anger and allowed it.

"You!"

Ohdra-Hun turned at the sound of a human female screaming and watched as the creature came forward. It dropped the small child's body.

The female was old and bent at the back, dressed in rags. She hobbled toward the He-Kisshi with what could have passed for malice in a younger human.

"What have you done?"

Most tended to back away from the He-Kisshi when a warning was offered. "Leave here before I destroy you." It spoke with little malice but turned to face the old crone, the better to let her see what she spoke to. A casual glance saw a human in a hooded robe. A closer examination did not make that mistake. Ohdra-Hun made sure to rear up properly to show the inside of its "hood."

Instead of fleeing, the woman backed away and let out a shrill whistle. Her left arm shook and a long blade slipped into her hand. Despite her age, she had nimble fingers.

"You would threaten me?" The anger came back, a tidal wave of fury. Ohdra-Hun stepped closer, reached out and grabbed the old woman by her neck. She tried to gasp, but Ohdra-Hun's fingers crushed down, claws slicing easily into the flesh at the back of her neck.

The first arrow drove deep into the muscles between Ohdra-Hun's shoulders. It screeched, but did not let go of its prey. Instead it looked around and swung the old woman in its grasp. The He-Kisshi were called many names, among them the Undying. They were also called faster than the wind, stronger than steel and savage. Ohdra-Hun saw the arrow coming and used the old woman as a shield. She shuddered as the arrow pierced her lower back. She'd have screamed if she could, but her airway was ruined.

Still, she drove her blade into Ohdra-Hun's wrist and it felt its grip on her loosen.

Looking around it saw humans coming from the alleys and from the rooftops, all of them armed and ready to defend one of their own. They would kill if they could. So would Ohdra-Hun.

The next arrow came down like a lightning bolt and drove into the side of Ohdra-Hun's head. The point went through meat and struck the host body it surrounded. Deep within Ohdra-Hun's body, the sacrifice that gave the He-Kisshi true life jerked and thrashed. She would not last long against a sustained assault.

Ohdra-Hun did not flee. Instead it called upon the elements and attacked. The winds came from everywhere and roared through the alley. Arrows in mid-flight were thrown aside and the fools standing on the rooftops learned how powerful a weapon the wind could be as they were hurled through the air and then dropped.

Long fingers reached out and Ohdra-Hun focused the power of the storm. Rains crashed down in heavy sheets, instantly soaking each person in the alley. Where there had been winds, a sudden calm fell and brought with it a fog too thick to allow mere humans sight. They chattered among themselves, suddenly afraid, as they should have been from the beginning.

Ohdra-Hun did not take its slights as lightly as its brethren. While they stumbled in the sudden fog, the He-Kisshi moved among them, claws groping and cutting at fragile, human flesh. The poor wretches saw only with human eyes and were limited to two. Ohdra-Hun saw colors they could never understand, and saw with a hundred eyes.

A boy stumbled close to Ohdra-Hun and it reached out, crushing the skull between its fingers until it ruptured like an overripe fruit.

Blood flowed from the wound in its back, from the wound in its head. There would be no more wounds. Ohdra-Hun had a mission from the gods and it would serve as it was meant to.

Still, there were offenders to kill and it took its time hunting them down through the fog.

"I've no bloody idea where this madness is coming from." Rik shook his head and moved through the alley by memory as much as by sight or any other sense and Tully was right there with him. To say she knew the alleyways and gutters of Hollum was to say she knew the shape of her hand. She had dealt with both for just as long.

The fog he spoke of had come from nowhere and come in fast. Fog didn't happen that often in Hollum and even when it did it normally stayed near the riverfront.

"Rik, I need to be gone from this town and soon."

"You've said that four times already. I told you, I'll take care of you."

They'd grown up in the same coven, that is to say, the same group of orphans. They were siblings in all but blood. They'd been trained by the same teachers, fed by the same cooks and paid their allegiance to the exact same masters in the Union of Thieves.

Rik said he'd take care of her. Niall, despite his nervous nature and penchant to browbeat himself into submission, actually had taken care of her. For all the good it had done. They were as hunted as before.

"Rik, you can't take care of me. Not in this case. I've very deadly things after me and I don't want to draw their attention while I'm here. I have enough problems in

Hollum without that."

"I should say. Theryn wants you skinned alive."

"I didn't take the box from her room." Tully shook her head and did her best not to look guilty. Her innocence be damned, at the thought of Theryn she felt guilty in her soul.

"And yet you know that's why she wants you dead."

"I told you, the Grakhul took me."

"How did you get away? What do they really look like? Is it true they drink blood?"

"I slipped the chains they caught me in and ran. Had help from a man named Niall. If he hadn't been there, I'd be dead." She shrugged. "They look like, well, they're like everything Theryn used to warn us about. And I don't know if they drink blood, but I'd not be surprised. They can fly like bats."

"Gods. I hate bats. Creepy little bastards."

"These are closer to seven foot tall and creepy. And they have claws."

Rik made a face that expressed his revulsion better than words ever could. He'd never been much good at talking, unless he was telling stories of how much he'd managed to get from a careless person with a large purse. Rik was a cutpurse; Tully preferred to burgle.

Somewhere nearby a cat made a noise and an instant later a rat let out a scream. It was not an unusual pair of noises in Hollum.

The sun was up. It was closing in on noon, but Rik had kept Tully moving with a promise to help her gather her belongings. He'd stolen most of them when Theryn came calling. The woman would have claimed them as tithings, and Rik was good enough to know that Tully would have never left her possessions behind by choice. None of them would. They worked too hard to earn them.

It was a sign of trust that he led her to his home. It was a sign of being a thief that he led her there through a dozen back alleys and roads he hoped she would never remember. They were family, but only a fool trusted a thief.

Finally, they reached a door that was barely visible in the fog.

Rik didn't bother to knock, but was very careful when he opened the door. One never knew.

Tully followed and felt the fine hairs on her neck rise. Rik was family, but there was something amiss here. She just couldn't figure out what it was yet.

The stairs led up to the third story of the building he called home. The apartment was small, just as she would have expected. Thieves seldom made enough to have a larger place and even if they could afford it, they'd never consider renting one. Might as well ask to be burgled.

Rik stepped out of her way and let her see the inside of apartment at the exact same time she realized what was wrong. He hadn't unlocked a door or unset a trip wire.

"Shit, Rik. I can't believe you."

"Don't blame him, Tully," came the voice from within. "I hardly gave him a choice and the reward for you is large enough to tempt anyone."

Theryn stood in the center of the room. She had two of her cutthroats with her. Both of the dark garbed killers had weapons drawn and were looking at her as if she were a mouse and they were hunting-cats. Theryn waited to see if she would run. She couldn't. Rik was between her and the door and if he'd turn her in for a reward he'd certainly be willing to stop her from leaving.

"I didn't take anything from you."

"That's a lie and you know it."

"I mean, I was going to try, yes, but I didn't have a chance. The Grakhul caught me."

Theryn was not pretty. She was not handsome but she

had been once. She had an angular face that was too broad for pretty, with a very deep scar running from her nose down to her chin from a time she was caught trying to pick a pocket and failed. Though she was bundled up and wearing leathers, Tully knew that Theryn's body was muscular, hard. She had seen the woman walk up the space between two buildings to a height of almost fifty feet in a matter of seconds. That was because she was incredibly strong and skilled enough to manage it. Tully had tried a few times and succeeded twice. She normally carried hooks and ropes for that reason. She was not anywhere near the physical equivalent of Theryn the Blood-Mother and she likely never would be.

Theryn stared at her with dark eyes. "Well, someone took a very large supply of my gold and made off with it. Same day, you leave town. The Grakhul had you, you'd already be dead. I know. I've seen them take our kind before."

It was like speaking to a stone. The words fell on ears that would not listen. "I escaped! Gods, I've had one of the bastards after me ever since. He's been hunting me like a fucking hound."

Theryn barely ever blinked. She asked, "If I did believe you, who would I blame for stealing my gold? Who would have had a reason besides you?"

"Why would I steal from you, Theryn? What possible reason?"

The Blood-Mother answered, "To prove that you could. To pay me back for demanding tribute. To make me look weak in front of my children."

"I'm one of your children. I've always been faithful."

"You've challenged me a hundred times, Tully."

The two assassins were still standing in the same spot, but they'd relaxed just a bit. Most every soul she'd met would relax when tongues started wagging.

"Course I've challenged you. You told us to challenge you and everyone else who would try to stop us. All my life that was the lesson you offered."

Those hard features softened just a bit. "Aye, and you learned it better than most. Tully, my girl, I don't want to punish you, but you're the only suspect that makes sense. You left town and came back when you were done spending what was mine, it's the only tale that fits."

"Spent it on what? I've barely clothes to my name. My boots are the wrong fucking size." She hauled up her shirt enough to show her belly and ribs. "I've not been feasting on pastries and meat pies, I can tell you that bloody much."

Rik said, "She's a point there, Theryn," and immediately flinched when Theryn looked his way.

There was one door. There were two narrow windows. They were on the third floor and Tully had no idea at all what was beyond those windows. Could be a lovely balcony. Could be a wall close enough to touch. Could be a fall to the damn cobblestones thirty feet down, and while she was a good sneak she had no desire to see if she could land like a cat from that sort of height.

There was no way to find out, with three people between her and the windows. Rik she might be able to handle – though he had blades and she did not.

She managed not to jump out of her skin when she felt Rik's hand touch hers. The package he settled was worn, soft leather. She knew the feel of it well. Her fingers took the collection of knives and thieving tools and much as she wanted to kiss him just then, she knew that would get them both killed.

So instead, she spun around and kicked him in the guts as hard as she could. Tully was small, but she was also muscular and her foot in his stomach sent Rik falling down the stairs in a clatter.

Theryn cursed and started forward. Her cutthroats charged like dogs let loose from their pens and Tully turned and ran down the stairs, her eyes on the steps, her hands moving over the leather packet her brother had saved for her and given back in her hour of need.

Rik was wincing on the stairs, holding his belly and coughing very convincingly. He had rolled as he fell and likely wasn't badly hurt, but he had also saved her life and she doubted that not in the least.

She hoped he wasn't hurt. She hoped his fall convinced Theryn.

She hoped that the next time she came to the miserable fucking town of Hollum she still had a brother left to thank.

Tully hit the street and ran, moving through a fog too thick to see through and hoping it concealed her from the Blood-Mother and her assassins.

It did not.

Tully felt a pain spike into her calf and fell down, stifling a scream. She saw the blade and pulled it out as she rolled across the cobblestones. What Rik called a stinger, just large enough to trip a person and cut the meat of the leg, but not enough to bleed them badly.

Another thing to worry about. Now she had to hope it wasn't poisoned.

She was back up and running and heard Theryn's tread behind her. Tully had been raised by the woman. She knew the sound of her walking, the sound of her breathing. She knew she was as good as dead for fleeing.

"There you are," said Theryn.

"I've found you," said the Undying at the same moment, as it lunged through the shadows for her.

Tully twisted sideways, ducked low, slid in the muck and bruised her backside, but managed to squeeze between the two nightmares trying to end her.

Theryn let out a squeak. As a rule, the Blood-Mother did not squeak. The Undying seemed to have that effect quite often. The alley she drove down was filled with obstacles that were shadowy and hard to see in the heavy fog. Tully hurdled what she could, crawled over what she had to, and did not once stop to look back. She'd been a burglar for years and she could move when she had to. The wound in her calf hurt, but not enough to make her stop running.

Behind her, the sounds of combat began.

Temmi frowned. "So you're saying you see no difference between slavery and delivering food and supplies?"

Stanna shook her head. "Aside from the fact that all I can do these days is deliver slaves that have been previously purchased or born into slavery, no."

Niall watched the two of them like a man watching a proper joust. All around them people hawked food and trinkets, blankets and jugs for holding water. So far he'd spent money on a knife, a jug and what may or may not have been roast boar. He wasn't sure but it tasted good and sometimes it was best not to ask.

"Look, Stanna, I like you, I do, but let's not go around thinking that what me and my family have done for generations is anything like what you and yours are doing now?"

"How are they different then?"

"Well, for one thing, we never once delivered a person in chains and told them they had to work for someone else for the rest of their lives."

"That's true enough." Stanna nodded. "All you did was knowingly deliver supplies to a people who have hidden themselves away and regularly committed murder."

"Oh, come on! That's hardly fair."

"No, no, hear me out. You took food to a people who

couldn't actually grow their own supplies from what you've already said, people who hid behind areas where, if a person walks the wrong path, they suffer from a rotting disease and shit out their own insides. Those are your words, not mine. Without proper training you could have never gotten to this place. And the people you got the food for regularly bathed, anointed then murdered four people every season to appease gods that may or may not even exist."

"Well of course they exist! They're the gods!"

Stanna shook her head. "They aren't *my* gods. Fuckers took my mother when I was young. I'll not worship them or follow their desires."

Niall nodded. "To be fair, I've no particular desire to worship them myself. They did choose to take me as one of their sacrifices."

"Oh, please! Gods need sacrifices!"

Stanna crossed her amazingly thick arms. "What for then? To answer prayers? I prayed to the fuckers to have my mother back. Still dead, thanks. I can say with sincerity that in all my life I've never once seen any god answer the prayers of any slave. If they had, the slaves would have run free across the land and I'd likely be long dead."

"Well. I suppose they need them to keep the world from spinning away."

"I don't ever recall hearing that the gods kept the world in place."

"Well, they made the world, didn't they? So I suppose they must have the final say on where it spins."

"Never heard that they created the world. Only that they demanded sacrifices."

Niall added, "According to my old teacher, the gods killed an entirely different group of gods who had, in fact, made the world."

Stanna looked at him and frowned. "Truly?"

Niall nodded his head. "That's what he said and he's a very wise man."

"Well then, there you have it. The gods created nothing, they just killed those that made the world and stole it."

Temmi jabbed a finger into Niall's chest. "Stay out of it, you."

"I was unaware I couldn't speak on these things. Very sorry." He wasn't really. It had been a long afternoon and the conversation was at least amusing in an offhand way. The fog around the city was so damned thick he couldn't see far beyond the dead man in the street.

"Run." The voice was very small.

"Did you hear that?" He was speaking to either of the women in front of him, really, but they were already debating the ethics of slavery versus selling food to murderers again.

"I can't see them as the same thing. We shipped food to people who would starve."

"I ship slaves to people who need laborers. Walls have to be built, houses cleaned, fields tended and crops gathered. In fact there's a goodly chance that slaves handled the very supplies you delivered."

"That has nothing to do with what I'm saying."

"Run. Run. Run."

"Ladies, I think someone's trying to tell us something."

Stanna ignored him and continued, "That has everything to do with what you're saying. Slaves are purchased. Some of them work the fields, harvest the crops, bake the breads, slaughter the animals, salt the meats that you were bringing to the murderous bastards that were killing people, some of who, by the way, were slaves."

"Ladies! I must insist–"

"Run!" Tully suddenly barreled through the haze at a speed that was unsettling. Temmi blinked and stepped back. Niall stared as the girl hurdled the dead man and moved across the street, a dagger in one hand. She did not look like she wanted a fight. She looked like she was desperate to escape. "Run, you damn fools! It's after me!"

Even as she said those words, the fog rippled and swirled violently and the shadowy cloaked form of the He-Kisshi tore through the air after her.

Everyone reacts differently in a stressful situation.

Niall stared.

Temmi backpedaled, her eyes wide. Despite her obvious hatred for the thing, she was also terrified. It had killed every member of her family, who could blame her?

Tully was already in flight.

Stanna drew her sword in one smooth, frighteningly fast gesture and cut through the Undying's arm and wing as it chased past her on its mission to kill Tully. The great shape immediately fell to earth, tumbling across the cobblestones and roaring in pain as its arm fell away and took a portion of its wing in the process. The slaver did not wait around to see if she had killed the thing, but instead charged forward and drove her sword through its skull, pinning the obscene head. Had anyone ever looked so cold while killing a creature? Niall did not know and did not want to. Stanna was terrifyingly efficient and at that moment the most beautiful woman he'd ever seen.

The hellish thing stood and slapped her backward as if the sword was merely an insult. Stanna rolled with the blow and came up in a defensive posture.

Despite the blow it offered, the Undying was in bad shape, bleeding heavily from the massive wound and, unless Niall's eyes deceived him, it already had three arrows jammed into different parts of its body. The thing should have been dead. That was, of course, why it was called Undying.

Stanna was unimpressed. A heavy dagger came from the slaver's belt. Her heavily muscled legs wrapped around the waist of the creature and both of them fell to the cobblestones again. The He-Kisshi screeched and thrashed, trying to dislodge its opponent, but Stanna grunted and locked her legs tighter, letting out a yelp of pain when the clawed hand of the thing dug into her forearm.

"Enough of you!" She roared the words like a battle cry and started stabbing the thing in its chest. The sounds of her blade striking were wet and mingled with the creature's cries of agony. When it stopped moving she hacked into its neck, working hard enough that her muscles became cords that shook with effort. In short order she pulled the vile head from the He-Kisshi and tossed it aside.

The woman was panting and shaking with exertion, bloodied and wounded, yet still she smiled when she rolled off the corpse.

"Undying." Her booted foot kicked the bloody skull of the creature away from the body and she spat on the corpse. "That's for my mother, you foul piece of shit."

The free hand of the He-Kisshi reached up to a token around its neck and clutched at it. Niall watched it happen. He was almost curious enough to examine the situation but decided against it. The hand uncurled a moment later and there was nothing there.

Tully looked at the resident giantess and eyed her dubiously. "You're a monster." When Stanna glared she raised a hand. "I mean it as a compliment. Me and three others took on that thing and all of us together could barely drive it away. You killed it. Flat out killed something called Undying. That is impressive."

Stanna didn't actually preen, but she came close.

"Burn the body!" Temmi snarled the words.

"No time. I've rather a large number of people want me dead right now." Tully shook her head and headed for the bridge to the other side of town. "And I mean they plan to kill me. So if we could just hurry along I've got a place to buy horses and I've got your map, Niall."

Niall nodded. "Well then, we should be off." He smiled as he saw that the fog was finally lifting.

Temmi shook her head. "Go on then. I'll catch up."

Stanna shook hers. "Go with your friends. I'll handle this."

"Are you sure? I thought you might join us." Temmi frowned and actually pouted a bit.

Stanna smiled. "I will, but I've a friend of mine I have to check on first."

"Do you know your way?"

"I know my way and I'm faster than you. We'll catch up long before you reach Edinrun."

Temmi managed a weak smile and nodded before following Tully. Niall nodded as well and then followed after the both of them.

Stanna looked at the body and shrugged. So far it hadn't gone about the business of coming back from death, but Temmi knew more about the things. If she said it would come back, Stanna would accept it as truth.

Several of the people running the local stands – she couldn't quite bring herself to call it a market – watched the entire sordid affair and did nothing. Then again, they hadn't done anything about the body festering in the corner, either, so what could one expect?

Lexx came her way with all of his swagger intact and his face looking much better than it had a few hours earlier.

"Thank you." He said the words easily. That was a good thing. Had his words been mangled she'd have had to go after the healer and kill him.

"You look well. How do you feel?"

"Better than I have any right to feel. I owe you for that."

"No. I took the gold from your purse to pay the man. I merely found the man to do the work."

"Just the same, I am in your debt."

Stanna shrugged. "Fine. Help me get rid of this and we'll be even."

"What is that thing? Is that the beast that whipped me?"

"One of them."

"What did you do to it?"

"I killed it, of course. Now we have to get rid of it before it heals itself."

Lexx looked down at the corpse and sneered. Just the same when he tapped the body with his boot he did so cautiously. "I don't know if you can heal from a beheading."

"I've been told they can. So I am supposed to burn it."

Lexx shook his head and grunted. "Throw the body in the river. Burn the head. It's easier to do."

Stanna frowned and considered that. The river was rather close and she could see his logic.

To make his point Lexx grabbed the head and headed for the closest meat vendor. He drew his hand back sharply and shook his fingers and she saw a few drops of blood spill from their tips. He reached out a second time and was careful enough to grab the arrow shaft stuck through the back of the hood. His expression of disgust when he saw the mouth he'd reached into was priceless.

Meat vendors nearly always had a fire going and though she could not hear the words, she saw him talking with the woman at length. The woman looked dubious until he reached into a pouch and pulled out a coin. After that the business was handled. The vendor moved the grating from over her fire and he dropped the disgusting head of the Undying into the flames. Sparks rose and there were a few sounds that could have been fat burning, or that head trying to hiss without lungs. Either way she felt her skin creep around at the notion.

Stanna looked at the decapitated body. It was disgusting. Fat and bloated, scarred and furred. The claws on the feet were long and the toes of the feet even longer. The hands of the beast were just as bad, with wickedly hooked claws on each long finger. The hand close to the body was burned in the palm, badly enough that it exposed bones. Just to the side of that hand was a heavy gold chain. She took that without hesitation and stuffed it into a pocket.

In any event it was dead. She grabbed the feet at the ankles and started pulling the grotesquery toward the bridge. Thanks to Lexx she had kept her word well enough. He came back her way, his usual swagger still in place.

Without saying a word he looked down at her prize and then grabbed the corpse at each armpit.

"Heavy bastard." She seldom complained about the weight of a thing, but the thing that should have weighed as much as a man seemed three times as heavy.

"Aye." He nodded and together they carried the corpse to the edge of the bridge and heaved it out into the waters. It hit with a hard splash then immediately sank into the depths.

Ohdra-Hun did not die. It could not. It was Undying.

Instead the body fell like a stone and settled at the bottom of the river.

In the waters of that river the Grakhul swam, all of those he had seen the slavers free. Several of them approached Ohdra-Hun's body and after some consideration they reached for the feet and pulled the corpse along as they followed the course of the river. The current was strong and they used that to their advantage as they left behind their time as slaves, and the human world. They had so very far to go in order to reach the Sessanoh, and as with the rest of the Grakhul, they knew that time was moving too quickly.

Back on the shore, Lexx looked at his fingers and sucked at the wounds.

Rather, his body did. Lexx was dead and currently Ohdra-Hun wore him as yet another form of body.

It will aid you only the once and you will know when to use it. The children are nearing Hollum. Your prey goes to the same place. Do not disappoint.

The children had been freed, though through no actions of its own. Still, it was now released from its obligation and could pursue those who had tried so many times to kill it.

The woman, Stanna, she would die as well, but not before she led Ohdra-Hun to the rest of them. They had names. Niall, the male. Tully, the one that had strangled him to death. Temmi, the one who raged and attacked as if driven to madness by Ohdra-Hun's very appearance. Had it killed her family? Possibly. Most of the humans meant so little that remembering their faces was a wasted effort. It had taken humans for sacrifice for as long as it had existed and that was a time measured in tens of centuries.

There was enough time. There had to be. The gods were both generous and kind. Still, it could feel the host body starting to die, cell by cell. There would be enough time, yes, but it would have to work quickly.

It had to play its part.

"What happened to the slaves?" Ohdra-Hun already knew, but the Lexx-body did not.

Stanna frowned as she replied. "The thing I killed? There are more of them. They would come looking for the slaves so I free them. I know you disagree, Lexx, but the way I see it, the loss is all on Beron. We would be paid for our efforts, but I don't intend to die for another slaver's profits."

"Then where is everyone else?"

"I sent them on to Torema."

"So we're to go to Torema?"

The woman shrugged he shoulders and shook her head at the same time. Ohdra-Hun studied the way her body moved and contemplated where it would cut her first. It wanted the sword-wielding animal to suffer. "You can if you like. I'm going to meet up with a few new people and explore Edinrun for a while. I'd like Beron to have a chance to calm down before we cross paths once more."

What would Lexx say? It had to think about that for a moment, but the answer was there. The gods allowed only one attempt to get revenge and they were good enough to allow Ohdra-Hun to know facts only Lexx could know.

"I'm in no hurry to debate anything with Beron. I'll stick with you."

"I have always said you were a wise man."

"I have always said you should learn to judge men better." Ohdra-Hun made itself smile with the tiny, insignificant mouth these humans endured.

"I judge men very well. That is why we are not going to meet up with Beron just yet."

Ohdra-Hun smiled with Lexx's mouth a second time. "Perhaps the winged things will kill him and save us the troubles."

"That would be lovely. I know where he keeps his monies and I have papers upon which I could fake his mark."

"Enough gold to buy an empire, even with all that he's lost."

"Aye, unless he spends it all on revenge."

Ohdra-Hun contemplated the words again. The name Beron brought with it an image of a dark-skinned man with a penchant for raw brutality. Ohdra-Hun was not worried. It would kill the woman, kill the others and leave their rotting corpses long before this Beron could hope to find them.

Besides, the others would likely kill Beron soon enough.

CHAPTER THIRTEEN
Beron

"I will see them all dead. Every last one of them." Beron was talking to himself as he did from time to time. Sometimes the only good company he could find was himself and that was especially true when it came to intelligent conversation.

The weather had continued to worsen, but they were making progress. They were south of Hollum and a few more days would see them finally in Torema.

He was considering the city where every vice was yours for the asking, when he spotted the riders. He should have been happy to see new faces, but he was not. Their appearance made him leery.

A sharp whistle escaped his lips and a moment later the archers were ready. The damp had done nothing to make his soldiers happier, but they managed just the same.

Levarre rode closer. "Who's coming?" The man had found him, brought another hundred sell swords along too, and fresh supplies besides. Levarre was a good man and trustworthy.

"No idea. But they are far away from any kind of civilization. Either they bring a message or I kill them."

"Do you recognize them?"

"Too far away." Beron shrugged.

"I actually came to tell you that one of the guards says he saw the Undying heading for us."

Beron nodded. "Prepare the oil. Prepare the arrows. I will handle what comes before us. The guards are better used taking care of the Undying. We will not let them win against us."

Levarre nodded and turned his horse. Beron was glad to see the man was armed and ready for combat.

He rode toward the approaching group. They were not familiar to him and so Beron made certain his sword was in easy reach.

They were darker than most of the people he'd dealt with for months. Their clothing revealed them easily enough. They were from the Kaer-ru, the islands.

The first held up his hands. "We mean no harm. We are seeking Beron, lately of Saramond."

"You've found me."

The man speaking was tall and lean and dressed like an island man. If the cold bothered him at all he hid it well. His hair was long and woven into a heavy braid. He had sword hilts showing on both of his hips.

"We have come to warn you. Your father sent us. He says if you do not change your path, you will die here soon. Die, or worse."

"My father is dead." Beron smiled, pleased to have caught the man in a lie so early on.

"Yes, I know." The man nodded. "That does not mean he does not look out for his son."

Superstitious nonsense. Still, a chill walked through Beron's body.

"You have given your warning. Was there anything else?"

"You misunderstand. He means now. Physically. You should change your path or you will suffer greatly."

"My path is chosen. I have a great distance left to travel

and diverting would only make the challenge of arriving at my destination greater."

The lean man sighed. "I have offered the warning. May the gods be with you."

"So far, of late, they have not been."

Without another comment the four riders turned and started away and that, more than anything else, made Beron reconsider their words.

"Wait!"

They stopped but did not turn back, leaving Beron no choice but to ride to them.

"You claim you have spoken with my dead father. You can see this might be a challenge for me to accept, yes?"

The man looked his way and nodded once, curtly.

"You came all this way just to convey that message?"

"It is what we do." The winds were increasing, and the rains started to fall harder.

"I have traveled a great distance to reach this point. I need to know what is supposed to happen."

The messenger spoke. "Ten times the gods have punished foolish people for disobeying them, just as they punish the world now. In past times the punishments were smaller. Rather than threaten all life, they removed life from places that offended. They allowed demons entry into this world then sealed the gates of the worlds behind them. Those demons are confined to small areas, but they are real and one of them is near."

Beron thought about that. Demons. He'd heard of the things, of course. Demons were supposed to be very powerful and capable of great punishment and great deeds alike. Though they sometimes offered help there was always a price to pay.

He bowed his head. "I thank you for your message. May I repay you?"

The thin man bowed his head in return. "That is unnecessary. We are rewarded by our work."

The concept of not offering payment went against his nature. Beron always demanded payment, thus allowing that he was never in anyone's debt, or they in his. "Perhaps with food and wine at least? You have a long ways to go."

"You are kind, Beron. But we have sufficient supplies." The thin man smiled as he rode away. Beron did not follow. He had offered payment and it was refused. His ledgers were clear of debt. That was what mattered.

Behind him the screams began. Beron turned and watched the arrows dipped in burning pitch rise into the air. Some struck true and others plummeted to the ground.

There were two shapes in the air, possibly a third. It was hard to say as the clouds were descending toward the ground and offering the Undying a place to hide safely.

Beron had two choices: go and help his companions, or find out what lay ahead and see what it truly meant.

The gods were now his enemies.

Could a demon be his ally?

One more sword against the Undying would make little difference.

Beron rode to where he had been warned to avoid and sealed his fate.

At first there was nothing, no difference, but after a few hundred yards the horse he rode refused to go further. He could have spurred the beast on, but he knew better. The horse would buck and throw him, and that was if things went well. Instead he climbed off the beast and patted its muscular neck. The animal did not run away, but snorted and refused to move.

Never let it be said that animals could not be trained and that included humans. The difference was that horses tended not to resent the training as much.

That his father would ever offer Beron a warning was an interesting notion. The man had trained him from the time he could walk, to be a slaver. No one in the business of slavery ever thought that meant a calm day.

When Beron disobeyed his father's wishes at the age of twelve, he was placed in the gladiatorial pits. Not as a gladiator, but as their practice partner. They were unkind in the extreme. The weapons were wooden, but they still hurt and they broke bones and they left scars just the same.

That was as close to being a loving father as the bastard ever came. Beron learned to fight and to understand slavery from both perspectives. His father never hid who he was from the gladiators. Several times they beat him within inches of his life. Each time he recovered and trained harder, until he earned their respect.

None of that mattered. The past was done. Still, the thought that his father would speak from beyond death to warn him was even stranger than the idea of demons.

Beron walked into the demon's lair without noticing the difference in the air. On his second step through the threshold he felt the sudden change in pressure. On the third, dread crawled into him.

He was a brave man. He had fought long and hard to build his empire. First he'd dealt with his father's associates, those who claimed he was not fit to rule, and then he handled the makers of laws who said he could no longer deal in the trade he had known since birth. Not everyone who dealt with him walked away intact and not nearly all of them walked away, but before he was done, Beron always got his way. It took inordinate courage and a stubbornness that bordered on fanaticism.

That was what kept him walking when all he wanted was to fall to the ground and cower.

The world made no sense. A moment before he'd been

walking in rain, crossing more of the nearly barren stretch of the plains. Arthorne was nearly at its end and he was soaking wet, dripping in the constant rain.

Yet here, the sky was blue, the air was dry and hot. Here there were plants of a thousand different varieties all around him, and there was a town. There were people.

No. Not people. Not exactly. They had been people, perhaps, but now they were mummified things, stretched out in a hundred different positions of agony, dried and preserved. They stretched on through the streets of the town overrun with plant life, buried under layers of ivy and trees that pushed up from the ground in places no tree should be. The city was there, but it was nearly lost beneath the plants as if it had been struck by a tidal wave of every imaginable sort of flower, bush and vine.

The smell of blossoming flowers was cloying. The scent of rotted flesh was merely an afterthought in comparison. None of which mattered at all when compared to the feeling that something massive was watching.

"You are here." The voice was not at all remarkable. Beron turned to face the source of the words and immediately regretted it. His eyes ached at the sight of the shape. It was not human, nor did it attempt to pass for human.

"I am."

The shape moved closer and Beron felt his vision swim.

"Why are you here?"

"Because I wanted to see you."

"Very few come here by accident." The voice did not judge. It merely stated.

"What happened here? Who killed all of these people?"

"They were killed when they disobeyed their gods. I was sent to punish them and I did. They were a godless people and they suffered for their actions, as your world is now starting to suffer."

"What are you?"

"You ask so many questions…" The voice did not change but the shape did. In seconds the aspects of the creature that hurt Beron's eyes were gone. Instead he faced a man who reminded him of the traveler that came to warn him. He was tall, he was lean and he was dressed in archaic garments. His eyes shone with amusement. His mouth twisted into the grin of a man with good humor and a desire to be entertained.

"This is more pleasing to your eyes?"

Beron nodded.

"I am me. I am here as punishment. I am here to punish. I am now stuck in this place for eternity as a way of making me behave."

The man gestured around. "I have my plants, but I tire of this place. You are fleeing the gods. You want to survive. You have angered them and even now their servants are killing your people and preparing to take your slaves."

Beron nodded again. "All of this is true. That is why I came seeking you. I would strike a bargain."

"What sort of bargain?" The tall man moved along, running long fingers over this plant or that flower, caressing them softly.

"I want it back. Everything I had. I want the gods to stop their attacks. I want to find and kill Brogan McTyre and Harper Ruttket. I want my money back. I want my world back." As he spoke Beron strode across the ground, treading on flowers, crushing desiccated flesh and bone beneath his boots. He waved his arms to encompass the world that he could not see, but knew was nearby. "I want a life that is less chaotic and more along the sort I've been fighting for my entire life. Do you understand?"

"You wish to no longer fear your gods. You wish to be stronger than any enemy. You wish to have wealth and power. You want what all people seem to want. The difference is, you have come to me instead of to your gods."

"They have never been my gods!" He glared his anger at the man before him, who seemed utterly unimpressed. "They take from everyone. They make demands without any compensation. They are what is wrong with this world."

"How do you mean, Beron of Saramond?"

"When I owe a debt, I pay it! When I am owed a debt I make sure that I am paid. They have taken for centuries but offer nothing!"

"Did they not keep your world safe?"

"Is it safe any longer? They are angry at Brogan McTyre and they take out their fury on everyone else. If they are gods, could they not merely grab him in their hands and crush him?"

"Of course they could. They demand fealty. They demand that they be obeyed."

"I will not obey the filth that take from me when I have done nothing wrong!" Beron's voice cracked. He had held his anger at bay and now it wanted out.

"What would you do if you could fix this?" The lean man walked beside him, smiling still.

"I would find Brogan McTyre. I would find Harper Ruttket. I would take them to King Parrish of Mentath and gather my reward. I would see the world saved."

"And then?"

"Then I would rule this world justly! And I would kill my enemies."

"What would you offer for this?"

Beron stopped and thought about that. "I do not know."

"Your gods demand four sacrifices with each season. They demand that the sacrifices be sanctified and offered in just the right way, not because they need it done that way, but because they like their rituals. Would you offer the same to them if it stopped all of the troubles and made you a king?"

Beron looked at the smiling man. He held a thick bloom in his hand that seemed made of a thousand petals. In the center of that bloom was a small, round fruit.

"No. They are too easily angered. They are too quick to punish. They are too old, and set in their ways."

"If I aided you in reaching your goals, would you offer me a similar deal?"

"I would offer you the blood of my enemies. I would offer you their flesh."

In an instant the man stood next to Beron, the fruiting flower still in his hand. Up close the bloom was intoxicating.

"Give me this. Give me the three who currently slaughter your people. Offer me the slaves you have with you, and I will give you power. I will aid you when you need me and I will help you achieve your dreams. When the gods have been defeated I will raise you up as the king of these lands."

Beron closed his eyes. He had never followed a god before. This one, at least offered him rewards for his service.

"If I fail you?"

"Then you do not get my aid."

"No punishments?"

"You have the very gods to handle. You must capture your enemies and surrender them for sacrifice. That is punishment enough. We barter, you and I. We make promises in good faith. Failure means you have no rewards. Success means you achieve all that you desire."

The man pulled the small fruit from his blossom and let the flower fall. The fruit he tore in half with his fingers. Sweet juices coated both of his hands and half of the fruit he offered to Beron.

"Give me these things, Beron of Saramond. Kill your

enemies in my name and bear my mark and you will be a' king."

Beron took the fruit. "Done."

He placed the sweet section into his mouth and chewed and watched the other man do the same to seal their arrangement. The fruit tasted as fine as anything he had ever consumed.

"Great men should have great weapons. I give you these."

Where they came from, Beron could not have said, but the sword and spear were heavy in his hands when he hefted them. The spear ended in a long blade that glistened as if wet, though when Beron touched it the metal was dry. The sword was a different matter. Wonderfully balanced, as black as midnight and marked on blade and hilt alike with a round symbol that hurt Beron's eyes all over again when he looked too closely.

"I am Ariah. I am your god. Serve me well and I will reward you with all that you desire."

"I am Beron. I am your servant."

"No, Beron. You are my priest."

Beron took three steps and found himself once again on the Plains of Arthorne, once again soaked in rain. Not far away his people were fighting with the Undying and winning.

The spear felt good and tight in his hand as he jogged toward the battle. One of the Undying was down, bloodied and cut deeply. The others were engaged in their fights, slashing with claws and throwing Beron's people around with too much ease.

Levarre roared orders and led the battle, as Beron had known he would. The man was heavy, but he was a fighter and he knew enough to keep the men alive in most cases.

Mud slapped at his calves as Beron ran and he took careful aim, charging toward the closest of the Undying and raising the spear with both hands. He did not hurl the weapon. He could see that the Undying had an unnatural command of the winds.

Instead he charged forward and rammed the blade into the side of the closest enemy, driving the point deep into flesh and muscle, past bone.

The He-Kisshi shrieked and tried to pull the spear free, but could not reach. Beron lifted the heavy thing into the air then slammed it into the mud, growling as he did it. The creature shuddered and coughed a thick, black blood.

He pulled the spear free and struck the thing in the head with the butt end several times.

Levarre focused on the other one, wielding a weighted chain that smashed into the creature's arm and slid down its vast wing. The blow was enough to take it from the air and that was enough to allow a few of the men working for him to throw a weighted net across the thing.

Beron smiled grimly as the men fought with the beast, lashing ropes over the net, beating it with poles to avoid getting cut by savage claws.

"We have them, Beron!" Levarre patted him heavily on the arm.

"I'm sorry I was gone so long, Levarre. I have found a way for us to get out of this with more than our pride intact."

"Gone?" Levarre frowned. "You were lost to us for only a minute. What plan do you have to make all of this right?"

"I need your help to gather the Undying. You and you alone. I need to introduce you to someone."

Levarre, who could often be obstinate and argumentative, was not foolish enough to debate the matter. Instead he nodded. "I'll get a horse to help haul them along."

Beron frowned and looked for his own horse, happy to see that it was still nearby, if not exactly close enough to pet.

"Aye. That's wise."

Levarre called out to the men and they immediately began tying the two creatures securely. Say this for slavers, they know how to bind a thing. Inside of four minutes the Undying were completely restrained and tied to the back of a draft horse.

"Levarre, we are going to lose the slaves."

"Say again?"

"We are going to lose the slaves. I have been assured that we will gain a return three times that which I invested. We will not need them."

Levarre stared long and hard, studying Beron carefully, as well he should. Beron was not known for letting any slaves escape him for long and had often spent a great deal of money to ensure the capture of any who did so.

"Just letting them go?"

"Not quite. We have been offered a chance to get back all that has been lost and more and I intend to take that offer."

"And you need the slaves for that?"

"The slaves and the Undying. Come along. I'll show you."

Ten minutes later, the horse shied away from where they were going and the two of them were obligated to haul the winged creatures through the spot that wasn't there, and into the garden of death and endless blooms.

Levarre handled himself well enough. He did not scream or cry when he met Ariah. He was shaken, but being a sensible man, he understood Beron's temptation to deal with the creature.

What choice did he have, really? Levarre agreed.

It was Levarre who marched down and called for the wagon master to lead the slaves toward Beron. For the space of a heartbeat he'd been certain the other slavers would rebel against their new plan. He too might have considered it, but finally the pale women were brought to the city of blooms and men took the place of the horses that refused to go farther. Another hour or more lost to the efforts, but well worth it.

Ariah watched on and nodded his approval as the pale women and the Undying were delivered. Without hesitation he gifted Levarre with a long dagger and a short sword that bore the same unsettling mark as Beron's.

After the promised delivery the demon pointed toward the north. "Your enemies, Brogan McTyre and Harper Ruttket are there. You must find them, bind them and deliver them, along with the other men who have created this turmoil. In the meantime, I will discuss the ways of the gods with their faithful followers."

As he spoke Ariah's visage changed and once more became nearly unbearable. Beron and the men were glad to leave.

"What have we done, Beron?" Levarre's voice was shaken as it had every reason to be.

"We have broken from the gods that have punished us and become the priests for a new god, one who would see us put into power over all we survey."

"The gods will be angry."

"They are already angry. They are destroying the world. We will become the saviors of this world, Levarre, and the people will be grateful for all that we have done."

Levarre was silent, but he nodded his head.

He would come around in time. He was a good friend, which was why Beron had offered him a part of the pact.

Besides which, if Levarre failed him, he would be sacrificed to Ariah. Beron was new to the idea of worshipping a god, but he intended to do it the right way.

Messengers were sent, calling for more forces. The slavers wanted to be paid? They'd come and serve. As a rule, slavers liked to be paid.

Then it was merely a matter of following Ariah's guidance. They rode west, toward the distant mountains, and veered lightly south as that was the direction Ariah said they should go.

CHAPTER FOURTEEN
Where the Rains Go

Myridia looked out at a land as different from her home as any could be. On the other side of the mountains waters flooded the land. On this side the river poured steadily through the vast crystalline cave, but there were no storms, no raging winds, and no rains soaking everything.

So far, there was peace. It would not last.

The night people had not done anything yet, but she could feel them as surely as she felt the pull of the Sessanoh. There was an urgency in her guts. She knew the others felt it too, or at least some of them did. The gods did not speak to her. They had never spoken to her. She was leading, but in this she was alone.

Lyraal was walking the perimeter of their small camp. She carried her sword over her shoulders and whistled softly as she eyed the world around her. Lyraal was not trusting. She would have made a better leader but refused.

"Fine, then." Myridia almost spat the words. "I'll lead."

Even as she said those words she felt the first cold touch of air from a place that she sensed but did not see.

Once there was a city that could only be seen at night. Garien and his people paid the price for visiting. It was not a temptation she could permit.

"Up!" The sun was just rising and the others were sleeping, exhausted. That did not matter. She had led them into danger with the troupe and the things that followed. The troupe was gone, perhaps, or merely joined with the night people. In any even they had to be avoided and failing that they had to be cut down.

Her people had lost so much. She had wanted to let them have time to adjust, even knowing that time was a precious commodity. No more.

"Up, I say! We have a long way to go and we will do what the gods demand."

Lyraal walked through the camp, kicking at the legs of anyone too foolish to stir. She did not want to lead, but she was an excellent means to make others obey.

The other woman nodded and offered her a small grin of approval.

It was enough for now.

The Sessanoh waited. According to legend there were more of their kind waiting at the Mirrored Lake. They would find out.

Myridia looked over her shoulder, back toward the mountains once again. Somewhere behind her the night people did whatever they did in the daylight hours. She'd keep her distance if she could. If not, she and hers would endure whatever happened. That was all the choice they had.

Edinrun was called by many names; most were complimentary. In the finer arts there was no greater city. Universities and colleges were in abundance and, if one wished to learn, one merely had to observe a few rules and possibly offer coin in exchange for lessons, mundane and arcane alike.

The great storms had not reached the city yet, but they

would be on their way shortly – seers and charlatans alike agreed on that. From the great wall that surrounded and on occasion protected the city, if one chose to take the time, one could see the towering black clouds as they rose higher and higher in the distant north and spread to the west like a vast shadowy wing. If that were a wing, however, the beast that spread that limb would indeed be godlike in its expanse.

Some were already saying it was the end of the world, even among the enlightened who no longer believed in gods.

It was to this place that three of the He-Kisshi came. They drifted down from clear skies and alighted themselves on the great wall.

Like penitents at prayer, they marched slowly along the wall, ignoring the awkward silences and the fearful stares cast their way. They were not there to speak to humans. They were there to do the will of the gods.

The First Tribulation was Storm. In time, if not stopped, the winds and rain and furious lightning would shatter the world, but it would take time. To the north, few doubted the anger of the gods.

In order to make certain that the south understood the anger of the gods just as well, the He-Kisshi came to deliver a message.

Words would not suffice. They seldom did.

And so it would be action.

The Second Tribulation was released into Edinrun.

The Second Tribulation was Madness. The gods watched their servants at work and knew that it was good.

The rains were not stopping. Brogan shook his head and spat. He'd never run across so much rain in his entire life and he wondered if it was possible to flood the whole of the world.

Beside him, sitting on a pile of oilcloths he'd be assembling into a tent soon, Harper sucked contentedly at his pipe, the aromatic smoke drifting around him lazily.

"Will you ever stop puffing away on that infernal thing?"

"Not likely. I find comfort in it."

"Wine is cheaper."

"Weighs too much, and too many people want to have a nip of it."

"You should quit it anyway."

Harper eyed him and smiled. "You kill those gods, I'll quit smoking my weed. Until then let's just say it calms my nerves."

Harper looked to the distant eastern horizon and continued smoking.

"Your nerves need calming?"

"There's trouble coming from the east." Harper tapped the ashes from the bowl of his pipe against his boot heel and watched the embers die in the rainwater.

Brogan saw what approached and was not certain what to make of them. They were female, to be sure. They were pale, absolutely.

For a moment he thought the creatures were the slave women he'd sold off. But their faces were bestial, with large, dark eyes and mouths full of sharp teeth. Their hands were clawed with long fingers and what looked like webbing between those digits.

They were heading for the camp and coming along at a hard run.

Brogan gave a sharp whistle. Harper did the same and the men with them that had been setting up camp immediately went for their weapons. Some didn't even bother to look for what was attacking, but instead prepared for the attack.

"Archers!" Brogan reached for his own bow. He wasn't the world's greatest bowman, but he could live on what he hunted and that meant decent accuracy.

The winds were light. The rain was heavy. He drew an arrow, nocked it and released as the first of the white things came within range.

Not ten feet away from him, Harper was doing the same. Arrows rose without military precision, but they flew high and fast, and when they dropped again most of them drew blood. Seven of the white women fell to their injuries. The rest moved faster, coming in on hands and feet in some cases or simply running in others.

Brogan's second arrow missed. The third punched through one of those large, dark eyes and dropped the creature in the mud. Two more arrows, two more hits before the enemy was too close to allow for many ranged attacks. There were a few of the lads who were better at archery than he was and who continued to fire arrows at a terrifying rate. From this close the impacts dropped the women with arrows doing horrific damage, often punching completely through bone.

Brogan took up his axe and met the charge of one coming his way. She slashed with webbed claws and her speed was impressive but her strength was obscene. Had it not been for his cloak, the fingers of the creature would have cut him apart. Instead she was tangled long enough that the head of his axe bit deep into her chest and sent her staggering back. The second swing carved away a large section of her face and left her down and screaming.

They were not fighters. Whatever they were, strong as they were, the things were not trained at all. They flung themselves clumsily at their enemies and made wide swipes with their claws in the hopes of hitting something. They were fast enough that a few of them did, in fact, cause great harm, but they were the exceptions.

The mercenaries, by comparison, were hardened fighters.

Most of them had been soldiers at one point or another, and even those who had not served in armies had been trained with swords, with axes, bows or spears.

Harper took his usual stance at Brogan's side and they advanced together, watching each other's flanks as they cut into their enemies. The white women were terrors to behold: exactly far enough away from human that it was hard to accept they were real. Exactly fast enough to make up for their lack of skills. One of them cut three fingers deep into Brogan's arm even as he drove the tip of his sword through her throat and shoved her back, choking on her blood.

Beside him Harper moved grimly and quickly. Several of the things screamed at him in a language that Brogan could not understand but had heard from the white women and the men who killed his family.

Four of them came for him at once, pouncing like feral cats. One he kicked in the face as it dropped low. Another he slapped with the flat of his sword. A third got the axe in her side as she tried to twist away. The fourth knocked Brogan off his feet and sent him sliding through the mud.

The sword slid away and he scrambled for his knife.

She came at him again, sliding through the mud herself as she reached out to grab at him. The knife cut into the palm of her hand, carved halfway through bone and lodged there. Brogan twisted, pulled at the handle of his axe and tore it free from the one he had stuck it in. The she-thing hissed and lunged and Brogan's axe cut into her neck and shoulder alike as he swung.

He had to kick the dead thing in its face to get his axe back. By the time he was standing the majority of the white women were dead or dying. Laram had one pinned in place with a spear and it screamed its agonies into the wind. Desmond stood over one that he had literally cut in two with his axes. Sallos was panting and holding his arm, which was bleeding freely enough to be a bother. Anna was already next to him, urging him over to where she could sit him down.

Harper said, "They did not stay slaves. I don't know if they escaped or if they were sent after us, but they did not stay slaves."

"These are the Grakhul?"

"I wouldn't have thought so, but they called me by name and they accused me of killing them." He lowered his head a moment. "To be fair, I did."

"No, Harper. You did not act alone."

His friend looked at him. "I made a choice, Brogan. I will accept whatever stains it leaves in me. I would do nothing different, given a second chance."

That was one more reason to strike down the gods. The very notion should have terrified him. He had seen their power from a distance, had seen their servants, both the He-Kisshi and the Grakhul. The gods had condemned him and challenged him and even now there were armies gathering to hunt him down. Even so, he was gathering an army of his own. It was a small army but they were loyal enough. Those that knew him understood why he'd committed his sins, if sins they were.

Still, he looked around at the dead women and felt no guilt over the kills. He thought of the thing in his saddlebag, the fur that continued to move, to struggle to be free to the point that every night he settled the matter by wrapping it in yet another oil cloth and nailing that cloth to the ground with tent poles lest it try to escape.

The very notion of that, when he let himself dwell on the situation, was nearly enough to make him want to scream and run off into the night. Dead should be dead.

Surely his family was dead enough. They were not

afforded the luxury of coming back from what had been done to them.

Brogan lent himself to the task of stacking the dead to one side of the camp. He studied them carefully, the webbing on their hands, the odd, scintillating scales on their flesh, small enough to go unnoticed at first. They did, indeed, have different teeth, but only in that they were sharper than he'd expected. A close examination showed that the sharper teeth had actually slid down over perfectly normal ones, like a second set that acted as a shield. They had hair. They were adapted for swimming, he supposed.

"What the hell are these things, Harper?"

Harper stared long and hard, then shrugged. "They are dead. That is all that matters."

Brogan could not argue with that.

"Why did they attack us?"

"Because everyone on this planet wants us, Brogan." Harper scowled lightly. "The only good news is that they want us alive for now." He paused then added, "Whatever it is you plan on doing, it has to be soon. They'll keep looking for us and I know some are loyal, but sooner or later one of ours will aim to take us for the rewards being offered."

"What rewards?"

"Don't be a fool, Brogan. There are always rewards."

"Aye. There's that."

"So what are we doing?"

"I've already said. We're going to find a way to kill the gods."

"How?"

Brogan nodded toward the bundle he'd already nailed to the ground. "There's the first step. We have other places we need to go. There's a cave inside the mountains that I need to visit."

"A cave? What sort?" Harper looked at him and scowled.

Brogan pointed north. "There. The Broken Swords. Somewhere in that madness is the secret of what I need next. The challenge is finding it."

Harper stared at him as if he were losing his mind. "It's only a legend, Brogan."

"I thought so too, but the Galean said otherwise. Whatever the case, I'll try to find what I need and I'll finish what has been started."

"Brogan, it's a madman's game."

"Harper, it is the only game left. We fight or we die. I fight or I die. The gods want me dead. The feeling is mutual."

He looked at the distant crystalline shards that ran through the mountain range.

"One way or another, this is all that is left. Live or die. Win or lose. I have no intention of dying. I will not let the gods win. All that they have taken from me, I will take from them."

On the other side of those very mountains twelve of the Grakhul continued their quest to find the Mirrored Lakes, the Sessanoh, so that they could prepare for the sacrifice of Brogan McTyre and his cohorts.

Directly to the east a band of slavers was coming for the same man, intent on capturing him and torturing him for as long as they could before he was surrendered for sacrifice. They did not follow the gods, but instead followed a new deity, a demon that promised them all they could desire.

To the south several groups were gathering, drawn to Torema and to Edinrun. There they would find their world was already changing more than they wanted to know.

Four of the Undying were dead or missing. One hid itself among the humans and another was bound and sealed in a package carried by none other than Brogan McTyre.

In a distant place, where once the Grakhul offered sacrifices to the gods and dwelled in a city called Nugonghappalur, the ground was shattered and crumbled into the sea. What was left was a collection of harsh, jagged stones that rose out of the waters when the tide was low and hid beneath the waves when the waters rose. Half a league off what had been the shoreline a great arch of stone seemed to rise and fall with the tide as well. That archway, that portal to other places, seethed with electricity. Lightning caressed the stone and never did the least bit of damage. At certain times, as it had always been said by the Grakhul, the gods would make their presence known, sometimes even entering the world of man to mete out their justice. Mostly, however, the gods merely watched and passed judgment from afar.

There were Five Kingdoms. One was under water, the last of the towns and cities were drowning in the waters drawn in from the sea as the land was shattered and the oceans crept closer.

Above the north and eastern skies the clouds grew in a slow moving tempest, eating the land and spitting out the corpses of those too slow to escape the wrath of the gods.

In ten places around the land, there were hidden doorways to other realms, prisons created by the gods to keep demons locked away, secured and hidden from the world after they served their purpose and punished those who defied the gods.

It could be said with truth that the demons did not like their lot in life. Some of them even planned to change the way the world had always worked. They would break the rules if they could and they would gather new servants and worshippers along the way.

According to legends the gods had once been lower beings before they slaughtered their way to the very top of the universe, where they could look down on all of creation and feast as they saw fit.

There had been other gods, cut down, cast out, destroyed

or buried, who could say? Perhaps the only ones who knew for certain were the gods and if they knew they did not share that knowledge.

Five kingdoms hunted a man. Five gods wanted that man dead. Armies gathered both to defend him and to capture him. They gods said he had sinned and the people believed them.

Brogan McTyre rode with a small army that would grow soon enough.

Brogan McTyre rode alone.

He carried with him one sword and one axe, and the hopes that before he died he would see the gods themselves destroyed.

Time would tell all the secrets of god and man alike.

Adventure calls...

twitter.com/angryrobotbooks

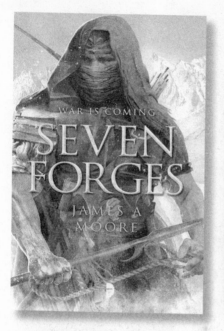

WAR IS COMING

SEVEN FORGES

JAMES A MOORE

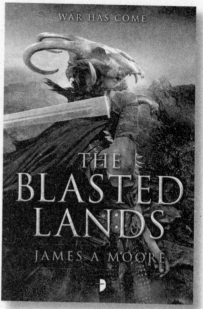

WAR HAS COME

THE BLASTED LANDS

JAMES A MOORE

War is coming... Join the fight!

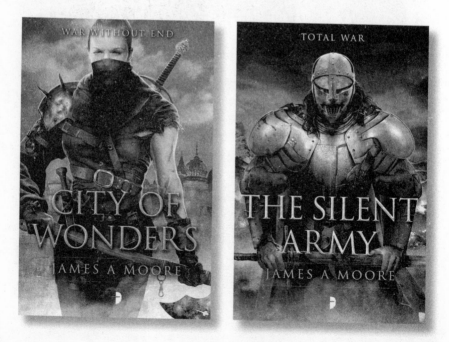

WAR WITHOUT END

CITY OF WONDERS

JAMES A MOORE

TOTAL WAR

THE SILENT ARMY

JAMES A MOORE